WRATH *of a* MINOR GOD

Other Books by Anthony Hains

WRATH *of a* MINOR GOD

Nightshade Chronicles
Book 4

Anthony Hains

Wrath of a Minor God

Published by PCNY BOOKS

Cover design by Elderlemon Design
Book interior by Cover to Cover LLC

ISBN: 978-1-7323880-8-6 (Ebook)
ISBN: 978-1-7323880-9-3 (Paperback)

To the book club

Contents

Acknowledgments

MANY THANKS TO SUSAN WENGER, my editor, and Kealan Patrick Burke, cover artist.

Thanks to Brent Gregory and John Phillips, who provided feedback on an earlier draft.

Finally, thanks to my wife, Ann, for supporting my extended hours in the alternative world of Cole Nightshade.

1

Remote Viewing

October 1977

"AGENT NIGHTSHADE. THANK YOU FOR coming in."

Cole turned his gaze from a painting of a sailboat on a calm sea, reminiscent of every piece of mass-produced artwork he'd seen hanging in cheap motels across America, to a tall, pudgy man in a white lab coat. The researcher extended his hand.

"No problem," Cole returned the handshake. While it hadn't been a problem to keep this appointment, it also wasn't an option. He'd been ordered to cooperate.

"I hope you haven't been standing out here too long." Placing a hand on Cole's left shoulder, the researcher ushered him down the hall, away from the reception area. The secretary had offered Cole a seat when he first arrived, but he preferred to stand.

"I'm fine. The drive from Fredericksburg took a little longer than I expected. I needed a stretch."

The nondescript building came as a bit of a surprise given the classical architecture that graced the rest of the

UVA campus. Thomas Jefferson had likely rolled over in his grave when the plain cinderblock structure was constructed among the columns, curving brick walls, and sweeping lawns. The building directory indicated that Vector Labs was on the second floor adjacent to the Reincarnation Sciences office. Cole hadn't perused the other groups residing in the building but noticed that the entire place fell under the umbrella of the Center for Perceptual Insights.

The second-floor walls were nicked, marred with scratches, and in desperate need of a paint job. The overhead lighting provided by dismal fluorescent tubes cast an unhealthy glare along the main hallway. The Vector Labs office proved equally disheartening. Its walls were a drab white, or maybe a cream, it was hard to tell. The shag carpet had been smashed into a threadbare path by past users.

Hard to believe Vector Labs was a CIA operation.

The researcher escorted Cole into a small office slightly homier than the hallway he'd just traveled. While only about ten by twelve, the room was lit by a floor lamp that cast a warm glow and contained newer-looking wall-to-wall carpeting. There were no windows.

"Please have a seat."

A wooden desk stood off to the side with a padded desk chair. Cole stepped toward a spartan metal chair to the side of the desk.

"No, no," the researcher said, smiling. "You get the seat of honor. Such as it is."

Cole nodded and took the comfortable chair.

"Ah, my manners." The researcher sat beside the desk. "I'm Dr. Bruce Rudyard, principal investigator on the project. I've been hired by the agency to investigate the potential of psychic phenomena for national security."

Dr. Rudyard had a shortened mustache which, in combination with his weight, gave him more than a passing resemblance to Oliver Hardy of Laurel and Hardy fame. Or was it Stan Laurel? Cole could never remember which was which despite having seen their movies hundreds of times on TV.

Not knowing what to say, Cole remained silent. Rudyard went with the benefit-of-the-country speech right out of the gate.

"You have a history of displaying a unique set of psychic skills, Cole. May I call you Cole?" The guy was probably old enough to be Cole's father and then some.

"Sure."

"Excellent. We're excited to have this opportunity to assess your talents. The reports have been eye-opening to say the least." Dr. Rudyard rubbed the palms of his hands together briskly as if cold.

"Sometimes the written record is inaccurate."

"Oh, I understand completely. This'll give us the opportunity to evaluate you and judge for ourselves."

The evaluation component made Cole uncomfortable. He was aware of his "talents," as Rudyard called them, and he'd learned to deal with them as they bubbled to the surface. His abilities proved valuable and even lifesaving at times, but the last few years had brought him attention he'd rather not have.

For instance, his unit chief recommended—no, call it what it was—required him to participate in some parapsychology research being conducted at the University of Virginia. This wasn't a trite academic study being conducted by undergrads trying to identify hidden designs on ESP cards. No, this was a massive project organized and directed by the CIA, not only at UVA but also Stanford.

Cole wished these people had something more important to study.

"Now, let's see." Rudyard opened a nondescript cream-colored file folder containing an inch-thick pile of paper. He fumbled through the pile, and Cole caught glimpses of his high school graduation photo and his discharge papers from the army. Then came medical records—there were plenty of those—and a recent psychological evaluation.

Rudyard continued shuffling to the end of the file and returned to the front of the stack. Here, the papers were engraved with *Vector Labs* in bold royal blue. Then the file was closed. There was no way Rudyard could've read anything during this cursory review. That meant he had examined the contents before.

"So, let me see. You're twenty..."

"Twenty-seven."

"Ah, yes. And you grew up in New River in Southwestern Virginia."

"Yes, sir."

Rudyard pursed his lips. "A tour in Vietnam, then a degree in psychology and criminal justice at Virginia Tech."

Cole glanced at his watch. "You have all this information in that folder with my name on it. I went over it with your assistant on the phone."

The researcher frowned but otherwise ignored Cole's comment. "You've been with the FBI since graduation."

Cole remained quiet.

"The Behavioral Science Unit."

He offered Rudyard the briefest nod.

"This may feel like a waste of time, but I need to get a feel for the terrain, check to see if anything jumps out at me."

Cole stared at the man. "Has anything jumped yet?"

Rudyard smiled briefly and opened the file again. "You've had vivid telepathic and clairvoyant experiences since you were a small child. Most with deceased individuals, although at times with other telepathic individuals. Live ones, that is."

Groundwork was being laid and Cole didn't quite see where it was headed. "That's correct."

"In fact, the experiences around your twelfth birthday were nothing short of spectacular."

"That's not a word I'd use to describe them." Cole wondered if Rudyard was aware of what had happened at Saint Edwards. Most people weren't.

"Stunning or astonishing, I meant."

Cole acknowledged this with a tilt of his head.

"Those served two major purposes. One was to inform you of the nature of someone's death. You were able to solve a mystery or acknowledge the past presence of a forgotten soul. The second provided protection or a warning."

"Yes." Again, probably in the reports.

"Then, the occurrences in Vietnam. These definitely were protective. You saved the lives of your squad mates more than once, I take it. During your deployment, there were hardly any casualties in the squad."

Cole thought of Sergeant Lewis and D-man and grunted. "One guy died and another lost a foot and part of his leg."

"Yes, well. That's limited, relatively speaking."

From the hall came the sound of quiet footsteps, most likely the receptionist. The room was cool, although Cole didn't notice that until the hot water radiator clanged.

"Sorry, I don't mean to be rude, but I'm struggling with my role here. You must be quite busy, and this is basic material from a file," Cole said.

Rudyard's eyebrows lifted. The little mustache wiggled on his lip. "No one explained it to you?"

Cole shook his head.

"Goodness. Let me cut to the chase, then. Your ability to receive communications from people about something they've seen in the past is what we call retrocognition. The impressions you receive from the past related to the deaths of individuals also serve as a warning. Meaning, you're capable of seeing the future. That's precognition.

"Lastly, you've reported conversations with other telepaths since your childhood. Ongoing, live conversations. Another extraordinary skill." Rudyard looked smug.

"There must be others who can do that," Cole said.

"Not that many. We've been looking. You, Cole, possess the telepathic trifecta. Your country needs you."

Cole couldn't help snorting. "I already serve my country."

"Yes, yes. You served in the military. And you've done fine investigative work as a federal agent—something you will continue to do. After your work on the Tompkins murders, the FBI won't give you up. But your talents may be used in other ways at other critical junctures." Rudyard sat back, folded his arms across his ample belly, and smiled.

"Which are?"

"Have you ever heard of remote viewing?"

Cole searched his memory. "No."

"It's a specialized telepathy. A sender goes to a location and observes targets of interest. The sender projects a picture of that target to a viewer who possesses the requisite telepathic skills. The viewer receives this detailed impression even though he is not present at the site."

"Why? And for what purpose?"

"The devil is in the details, Cole. What if the sender is

observing enemy troop movements or a heretofore unknown nuclear facility in the Ural Mountains or the hideout of an international terrorist? The viewer receives the information from the sender, and the agencies take appropriate action."

"Psychic spying."

"If you like."

Cole was troubled. He shifted in his seat. "Ultimately, you're wanting to weaponize these skills."

"Young man. The Soviets are already pouring millions of rubles into psychic ops research. We're behind. Dangerously so."

Cole stood, then walked to the back wall. He leaned against it and stared at Rudyard. "My experiences, as you call them, have never fit the pattern of purposeful execution that you're looking for. They're short. Fleeting. And spontaneous. I can't predict when they'll happen or conjure up a—a vision."

"I understand. But we really won't know whether intentional remote viewing efforts work until we try, will we? Right now we have three individuals who've displayed certain paranormal talents. You would be the fourth. Stanford has numerous test subjects they're assessing. I'm kind of envious, really. But that's California, after all. Land of fruits and nuts." Rudyard chuckled at his own joke.

Cole pinched the bridge of his nose.

"We're just at the initial assessment phase," Rudyard said. "But can you imagine our excitement when the scuttlebutt about you came to our attention and we learned we had a potential test subject in our midst, working as a federal agent? A few queries were made, and a request from one agency to another, and you were loaned to us for the day for some tests. They won't take long. Then you can have the rest of the day off. If things look promising, we'll call you back. Maybe in a week or two at the earliest."

Cole's psychic experiences were frequently jolting and terrifying. War casualties died repeatedly. Young women flung themselves from upper stories of an asylum. Once in a blue moon, though, they could be affirming. Meeting his mother for the first and only time—that memory had been forever etched into Cole's being.

Either way, though, the events tended to have some personal connection. Cole was able to act on the knowledge. Hell yes, he saved his squad, found the missing, or helped solve a murder. That's what he was meant to do.

But this?

"I'm skeptical," Cole said to Rudyard when the researcher returned to the room after excusing himself to confirm that they were ready to proceed with the assessment.

"Of course." Rudyard grasped the back of his chair and moved it around the desk to sit directly in front of Cole. "That's not uncommon. We can only try, though."

"I understand. But when it happens, it's usually spontaneous, as I said before. And there's some kind of urgency involved. I'm not just waiting to receive a message. This"— Cole motioned to the space in the room—"is artificial."

Rudyard lifted an open briefcase containing audio-recording equipment from the floor along the wall. It had been out of Cole's line of sight, and he hadn't noticed it. "Think about it, Cole. When you received these messages in the past, maybe you were ripe for listening. You were prepared based on some cues in the environment or an internal emotional state. You weren't sitting at a desk in a lab, maybe, but you were certainly prepped." Rudyard continued to set up the cassette recorder.

A flash of a memory from seven years ago. Cole couldn't help grunting.

"What's funny?" Rudyard asked. He completed his task with the recorder and sat down.

"Someone told me something similar once before. That maybe I have an extreme emotional sensitivity to certain situations involving trauma."

"That is a viable hypothesis," Rudyard said.

"It is, I suppose. Not necessarily a psychic phenomenon, according to him."

"Still, intriguing." Rudyard shifted in his seat as if to move on. "Sounds like someone I'd like to meet."

"No, you wouldn't." Cole deadpanned. "He's a serial killer who's still at large. When I knew him, he had a thing for abducting families and murdering them. Slowly."

Rudyard blinked. "Charming. We don't have anything in store for you remotely like that."

"All by way of saying, I'll give this my best shot. I'm just not expecting much."

"That's all we ask." Rudyard said. "Let's give this a go, shall we?"

A stack of paper appeared on the desk, followed by a fistful of writing implements. Rudyard deposited multiple number two pencils, three ballpoint pens—black, blue, and red—a couple of felt-tipped pens, and a lead pencil.

"Here's the procedure. We have a sender who's currently at a location and will be directing messages to you about the location. Your task is to attempt to pick up these messages using whatever means necessary. For most people, this would involve sitting quietly and attending to flashes or pictures that may crystalize, either gradually or immediately, into an image of the location."

Cole sat taller in the chair. "This person is ready to go?"

"We'll get confirmation of that soon. Let me describe the experimental controls and methodology before I check. First, we've already taken photos of seven locations around the Washington DC area. The photos were developed as five by sevens and mailed to an attorney at Langley. He, in turn, placed each of the seven photos in separate unmarked envelopes and sealed them. This happened yesterday. Our sender arrived at the attorney's office at noon today, chose one of the sealed envelopes, and returned to her car. Once there, she opened the envelope and learned of the location. She's already checked in, so we know she's in the vicinity. We're just giving her some time to reach a good vantage point. She'll start sending around two o'clock."

"Will this be a historic place?"

"Not necessarily. I mean, it could be, but it could just be a side street or a park."

Cole nodded, still skeptical.

"Your task is to clear your mind and attend carefully. As the impressions become clear, start drawing what you see. It may come piecemeal over time. You may only see lines at first, or other shapes. Keep drawing. If you feel you need another sheet of paper, I'll give it to you. I've had people draw their impressions on as few as two sheets to as many as thirty-seven. Whatever is natural for you is what you'll use."

"How will I know when I'm done?"

"You'll know." Rudyard offered his hands as if stressing the obvious.

"Will you let me know if I'm accurate?"

Rudyard smiled. "Not right away. I don't know what photo has been chosen either. Before I find out, I'll score your impressions to see if any of them—or any combination of them—are close to one of the actual locations. In fact, I usually try to figure which one was chosen based on what I'm given. *Then* I check to see what it is. We'll let you know, however. One way or the other."

Cole stood and stretched while Rudyard left to check on the sender. He had time to circle the room once before the researcher returned.

"She's in position. She will spend the next thirty minutes observing everything about the location—all the while concentrating her focus of the images toward our location."

How she was going to do that was unclear to Cole, but he decided not to ask.

"In addition, I'll be recording the session, so feel free to talk or make comments while drawing. We encourage you to provide any verbal information to help inform us as to what you're producing on the page. In fact, I may even ask you questions. But if at any time you find these questions distracting, please tell me to remain quiet. Understood?"

Cole nodded.

"Any questions?"

"Can I ask questions during the process?" Cole said.

"By all means, if you're unsure about anything, please ask."

They began right at the top of the hour. Cole selected a standard pencil and propped his elbows on the table. This resulted in him staring directly at Rudyard, which was distracting as hell. Averting his eyes, he noticed the cassette recorder. A red light indicated that it was recording. He sat back in his chair and crossed his right ankle over his left knee.

"Have you got a binder or a pad? Something for me to lean the paper on?"

Without saying a word, Rudyard produced a thick letter-size pad.

This would do. He closed his eyes and waited.

Flashes of his house and dirty dishes in the sink. Images of Cynthia naked.

No. These were probably not from the sender.

A pile of leaves by a curb, two high school kids walking to school, a morning commuter dashing into his car to beat the craziness on I-95.

Those were images from today's early-morning jog. Cole fought a flash of impatience.

An impression of a faint path within a wooded area. Flickers of light struggling to break through a canopy of trees. Dark shadows jostling for dominance over the sunlight as a gust of wind buffeted the trees.

Interesting. That wasn't him.

More lights and shadows. The trees swayed. Maybe it wasn't the sun breaking through the shade of the trees. Could it be lightning? Moonlight?

Cole opened his eyes and started drawing. He was not an accomplished artist. In fact, he'd disliked the subject when he had to study it at school. This made any interpretation of his drawing suspect. His initial efforts were the trees. Long lines indicated the trunks. Scribbled circles were the leaves. The entire thing looked shitty.

"Any comments?" Rudyard said softly.

"Quiet." Chatting would be disruptive.

Cole shoved the sheet aside. More images were trickling in, and they didn't fit well with the first drawing.

A second blank sheet materialized before him. An elongated square appeared on his sheet. His hand was moving rapidly.

"No not a square. A rectangle," he said aloud.

"You're seeing a rectangle?"

"Shut up." Rude, but necessary.

Dark, dark, dark. The rectangle was dark. And, damn, not really a perfect rectangle. An oblong shape? Maybe. But inside the shape...dark, dark, and cold. Dark and sickening. Dark and...final. Something inside but not inside. Was this a box? A container. No. no. Smaller. And jostling. Moving?

"Something awful here. But inside? No. I don't know." Cole heard Rudyard's intake of breath. He was going to ask something. "Quiet, please," he said, making up for his previous rudeness.

The second paper was shoved aside. Another blank piece appeared in its place.

A circle, dark. A perceptual change and the circle turned into a cylinder. No, that wasn't right.

"A pipe. Wait, no. Not a pipe. Shit. A tunnel." Again aloud, funny how that happened. Rudyard kept his mouth shut. He seemed to learn quickly. "Yeah, a tunnel."

His hands drew a circle and shaded the interior with the side of the pencil point. When the point broke within seconds, Cole threw it down and grabbed a second one. The discarded pencil was scooped away.

Cole uncrossed his legs and sat up at the table. He kept the thick pad to lean on despite the uncluttered surface.

Next to the circle, he changed the angle. A three-dimensional drawing of a tunnel.

"This is a tunnel. Even though it looks like a pipe."

Not right, though. It should be vague because the tunnel wasn't solid. Shit. He pushed the piece of paper aside. Another appeared. This time he drew the 3-D image with dashes. "It's not solid. It's abstract. Spiritual."

What the hell did that mean?

Shadows moved within the pipe. Were these people?

He drew them as blobs within the tunnel.

"Shadows. They may be people."

A pause. It was like a filmstrip broke. An unfilled white light.

Then, of all the dumbest things. A bag of potato chips. Cole snickered. "Potato chips. That can't be right."

He didn't draw it.

Then canvas. A stone color, earthy. A shape, common enough, but he couldn't place it. A bag? He drew a bag. Gave it handles. Then it was lost.

Timothy Augustine. The quickest flash. Cole smiled again. "My nephew. Although he's really not my nephew." He didn't draw him, either. Timothy looked peeved.

Back to the tunnel. Except different. Flat flooring with sides and a roof. He was sucked into the opening. Swooshing down the length to an opening at the end. Trees, trees, and more trees. Farther on, a shelf. Flat and hard near the ground. A slab? Rectangle? Oblong? It's night, but he can see.

Then sucked backwards along the path. The effect was dizzying, almost nauseating.

He drew a house. It came out as a three-dimensional box—right next to the opening for the tunnel.

Then it was gone.

And he was done. Rudyard was right. He just knew.

He glanced up from the table. Rudyard sat with his elbows on his knees, his face intent on Cole. "How do you feel?"

"That was..." Cole searched for the word. "Intense." His right hand had cramped. A sheen of perspiration covered his face.

"I'll say." Rudyard leaned forward and turned off the recorder.

Multiple sheets of paper were piled at the left side of the desk. More than Cole remembered drawing on.

"How long did that take?"

Rudyard stared at him. "One hour."

"What? No way." It seemed like minutes. Fifteen tops.

"Yes, Cole. You provided us with, I think, sixteen drawings. We have our work cut out for us."

The previous Saturday, Cole had sat with Kenny at a booth with a half-filled pitcher of beer between them. The Allman Brothers sang "Ramblin' Man" from a jukebox. Filled with mostly college students, the bar had a typical bustling feel.

"Sounds like you kicked serious ass," Kenny said. "Major score for the psychic kid and behavioral sciences."

"Yeah, well."

"Jeez. You're too fucking humble, Cole. This is huge."

Yes, it was. Nailing Stanley Tompkins based entirely on a seeing incident. That was a stroke of luck.

"Did you actually see the bite in real time?" Kenny said.

"No, well, I'm not sure. I got the sense of teeth ripping something and then the image of front teeth pulling back skin from a hairy forearm." Cole sipped his beer.

"Now that's something you don't see every day. Though maybe you do. I can never be sure."

Cole grunted and then smiled. Kenny was one of a handful of people who didn't get uncomfortable dealing with Cole's extraordinary abilities.

"The thing was, since all the victims had been bound,

they would've been hard-pressed to fight back in any way. But when I saw the bite, I knew our guy had gotten sloppy. His arm just got too close to Wendy Fleming's mouth."

Wendy was the fifth strangled young woman to be found dumped in a random, off-the-beaten-path location in northern Virginia. All the victims had been securely bound and tied in a fastidious fashion. The knots were picture-perfect in their neatness. Forensic evidence was hard to come by as the bodies had been wiped clean.

Except in Wendy's case, there were remnants of blood in her mouth and in her lips—and more importantly, it wasn't hers. Then Cole saw why. She had bitten her killer on the arm.

The BSU already had a profile: a man who felt dominated by women. He was insecure and possibly browbeaten by female figures in his past. They also suspected a man in his late thirties or early forties—old enough to have a long track record of failure at social and romantic relationships, but still young enough and powerful enough to subdue a younger female victim.

"But what were the odds that you'd find him working in the very clinic you first investigated?"

"Not as remote as you'd think," Cole said. "I mean, three of the five had been patients at this very clinic. There was a chance that the suspect would have spotted them there. If he was familiar with the place, he'd likely go there for treatment of the bite."

Kenny shrugged. "You're impressive."

Two local cops accompanied Cole and his partner, Martin Westford, into the clinic to conduct interviews of staff. They weren't in the place twenty minutes when Martin said, "Well, fuck me blind" under his breath to Cole.

Cole turned in the direction that Martin was looking and saw the janitor, Stanley Tompkins, polishing the floor at the end of a hallway. A wide gauze bandage was wrapped around his forearm. He surrendered without a fuss.

"The one thing we had wrong was his age," Cole said. "He was pushing fifty. I would've thought ten years younger."

"Still." Kenny said. "They can't help but take you seriously now."

"They" were the powers that be in their unit. His fellow agents frequently kidded him about his visions and telepathic skills. A few still were leery of him. Colleagues who could deal with mass murderers were often spooked by his supernatural abilities.

"It's the occult angle," Kenny said more than once. "There's a lot of conservative Catholics in our respective professions. This freaks them out."

Their respective professions. Cole had been actively recruited by his mentor and current partner, Martin Westford, for the Behavioral Science Unit. Martin embraced and encouraged Cole's abilities as they prepared psychological profiles of suspects while hunting them.

Kenny Augustine, on the other hand, was in a different line of federal work. Ostensibly he was CIA. And yes, he did his share of desk work, combing through reams of evidence and data to search out whatever it was the CIA was looking for. But there was another side to his job. Kenny would disappear for days at a time on some covert mission that Cole would hear about thirdhand or never learn about at all. His friend could be deployed on a mission at a moment's notice and sent anywhere in the world. When he returned, it was without fanfare. Every now and again Kenny's absence would coincide with an uprising in the Middle East, the sudden death of a terrorist, or the dramatic rescue of a US national.

While Kenny never seemed to fear for his personal safety, these covert activities necessitated a sensitive juggling act between his personal and professional life. Kenny was a single father with a thirteen-year-old. Over the years, Cole and Cynthia had become surrogate parents for Timothy. Kenny could count on them to take the kid with little warning. They even had a spare bedroom dubbed "Timothy's room." But Kenny was blind to the emotional impact this had on his son.

"Where's Timothy tonight," Cole said. Cynthia was at the hospital, so Cole had all the time in the world to go out for a beer with his friend.

"Sleepover at his buddy's house. It's the kid's birthday, and there are six boys invited. Sounds like hell to me." Kenny finished his beer and grabbed the pitcher. He refilled Cole's glass and then his.

"How's he doing?"

"Fine. His grades are good. School's okay. You know. He's pissed at me, though."

"Because of Marilyn, I bet," Cole said.

Kenny had been seeing Marilyn for two months—a record for Kenny—before they broke up.

"He really liked her," Cole added.

"Yeah, but I told him I don't decide who I sleep with based on my son's opinion."

"Kenny, jeez."

"I know. Thoughtless. He told me to fuck off and stormed into his room. We made up later. Still, he's been moping a lot."

Awareness of other people's emotions—or his own—wasn't a strong suit of Kenny's. Cole worried about him, partially due to his tendency not to worry about himself. And there was something going on in his relationship with his son. Kenny was usually an expert at keeping the focus off his work and personal life when they got together socially, so the fact that he'd even mentioned their fight was interesting.

Cole wondered if the likely onset of puberty was making Timothy moody. Unlike his dad, he wore his emotions on his sleeve. The regular upheavals of his life that resulted from Kenny's work didn't help things either.

"Not to change the subject or anything, but when do you go for your mind-reading test?"

"Ugh. Wednesday, I think. Maybe Thursday. God, I can't believe they're making me do this. And it's not a mind-reading test."

"Fortune-telling test?"

Cole laughed softly. "Yeah, make fun, go ahead. It's some assessment of telepathy. Something *your* bosses are up to."

Dusk was settling in as Cole turned left onto the street where he and Cynthia rented their house. His thoughts wandered mindlessly until he jerked to attention at the abrupt appearance of a figure standing at the edge of the road. A young guy with slicked-back hair and a scruffy beard vanished as quickly as he'd materialized. Cole scanned his rearview mirror, looking for a trace of the guy, but saw nobody.

"Goddammit."

The man had looked solid, but he blinked out so quickly that Cole couldn't be one hundred percent positive. The supernatural episodes he experienced typically lasted longer. But it was a good example of how his telepathy skills operated. A spontaneous and unpredictable occurrence. Not like the controlled event Rudyard had tried to capture.

A ghostly entity or not, the whole thing was unnerving in a way he couldn't describe. The figure's dark hair, beard, and clothes naturally meshed with the increasing darkness of evening.

Cole pulled into his driveway. When his headlights swept across the front porch, Cole wasn't surprised by who he saw there. His ruminations about Kenny and Timothy on the way home hadn't been random free associations. He should've realized that.

Timothy sat bundled in a jacket, looking glum. His duffel bag, constructed of an earthy stone-colored canvas, sat at his side. An empty bag of potato chips lay between his feet. His bike was probably parked around back.

"Aw, shoot, Timothy. I've been in Charlottesville all day. Did your dad have to go out of town?" Cole walked to the front door, fumbling with his keys. Glancing in both directions to check on his phantom from moments ago, he stooped to pick up Timothy's bag. Timothy beat him to the punch and swiped it right out of his hand, then bent over to pick up the chips.

"Yeah. It was all of a sudden." Timothy brushed past him into the house after Cole unlocked the door. He wore a soccer uniform under his jacket.

"Did you have a game?"

Timothy paused in the living room. His duffel bag plopped to the floor. Without facing Cole, he nodded.

"How'd you do?"

"We won." A shaky whisper.

Cole shut the door behind him. "Did you walk here?"

Another shake of the head.

"Did you wait long?"

"Like forever."

Cole sighed. "C'mere."

A shake of the head.

"Come on."

Timothy turned but kept his head down. He wasn't crying, but he was close. Cole hugged him. He stood unresponsive for a moment and then returned the embrace.

"Are you pissed at me or your dad?"

A sniffle. "I'm pissed at Dad. Everybody else had a parent there."

"Phew. Thank God."

"And I'm pissed at you. Just because." He pulled away. Red-rimmed eyes belied his faint smile.

"Where'd he go?"

"Europe. Here. Read." Timothy passed him a note that he must've shoved in his pocket. It was bent around the edges and been folded and unfolded numerous times.

Cole, sorry about the lack of notice. This came up suddenly and we had just ninety minutes to get ready. Left a message at your office and I hope to get this to T. so he can hand deliver. Off to Europe to help save the world. It'll be a few days. You guys are the greatest. My love to C.

"Europe, huh? That could mean anywhere, though."

"I know. I tried to send you the message telepathically, but I guess you didn't get it." Timothy crunched up the chip bag in his left hand and grasped the handles of his duffel bag.

Actually, he probably had.

"Oh well," Cole said. "I'm starving. I don't know about you."

"Me too." Timothy's face transformed from glum to

beaming in the blink of an eye. This was the joyous face Cole had been used to seeing over the past seven years.

"You know where to put your bag. There's no food here, so we've got to go out. Go wash up and let's hit the road."

"Yay! Let's do Pizza Rut." Timothy ran from the living room to the back bedroom that was his when he stayed over.

"Pizza Hut it is," Cole called after the retreating figure, smiling at Timothy and Kenny's name for the place.

Two pepperoni pizzas with a couple of uneaten slices to bring home and a pitcher of Coke later, both settled back in satiated bliss. Timothy added an extended belch to cap things off.

"What makes Dad do what he does?"

"What? You mean being a federal agent?"

"That, yeah, but with all the extra danger and stuff."

This discussion could turn into a minefield. "I can tell you it's not all that dramatic all the time. Not a James Bond movie. No wall-to-wall action or hot chicks in bikinis hanging on your arm. A lot of time, your dad is sitting in an office filling out government forms or listening to long-winded bosses and politicians."

"C'mon, Uncle Cole. You're stalling."

Cole wiped his lips with a crumpled napkin, then tossed it on the table. "I am not."

Timothy glared at him through slit eyes.

Cole smiled at the expression. "Okay. You might as well ask me what makes your father tick. Your dad is fearless. And when you need someone like that on your side, he's the best choice. He also has little tolerance for authoritarian bullies and human monsters. He'll do anything to save anyone from them."

Timothy looked to the ceiling in reflection. "I guess. That's what he does when he disappears like this."

"That or something like it. It's usually in the best interest of our entire country."

"He's killed people." This wasn't a question.

Cole peered intently at Timothy. "I've killed people. We were both in combat. It happens."

"Yeah. You have nightmares, though. Dad doesn't."

"How do you know? Especially about me?"

Timothy smirked. "I know. I keep my ears open."

"What's going on with these questions?"

"Is dad a psychopath?"

"What?" Cole said. "Where did this come from?"

"Andy Schoemaker. He said his dad said that these secret ops guys are all psychopaths because they can kill without feeling guilty. That's why they're hired for the job."

"That's crazy. Andy Schoemaker's dad doesn't know what he's talking about."

The thing about Kenny Augustine was that he did have many of those characteristics. Kenny thrived on chaos and danger. And he'd killed when the situation demanded it.

Timothy shrugged, but he was clearly struggling.

"Listen, your father is the bravest person I know. He's taken dramatic action to save the lives of people, me included. He has to think clearly and decisively, often within seconds. But he also loves you very much, and he loves his friends. Most psychopaths don't do that."

Timothy nodded in reply. The issue was still a live one, though—not likely to die anytime soon.

The phone rang just when Cole was about to hit the sack.

"Sorry about the lateness. I haven't had a moment to myself. There was a multicar accident on the highway. Lots of injuries," Cynthia said softly into his ear. Currently on the trauma rotation at the hospital, she must've been calling from the emergency room. The residents went torturously long hours without sleep, and she'd be exhausted when she no longer was on call. Such was the life of a brand-new doctor.

"Sorry, hon. Sounds awful."

"At the moment, maybe. But in the long run...well, it's what I went to medical school for. Anyway, by now you know that Timothy is staying with us for the foreseeable future."

"You heard," Cole said.

"Yeah, Kenny left a message for me here after he couldn't reach you. How's our boy?"

"A little grumpy when I pulled up. He'd been waiting awhile. He was upset that no one was at his game."

"Poor guy. You're okay with me missing in action?"

Cole heard shuffling in the background and figured Cynthia was making notes in patient files. "Yeah, he got back on track when we went out for pizza. He took a shower and went to bed about twenty minutes ago."

More voices in the background. Cynthia talked to someone while her hand partially covered the phone. "Sorry. There's evidently an ambulance coming in. You're good to do this, Cole."

"Well, so are you. People did it for me when I was a kid."

"Yes, and you're doing it for others. I've got to run. I just wanted to hear your voice. I love you."

"I love you, too," Cole said to a disconnected line.

2

A Vampire Did It

October 1977

"ABOUT TIME," MARTIN SAID.

"Yeah. Sorry. Kenny Augustine went out of town."

Martin looked at him blankly.

"His son stays with us when he leaves. I had to make breakfast and get him ready for school. Not my usual morning routine." Cole slipped into his office.

Their unit's suite was comprised of compact rooms along the perimeter of a large open area with a conference table in the center. An interior space with no windows meant no natural light, and the entire setting had a dusty, gritty feel.

Cole's office was the same size as the other five but more cramped. He'd never thought himself as a pack rat, but it looked like he'd turned into one. He was slow to toss things in the garbage.

Martin remained seated at the conference table with multiple crime folders spread along the table, accompanied by official-looking reports. Cole didn't check these out on his way past, but figured he'd be called in soon.

"Cole? Drop your stuff and take a seat out here." Martin's voice carried easily into the office.

That took no time at all.

He riffled through a short stack of pink message slips across his cluttered desk. Nothing urgent, so he returned to the conference area. Martin was still shuffling the reports and looking at one in particular. The photos displayed a corpse partially covered with leaves and badly smudged. The smudges were likely blood smears.

Cole pulled out a chair opposite his partner.

"What happens when you go out of town and your girlfriend is stuck at the hospital?" Martin gently closed the folder on the report.

"You mean when Kenny needs us to watch Timothy? We normally have a little time to sort it out. Sometimes Cynthia's mom comes up, or more likely Flo. We work around it."

"Good." Martin said. He slipped a hand inside the folder nearby, pulled out two crime-scene photos, and handed the top one to Cole. "What do you make of this?"

A young woman lay on a pile of leaves among small bushes. Her clothing was rumpled but not removed. Bruising and broken skin raggedly crossed her neck, and a finger from her right hand was missing. Her ungainly position suggested she'd been dumped there carelessly. She was in her late teens or early twenties.

"And this." Martin handed over the second photo.

Another young woman discarded among some underbrush. At the edge of the photo was a slice of what looked like blacktop. Like the first woman, her throat was slashed and there were other marks on her neck. Cole looked closely at the picture and then examined the picture of the first young woman. Something with the necks. He examined the photo of the second young woman again.

"My initial thought was they had their throats cut. I mean, they did, but there's something more," Cole said. "They've been…"

"Go on."

"Jesus. Bitten. They've been bitten."

"Yeah, that's what it looks like. The girl in your right hand is Patricia Loots, seventeen, found near Michie Tavern where she worked as a waitress. She was from Charlottesville and a senior in high school."

Cole gazed deeply at Patricia's photo. Something was off.

"Shit. Her hand has been hacked off. And the other victim—"

"Is missing part a finger."

"Trophies?"

"That'd be my guess," Martin said. "The other girl is Nadine Rudy, nineteen, a sophomore at UVA. She was found two weeks ago off a trail in Pen Park. The locals have no idea yet who killed her or why."

"Forensics?"

"Nothing much. No fingerprints, so the killer likely wore gloves. No traces of semen on either victim. In the case of Nadine, a recent rain likely washed some things away. Patricia was found Labor Day weekend. It rained then too, if you recall. The weather worked against local law enforcement when it came to clues." Martin gathered the photos back into the folder. "Another victim was found yesterday morning outside Charlottesville. Same bite marks on the neck from what we can see."

"From what you can see?"

"Yeah. This time the trophy was the head."

"Shit."

"We've been asked to consult. So we're taking a ride."

Cole slumped in his seat. "Back to Charlottesville?"

"Back to Charlottesville."

⚲

"I feel like I'm being made into a parlor trick," Cole said, looking out his passenger-side window.

"A parlor trick." Martin kept his eyes on the road. The traffic wasn't bad midmorning. Puffy, nonthreatening clouds drifted through the sky, reducing the glare.

"You understand what I can and can't do. I don't have regular visions or anything like that. The information is incomplete and irregular—when I get it at all."

Martin nodded. "Sometimes your images seem like nothing more than hunches."

"I think that's why I was aggravated some yesterday. They're looking for me to perform on the spot every time. It won't happen. And get this, it's like they want me to give precise information from distinct locations." Cole trailed off and watched the scenery rush by.

"Yet you still gave them a lot of information that you weren't even conscious of. According to you."

"Yeah. That kind of freaked me out. The only accurate thing was seeing Timothy, though. The other pictures were pretty useless, I would think. Besides, I can't draw for shit."

Martin chuckled. "Well, just keep doing your job and everything will play out like it's supposed to."

"What does *that* mean?"

"I have no idea. It just sounded good."

When at a crime scene, Cole steeled himself to see or hear something paranormal. A ghost, disembodied voices, a sense of doom—all had made appearances in the past. He couldn't rely on it, though.

Martin was a good fit as a partner and teacher, basically a no-drama investigator. Whatever clues came in, he rolled with them. When one of Cole's apparitions provided information, he listened to Cole and considered it another piece of forensic data. Cole liked the arrangement. He never felt pressure to see something otherworldly. He was a valued team member with or without the psychic contributions.

"The body was found in a field just outside Fort Concord Military Academy," Martin said as they got closer to the destination. "A group of students from the academy stumbled on it. They were out jogging. It was early."

"So, no Charlottesville."

"Not the city proper. At least for now."

"What's this military academy?"

"One of those hundred-year-old ultra-privileged boarding schools where the rich send their teenagers. They're in a bit of a huff because the victim's one of their kids."

Cole scanned the landscape in front of him but couldn't see the campus. "I can see how this wouldn't look good from a marketing standpoint."

"Definitely not. Safe to say this won't make it into the brochure." Martin made a right turn onto a road that was well hidden among the trees.

"You seem to know the way."

"I almost went to school here. My father threatened me with it if I didn't get my shit together," Martin said.

"No kidding? What happened?"

"I got my shit together. My father's word was written in stone. If he said it, he'd do it. I ended up going to a private school near home. I wasn't shipped away. Ah, here we go."

A drive adorned with boxwood hedges bisected a perfectly constructed rock wall. A sign the color of raspberries, bordered with gold trim, stood parallel to the drive on the right side. The name of the school was painted with the same gold.

"The sign is…majestic," Cole said. "Impressive."

"Yes, they spare no expense."

Gathered around this opening were multiple cars and vans with the logos of network news stations. Photographers inched toward the car and snapped photos. Reporters yelled questions. Martin slowed to a crawl until the local rent-a-cops gathered their wits and pushed back the media. One photographer fired away with his camera and likely scored a close-up of Cole's face. The press pass hanging around his neck read *Richmond Times-Dispatch*.

Cole thought of his brother, Josiah, for a second before returning his attention to his immediate surroundings.

The drive to the main campus took another two minutes. Brick and stone buildings, complete with columns and gargoyles, appeared once they cleared the oak trees that bordered the driveway. A domed structure sat dead center—that had to be the administration building.

"This is a high school?"

"And junior high. Grades seven through twelve," Martin said. "We need to check in at the main office. The chief of staff, which I guess is the principal, is a Colonel Lee." He parked in a designated visitor space adjacent to the domed structure. "Colonel Robert Lee."

Cole smiled. "Tell me his middle initial isn't *E*."

"I didn't ask. Don't you, either."

The colonel must've been watching for their arrival. He appeared at the front door and walked down the two granite steps to meet them.

"Colonel Lee?" Martin strode forward with his chest puffed out.

Cole couldn't help smiling. Martin was trying to match Lee's military demeanor. His experiences in Nam and his covert work with the CIA during that time had provided him with genuine credibility.

"Yessir." Lee shook Martin's hand.

"I'm Special Agent Westford, and this is Special Agent Nightshade. We're from the FBI. We've been asked to assist the local authorities in the investigation of the death of one of your cadets."

Cole shook hands with the colonel and noticed him wince at "one of your cadets."

"Yes, yes. I understand. Although I do believe the coroner has taken the body into town."

Cole and Martin looked at the man.

"You're certainly welcome to look around," the colonel added quickly. "This has been a most unfortunate day. This type of thing never happens here. One of our boys…"

"I understand. It's tragic." Martin maintained a somber countenance. "This must be like a nightmare for you and your staff."

"And the kids," Cole said.

"Of course, your students too."

Lee nodded once. "Frankly, we were not prepared for something like this."

"No one ever is." Cole felt the need to normalize the man's reaction.

"True." Lee pursed his lips and looked down for a second. "We educate boys to become young men with the highest moral and ethical qualities. They are our future elected leaders, military officers, CEOs of America's great industrial complexes and financial institutions. Our alumni have graced the halls of power everywhere in our great nation. Then an event like this comes along to threaten our security—our mission." Lee scanned the grounds as if searching for assassins. "The presence of the media has made the situation even more complex. The story is out, and parents have been calling all day."

Martin glanced toward the direction of the front gate. "At least they've been herded to the entrance."

"Well, now they have. Before we had some photographers snooping around the grounds. The older boys corralled them, and with the help of the police, escorted them off the campus. They'll probably be a little sore tomorrow if they aren't already."

They divided their duties, with Cole examining the crime scene while Martin went to interview the students who found the body. Colonel Lee offered to have a staff member accompany Cole to the site, but he declined.

"I'd like to get my own perspective of the location if you don't mind." With directions from Lee and the specific path the boys took on their run, Cole departed, leaving Martin to ask Lee about the dorms.

Cole skirted the administration building and found himself on the north quad. To his immediate left, a paved sidewalk led to buildings that looked like they belonged on a college campus. Some had vines climbing the wall, others had ornate columns buttressing grand entrances. These had to contain faculty offices and classrooms. At the end of the path sat a huge athletic center. To the right were two rectangular saltbox structures common in Virginia. Both were dorms, with one called Primrose Hall—no doubt named after a benefactor. "Primrose" didn't exactly connote tough military standards.

It was Primrose where the murdered youth had lived and from which the joggers emerged this morning.

Cole found the side door where the boys exited and followed their route as they had reported it. More buildings, which Cole barely noticed. He stopped when he reached the playing fields. Cole had never seen anything like them at a high school. A football field complete with bleachers and a running track. A baseball diamond beyond that. On the other side lay a soccer field, or maybe a lacrosse or rugby field. The athletic building probably contained the basketball court, and God only knew where the pool was. There had to be one.

Athletics were a priority, clearly. Imagine the poor kid who wasn't particularly gifted in sports. Then again, that kid probably didn't go to school here.

Several boys were exercising, running, throwing footballs, or kicking soccer balls. Cole threaded a needle among the games while advancing to another rock wall fifty or so yards away. Beyond that were wooded lands ascending a mountain. Students glanced in his direction as he passed, whispering to one another. He overheard "Cop," quickly followed by "No, a fed."

A group of younger boys around Timothy's age played touch football on a smaller strip of grass.

"Simon, c'mon, man, get your ass in the game."

Cole looked in their direction and saw Simon staring at him. He was a gawky kid, all elbows and knees beneath his sweats. His eyes shifted from side to side, and he took a hesitant step forward. His Adam's apple bobbed up and down with an involuntary swallow. Cole could've sworn he hear the gulp.

"Simon, jeez."

Simon shifted his feet and ran toward his group.

The kid probably wanted to say something to Cole. Well, he'd be around for a while.

Cole approached the rock wall. So did a guy around Cole's age dressed in a military outfit generic enough not to fit any of the US armed forces.

"Sorry sir, that area's off limits." The staff member, probably an instructor, was barrel-chested, his thick neck nearly bursting out of his tightly buttoned collared shirt. As he came closer, Cole saw that his face was red and he was licking his lips.

"It's okay." Cole held up his FBI identification.

"Oh." He sounded disappointed.

"Have you been keeping the kids away?"

"Yeah, we've been taking shifts. They were sneaking down to look even though they'd been instructed to stay away. Then the fucking reporters started to swarm."

"Good. Smart move to keep them out." The crime scene had likely been contaminated, though. "Do you know if anybody touched anything?"

"Well, one kid from the first group leapt over the wall and nearly landed on the body. Shocked the hell out of him. Beyond that, I don't know. To be honest, I can't imagine people not touching. Not the body, I mean. The wall."

Cole nodded. "Do I need to climb over or is there an opening somewhere?" The wall wasn't too high, maybe five feet, but not easy to clear in a jacket and tie.

"There's a gate over here. About twenty yards down."

It was in plain view. Cole had just missed it. On his way around, he asked the teacher, "Did you know the victim?"

"Zachary? No, not too well. I never had him in class. He

could be a handful. High-spirited, questioned authority, tried
to push against the rules."

In a place like this, that could make him a pain in the ass.

"Was he liked by the others?"

"Yeah. I'd say so. I mean, he wasn't the kind of kid to be
on anybody's hit list. More of a clown than anything."

Zachary Tillman's body had been found on the ground
along the wall. He was positioned so that his head—if it hadn't
been severed—would've faced the woods. The remnants of a
human bite extended below the wound on his neck. He wore
a pair of gym shorts. A T-shirt had been tossed aside.

The area was roped off with crime-scene tape. The body
was long gone, of course, but dark smudges and streaks
weighed down the grass. Dried blood. A smear also streaked
along the wall.

"Do you need me for anything more? Can I help at all?"

"No," Cole said to the teacher. "Right now, I'm just
getting the lay of the land. See if anything strikes me. You can
go back to doing whatever you need to do."

The teacher left and returned to the athletic fields.

Beyond the rock wall, the ground sloped downward a
quick five feet and then leveled out. A worn footpath, increasingly devoid of grass, led from Cole's location to the edge
of trees that marked the beginning of heavily shaded woods.
The footpath continued into the dense tree growth. Students
obviously used it a lot.

The depth of the woods was unclear from Cole's vantage
point. The base of the mountain was somewhere in here, but
so were suburban neighborhoods that made up part of the
Charlottesville area. Cole walked to the start of the path by
the edge of the trees. He turned to look at the campus. From
this angle, the only part of the school visible was the upper

floor of the Primrose dorm. The rock wall extended quite a distance in both directions and likely marked the boundary of the campus. The victim's body had been slumped behind the wall in such a way that it wouldn't have been visible from the campus proper. Someone would have to come up right on top of him, which the joggers eventually did.

"Psst."

Cole froze and listened.

"Psst."

Okay, he did hear that. Turning slowly, he scanned in the direction he thought the voice was coming from. "I hear you."

"Over here." A faint whisper.

Cole stared and finally saw a head sticking above some bushes. Eyes darted back and forth.

"You can come out. It's just the two of us." Cole stepped carefully over the path, not wanting to frighten the kid even more.

The bushes rustled and a youth in sweats badly in need of washing emerged.

"Simon." Cole wasn't surprised, given how the kid had watched his advance through the athletic fields.

"How'd you know my name?" Simon wiped his brow. His hand was shaking noticeably.

"I heard one of your teammates call you up there." Cole motioned toward the fields with his head.

Simon blinked and let out a breath in relief. "Oh, yeah."

Cole waited a few seconds for Simon to talk. The kid wiped his forehead again, sniffed, and scratched his head

After a few false starts, Simon said, "Are you a cop?"

"FBI."

"Oh. Cool. Um…" Simon weaved and tilted his head in all directions as he searched the immediate area.

"I get the feeling you want to talk to me."

"Um..."

"Did you see something?"

"Uh-huh. I think I saw what killed him." Simon looked at the ground.

"You mean who killed him."

"No. I mean *what*. It was a vampire."

"A vampire." Cole's heart sank.

"Look. It sounds stupid, I know. But I saw it." The kid was near tears.

"Hey, it's okay. I've seen a lot of strange things. Tell me what you saw. Start from the beginning."

Simon exhaled loudly. "Okay. I like to sneak out at night. I mean, lots of guys do it, not just me. But me, I like to be alone. Just to get away. You know?"

Cole nodded.

"I like to explore. Things look different at night. I kinda make believe I'm like a spy or something." He looked at Cole. "Does that sound weird?"

"Not at all."

"So, okay. Snooping around the grounds is fun, but so's going into the woods here. I have a small flashlight, ya see? You gotta watch out for the other guys, though. The older ones, I mean. They sometimes come out here to get drunk or high. Or meet up with girls they know from town."

"Is it against the rules to sneak out?"

"Yeah. But that doesn't stop kids from doing it. And like I said, it's mostly the older guys. They don't want you sneaking up on them. I would never squeal on them, but still. There're stories, too, about some girls who like to hang out in the woods, and if you meet up with them, one of them will give you, um, you know, a blowjob."

Cole couldn't help smiling. "You know that's not true."

Simon looked downcast. "Yeah, I kinda figured."

"What about what you saw last night?"

"Yeah, um, I had just snuck out. I couldn't sleep. I think because I was worrying about my math test this morning. So I got dressed and snuck out the side door. They're never locked. I was just gonna walk along the edge of the fields, y'know? At the last minute, I decided to cut through the wall and take a walk in the woods. The moon was out, and it was kinda light. I had to be careful."

Simon paused long enough to scan the area again. Satisfied that no danger lurked, he continued.

"Anyway, I'm coming closer, and all of a sudden it's just standing there."

"The vampire?"

A vigorous nod. "Yes."

"What makes you think..."

"That it was a vampire? He was in black. Black pants or dark pants. I think they were sweats, maybe. He didn't have a shirt on. But his chest was covered in blood. So was his mouth. It was dripping off his chin."

"How do you know it was blood?"

"What else could it be? The blood was, like, shiny black in the moonlight. And with what happened to Zachary..."

"Did you see Zachary?"

"No. I mean, I didn't notice. My eyes were glued on the vampire."

Cole thought for a second. "Did you recognize the vampire?"

"No. I'd never seen him before."

"Could it be a student here? Or someone who used to be here?"

"His hair was too long for him to be here now. It was like below his ears. But I'm new—just in seventh grade—so I don't know anybody who left or graduated."

"Could it have been a girl?"

"No way. He didn't have a shirt on. There weren't any, you know, tits."

"Was he old? Young?"

"Young. Maybe twenty, tops. Looked like he coulda been in college."

Cole jotted down notes in a small notebook. Simon inched closer to see what he was writing. Cole leaned forward so Simon could see for himself. He didn't want to appear secretive. "Can you describe what he looked like?"

The kid scrunched his face. "Not really. I mean, he had long hair that was dark. Brown or black. His mouth was smeared with blood. He growled when he saw me. Scared the shit outta me. I took off."

"Did he chase you?"

"I thought at first he was. Then I looked back and he wasn't there. When I woke up this morning, I thought maybe that I had dreamt the whole thing. Then I heard about Zachary."

Cole sighed. "Did you tell the police this?"

Simon shook his head. "I got the feeling we should keep our mouths shut. In assembly this morning, Colonel Lee asked the whole school if we saw anything. Teachers were watching us like hawks. Who'd volunteer under those conditions?"

"You're very observant."

"Yeah, I am. You'd be surprised what you can find out just by keeping your eyes open. Most kids don't realize that."

"Did you know Zachary at all?"

"Not really. He lived in my dorm and all. But…"

Cole peered at him. "But what?"

"Um. Shoot. Okay, here goes. I think he liked boys."

"You mean he was gay?"

Simon looked skyward. "I mean I saw him kissing a guy once."

"What was this guy's name?"

Simon shuffled on his feet. "Um. Jamie Yokum. He's a senior too."

Cole made a note. "Anything else? Zachary didn't, like, proposition you or anything."

"No, man. Nothing like that."

Cole asked for Simon's full name. "I may have to contact you again. Or the police might. They may send over a sketch artist to draw the person you saw."

"The vampire, you mean?"

"Yeah, him."

Simon's shoulders sunk. "I sorta figured that might happen. But I guess it's my duty to report this."

"Yes, it was. Good man."

After Simon scooted off, Cole moved at a strolling pace down the path. The ground was dry and strewn with autumn leaves. If there were footprints, and Cole couldn't see any, they'd be well disguised by the countless other feet that used the path. If Simon and the victim made use of it, he could bet that just about every other kid in the school did the same.

It didn't take long to find evidence of frequent use. Remnants of cigarette butts considerably older than the murder lay scattered under a lower branch of a bush already blazing red. After about seventy-five yards, a sign pointing left indicated the direction of the "Horizon Hiking Trail up Mt Concord (elevation 2400 feet)." Cole took the path that veered right. He wasn't dressed for a mountain hike. Twenty-five yards later, the trees thinned out and he stopped near a country road. No traffic in either direction, but he saw two houses on the opposite side of the road, less than a quarter mile from his position. A glance told Cole that additional homes stood on a turnoff from the country road and extended around a bend.

So, despite the isolated feel of the school, there were neighborhoods close by as Cole had expected.

Cole returned the way he came. Three-quarters of the way, he noticed a scuff mark on the trunk of a bur oak tree. He moved closer. A small section of bark had been stripped away. It looked like someone had scraped his fingers or the tip of a shoe across the ridges and furrows and pulled or kicked away the bark.

A person trying to hoist himself up the tree could've done this. Maybe trying to get a foothold?

Cole scanned upwards.

Damn. This oak was tall, possibly sixty feet.

A higher vantage point might allow a perfect view of approaching visitors.

Cole removed his jacket and folded it over a bush. It was relatively new. Cynthia would be pissed if he wrecked it.

The ascent was not easy. Cole hadn't climbed a tree in years, plus he was in street shoes. He'd managed to pull his shirt out of his pants, and his tie was a nuisance. When he reached thirty feet, he heard two tearing sounds and had no idea what articles of clothing had ripped. Swearing, he was ready to call it quits when a clearing in the branches made him start.

He had an unobstructed view of the campus grounds, starting with the athletic fields and the school's buildings beyond. The direct path from the dorm to the fields to the crime scene lay right before him.

So, our guy could stay up here and clearly see who was coming and going.

Cole looked around his perch. Nothing indicating the presence of another individual. Then again, Cole wasn't the tracking type. He climbed up another series of branches and found a hefty branch where he could rest his butt.

On the trunk right before his eyes: *Dash lives.*

The words had been chiseled into the tree.

Who the hell is Dash?

A young man's face burst into his field of vision. Black hair slicked back and an unkept spotty beard. Red-rimmed eyes framed in a deathly pallor. His mouth sprang open with a low growl and spewed a rank spray on Cole's face. At the same instant, a searing pain flared deep in Cole's neck.

The combined impact jolted Cole, and his hands and feet jerked awkwardly in response. Branches wacked his back and chest as he tumbled, further yanking his shirt out of his waist. The face pursued him, leering. The remnants of a small broken branch caught the bare skin above Cole's beltline and tore his skin like a protruding nail.

One flailing arm caught a large passing branch. It was pure luck, but Cole stopped his fall.

"Shit. Fuck, Fuck." The sensation felt like a knife slicing his back. He'd also knocked his forehead on something on the way down, and he'd pulled something in his groin. "God-dammit."

The athletic fields, about forty yards away, were empty. Naturally. When he could've used some assistance, there was no one to be found.

A cautious head turn showed he'd almost fallen past all

the tree branches. Another five feet or so and he would've cleared them and crashed directly to the rocky soil. That would've put a real damper on things.

His dress shirt had pushed up nearly to his armpits. Blood dripped down his hip. The waistband of his pants was absorbing copious amounts of it.

"Shit." He carefully lowered himself to the ground. The pull in his groin was painful. Well, damn, everything was painful. He lowered his shirt and tried to look dignified for his walk back to the administration building. Cole grabbed his jacket, still hung safely on the bush, and limped his way to find Martin. His shirt continued to soak up the blood on his back.

"So, while you were lounging, I did some extra digging," Martin said as he pulled out of the emergency room parking lot.

"Shit. I still cannot believe it. Over two fucking hours." Cole leaned back in the seat with the back of his head against the headrest.

"More like two and a half, but who's counting."

Cole's right hip and his back in the kidney area were still numb, but the anesthetic would be wearing off soon. He already had a sense of pulling where the six stitches had gone in. His bandaged temple had also started to throb. He hadn't even noticed the bleeding from that cut until he approached the door of the administration building.

A secretary was the first to notice him. She let out a squeal that jolted everyone in the vicinity of the main entrance. Colonel Lee rocketed from his office, followed by a perplexed Martin—who immediately took control, much to Lee's annoyance. They entered the nurse's office within seconds.

"Could you leave us for a moment?" Martin asked the nurse.

She looked like she was ready to argue, but Martin said, "FBI business."

Cole looked somber and added a polite "Please," and she relented.

"What the hell?" Martin hissed.

"I fell out of a fucking tree. Just shut up for a second. There's a witness, and the victim may have been a gay kid."

"Well, who did it?"

"A vampire."

"Oh, Jesus." Martin closed his eyes and sighed. "What did you find out?"

"Not that much, for sure."

Cole filled Martin in on the details and arranged for a local cop still on the grounds to take him to the hospital.

"Anyway, after you were whisked away, I had a heart-to-heart with Robert E. Lee. I told him he cannot discourage the kids to talk to the law. I had no idea if he'd done that, but Simon hinted at it and so did some of the boys who found the victim. He started in on some bullshit about having to weigh the legal procedures and protecting the reputation of the school and, get this, the well-being of the students."

"God. This is a military school."

"I know. So, I called the detective from Charlottesville PD who led on the case, told him what we found, and he high-tailed it out to the school. He was pissed and let the colonel know that they'd be reinterviewing every kid individually."

"What about that kid, Yokum? You didn't single him out in front of everybody, did you?"

"No, what do you take me for? But I started with him, and he swore up and down that that'd been the one and only time he messed around with Zachary. In fact, he implied that Zachary came on to him and he was caught off guard. I tell you, that kid was about to shit his pants. He started crying and begging me not to tell anybody. His father would kill him and so on. I don't see him as our perpetrator. God help me if I'm wrong and I held back the evidence."

Cole shifted his back slightly. Some breakthrough stinging was making itself known. "The sex of the victim doesn't make sense. The previous two were female."

"If this is the same guy."

"If it's the same guy, sure. But how many killers who cut their victims' throats, bite their necks, and take a body part are there in Charlottesville, do you think?"

Martin grunted. "So, you're going with the vampire theory."

Cole paused. "God, I don't know what I'm saying. I've got to review those files again."

"My God, Cole!" Cynthia gaped at him when he entered the kitchen.

Timothy stopped sprinkling shredded mozzarella cheese on the lasagna the two of them had been preparing for dinner. "Whoa, what happened?"

Cynthia quickly rinsed her hands at the sink and approached, scrutinizing him from head to toe. "Seriously, are you okay?"

Cole hung the car keys on a small pegboard by the door. Removing his jacket made him wince. He also had forgotten how bloodstained his shirt was. "It's not as bad as it looks."

"God, you're always getting hurt." Cynthia shook her head and gently led him into the light.

For his part, Timothy remained frozen with the cheese still clasped in his hand.

"Timothy, finish sprinkling that cheese, or dinner will never get in the oven," Cynthia said.

"But man, what happened?"

Cole sighed. "Basically, I fell out of a tree in Charlottesville."

"I suppose there's a story here," Cynthia said. "But there's no way we're going to eat looking at you with dried bloodstains."

"Yeah we can." Timothy completed the cheese and placed the lasagna in the oven.

"No way. We've got an hour for this to cook. Cole, get cleaned up, and then you, buddy, need to do the same."

Like yesterday, Timothy hadn't changed out of his soccer practice clothes.

"Oh, man. Shoot."

As instructed, Cole showered first. While Timothy was doing the same, Cole gave Cynthia a brief overview. This included the bearded young man who'd startled him out of the tree.

"When you tell the story, you may want to leave out the details of the kid who was killed. Might freak Timothy out."

"I don't know," Cole said. "He's got a dad with a secret job. Who knows how his mind operates?"

"That's my point. He's aware enough to see the risks with Kenny's departures. And sensitive enough to take stories of death personally. I bet that's part of the reason he's been angry at his father lately."

Her perspective was convincing. Cole kept the emphasis on climbing the tree and his subsequent fall—blaming it on the stupid street shoes.

"Yeah, really. Stupid, Uncle Cole. You need sneakers to do that."

The label "uncle" was inconsistently applied. Cole couldn't figure out why Timothy used it when he did. He marveled at hearing it, though. There was always a little tug of emotion.

"So, a kid was killed?"

"Yes, and it's really sad. We're trying to figure out why."

"You will." Timothy helped himself to another piece of lasagna. "Oh, you may not want to hear this."

Cole and Cynthia's eyes met. She shrugged.

"Oh no. Why not?"

"Well, if Dad's not home by the weekend, I got a soccer match."

"That's not bad. I'll come if I can." Cole was puzzled.

"Um, but...it's in Charlottesville."

Cole groaned. "Oh, man."

Timothy seemed like he didn't know whether to smile or be concerned.

"It should be okay," Cynthia said. "Soccer fields are flat. No trees. And he won't have very far to fall."

Timothy grinned widely.

Hours later, in bed, Cole turned to face Cynthia. He could tell she was still awake by her breathing. "Sorry I wasn't home when you got here."

Cynthia turned toward him in the darkness. "I wasn't expecting to prepare dinner. Or babysit a junior high kid. It worked out, though. He was helpful and didn't complain."

"Still, I should've—"

"Yeah, you should've. But what? I don't know. It's this crazy life we lead. I'm exhausted. You are too. But you handle it better than me."

"That's not true."

"It is, Cole. I can't talk about it now. I need some sleep. I've only got a few hours."

He kissed her cheek and she was asleep a second later.

3

Retrocognition Rumblings

October 1977

THE MORNING ALARM ROCKED COLE into startled wakefulness. His heart rate must've skyrocketed to twice its resting level. Cole nearly threw the alarm to the floor to shut the damn thing off.

Sitting on the edge of the bed, Cole breathed deeply to reduce the pounding in his chest. He'd awakened earlier when Cynthia got out of bed, turning off her alarm before the scheduled time, to begin her day at the hospital. He also remembered her soft kiss and whispered "goodbye" thirty minutes later.

The intervening time was chock full of the damnedest dream—or dreams, Cole couldn't tell.

Pains had alternated in his neck and entire GI tract—even his butt—and on one level he thought maybe the lasagna wasn't agreeing with him. But then there was the imagery...being grasped by unseen hands and carried. Then...galloping— yes, galloping—down a wooded path, panting, screaming. A knife or blade searing through his neck. Images of a figure in black, teeth—oh, the teeth—glistening behind grinning lips. A bloody-faced figure with long hair, shirtless and staring. Eyes that flattened like almonds with a hideous smile. Blood smeared and running down the smiling face. And dripping off a straggly beard.

Cole shook his head to get rid of the mental pictures. Experience told him he'd seen something of importance. These were dreams, yes, but he'd experienced enough of his abilities to know there was more.

Retrocognition. That was the term he'd learned from the remote viewing researcher. Telepathic impressions from the past. From Zachary, most likely. Or maybe the earlier victims.

Cole stood on sturdier legs and cruised into the shower. Despite taking one last night, he felt dirty. He was quick and completed a better-than-half-assed job of changing the dressings on his stitches.

The clock in the bedroom said he was running behind schedule. Timothy should've been up and stumbling around, but Cole heard nothing. He went to the small guest room that the boy called home when he stayed. A quick rap on the door went unanswered. Cole knocked again.

"Yes." A weak reply.

Cole entered.

Timothy sat on the bed in his underwear with his hair mussed. A sweatshirt lay beside him, and his jeans were crumpled on the floor.

"Hey, kiddo. Time to get moving."

Timothy's skinny frame trembled. "Okay."

"Are you all right? Feel okay?" Cole stepped into the room with increasing concern.

"Yeah, I think." Timothy rubbed the front of his T-shirt in a wide circle. "I had these sharp pains in my belly. And a

bad dream. There was a scary guy. That's all I remember."
He retrieved his jeans from the floor and inserted both feet
while rocking onto his back. In another motion he hopped
forward and pulled up the pants. "I feel okay now. It was, I
don't know, just weird."

"Well, it's running through me too. Same pains and weird
dreams. Too much lasagna last night, I think."

Timothy pulled on his sweatshirt, messing his hair up
even more. "Nah, never too much lasagna."

"Whatever. We're running late. Go do your bathroom
routine and then snarf down some breakfast."

"I've got a couple of our officers interviewing the
students. We're starting with the most likely to have known
Zachary Tillman—seniors and close teammates. Romantic
relationships, sexual activity and preferences, risky behaviors,
you name it. We'll talk to that Simon kid to see if there are
any other nuts and bolts rattling around. And an artist will
come to generate a picture of the guy. I'm never too optimis-
tic about those things, though. Suspect drawings always seem
so generic to me."

The chief detective of Charlottesville PD, Walter
Dominici, had been inconsolable this morning. They'd
scooped him on the witness and the other clues from the
woods. But Cole wasn't concerned about who got credit as
long as they caught the shithead.

"Lab work?"

Dominici blew his nose. It sounded like an explosion
over the conference phone. "No prints at any of the crime
scenes. The guy had to be wearing surgical or medical gloves.
Or good at wiping things down. Blood, of course, and we're

checking samples to find someone other than the victim. Nothing from the first two."

"The bite marks. Anything stable for comparison?" Martin said. He and Cole huddled over the crappy conference phone device. The reception was flat and tinny.

"Nothing we've found. And the marks on our three vics were all distorted. Combination of deterioration and weather for the first two. The Tillman kid might've fought back for a second. Lots of tearing on his neck. In terms of the head lopping, the coroner said the tool was likely your standard axe that you can get at any hardware store. No rust or jagged edges, so it's probably in decent shape."

"What made the tearing wounds, then?" Cole said.

"Chopping a head off is not as easy as you think. He got his kill shot in with his regular knife, then went with the axe. He needed multiple attempts at it. Wasn't too neat with the effort. We took a cast on what remained of the bite, but it was kind of a mess. Plus, without something for comparison…"

"Anything on Dash? Or Dashiell" Cole said. When he'd asked Lee at the academy, the man said there was no kid enrolled with that name—first or last.

"Zip so far. We're extending into friends, relatives, neighbors behind the woods. By the way, we're recanvassing the neighborhoods within a one-mile radius from the woods. We're checking into deliverymen, drivers for utility services, mail carriers, whatever."

Cole leaned back in his chair. The discussion lagged for multiple seconds. Cole exchanged glances with Martin to see if there was anything to add.

"Let me ask you," Dominici said. "Outside of a real vampire, what kind of person is doing this?"

Cole inched forward again. "Frankly, we've got some

mixed data here. I would've expected our suspect to be consistent with the sex of the victims. Two females and one male make this unusual. Typically, such killers stick to their preferred sex. Was the male one of convenience? Or was he intended? Though we don't know for sure, our suspect is likely young. And likely appealing in some way. He had to feel comfortable controlling a young adult."

"So, strong and manipulative?"

"Not very helpful, I know."

After a quick lunch in the cafeteria, Cole returned to his office. He sat back in his chair after pulling open the middle file drawer on the right side of his desk. This was his favorite height for a footrest. He gathered the file for Zachary Tillman.

Who was this guy?

He consulted the demographic sheet on top. Eighteen as of three weeks ago, from a posh Richmond suburb. His father was some hotshot attorney who kept the wealthy descendants of tobacco company executives from going to jail and paying too much in taxes. The youngest of three kids. The older two were in college, also male.

Neither of his older brothers had gone to Fort Concord—instead they attended a private school right in Richmond. The sheet briefly hinted at "behavior issues" to explain why Zachary had been sent away.

Mr. and Mrs. Tillman must've caught wind of their son's sexual preference. So, off to military school to make a man out of him.

Zachary did well enough in his academic work. Mostly As with an occasional B. He seemed to have a cadre of friends, so no red flags there. He was, as the teacher on the athletic field had suggested, a bit of a cutup. Minor infractions related to the class-clown type of discipline issues. Nothing that would suggest anything more serious like drugs or alcohol—or sex with fellow students. Cole suspected that would not have been tolerated. Or maybe the administration looked the other way when it came to wealthy parents.

In sports, Zachary participated in soccer and track, the latter involving long-distance events.

His phone rang.

"Cole Nightshade? My name is Maryellen Otto. I'm a reporter with the *Richmond Times-Dispatch*."

Shit.

"Agent Nightshade, are you there?"

"Yes, I'm here. What can I do for you?"

"I got your number from your brother, Josiah."

Cole groaned.

"I'm calling to get your thoughts on an article I'm writing. Why did the FBI decide to bring you in to help with the Charlottesville murders? Specifically, one with your talents? A psychic. You don't often see this kind of a move from J. Edgar Hoover's group."

"Ms. Otto, is that what Josiah said to you?"

"He gave me a lot of your background. I'm calling to see what you're specifically bringing to the cases."

"I'm with the Behavioral Science Unit. We're assisting the Charlottesville Police Department. This is their case."

"Oh, come on, Agent. There's got to be more than that."

"That's all I have for you, Ms. Otto." Cole hung up.

Goddammit, Josiah.

When the phone rang again, Cole took his files and left his office to sit at the conference table.

Patricia Loots, the victim still in high school, had been involved with the theater and drama club at her school. No serious boyfriend but dated a kid for a few months until they broke up two weeks prior. Steve Brown, the boyfriend, was questioned, but he had been at a family wedding in DC the night of the murder. Neither he nor any of Patricia's family were aware of any new boy in her life. In fact, before Patricia left for her shift at Michie Tavern, she'd attended her younger brother's soccer game.

A scan of transcribed interviews of the waitstaff and diners at the tavern didn't provide anything useful.

Cole rubbed his eyes and rose from the conference table. He walked to Martin's office.

"This Michie Tavern. Is that a rough place?"

Martin chuckled. "I know what you're thinking. And no. You haven't ever been there?"

"Never heard of it."

"And you call yourself a Virginian. It's a historic landmark. It practically oozes Important Virginia History. Established in, God, I don't know, late seventeen hundreds. The actual structure was moved about fifty years ago to be near Thomas Jefferson's home. So, you know, there'd be a place for tourists to eat."

"You're saying killers never step foot in the place," Cole said.

"Well, not the rough crowd you were thinking about. Maybe some white-collar types. And no, the staff and customers didn't see anyone strange hanging around outside."

Back at the table, Cole reviewed the Nadine Rudy file. Information on her movements before her murder was sparse. She had been at the library studying. Her roommates at UVA hadn't been concerned when she didn't show for dinner. One thought she might've had a game, the others said she had a ton of homework and thought she'd worked through dinner.

Not that unusual for a college student.

Another girl from the dorm thought she might've seen Nadine talking to a guy on campus. He was tall and wore a baseball cap. She didn't know the team and thought the cap was blue. His hair stuck out from underneath, and it was brownish.

That was it.

Because Cynthia was on call that night, Cole had found a hiding place for the house key so Timothy could enter in case Cole ran late. He didn't want to drive up and find the kid sitting on the front steps looking gloomy again. They arranged for the key to be hidden within a cinderblock in the garage.

All the lights were on as Cole pulled in. Timothy was probably nervous about being alone in the house. The key was still inserted in the lock as he reached the door.

"Okay, you made it in," Cole said as he stepped inside. "Remember to bring the key in, though. No sense leaving it there for the robbers." He showed it to Timothy.

"Oh, shit. Sorry." His eyes darted around the kitchen.

Cole could smell something cooking. "You started dinner." He burst into a grin.

"I'm reheating lasagna leftovers. I hope that's okay with you." Timothy pursed his lips.

"Okay? Hell, yes, it's okay. I'm starving."

Timothy exhaled loudly. "I even made the salad." A large bowl of shredded lettuce sat on the table. He looked pleased with himself.

"Fantastic, kiddo." Cole wrapped his arm around Timothy's shoulders and squeezed. "Let me get out of this getup before we eat."

"No problem. I think you've got about twenty minutes anyway."

Cole changed in his bedroom. Cynthia, who was typically neater than him, had left a few items of clothing tossed over a chair. He wondered if they were dirty. Laundry on Saturday, and he'd need to clarify their status.

Then he remembered Timothy's game and realized he might have to bite the bullet and do the laundry tonight or tomorrow night. Shit.

The phone rang in the kitchen.

"Want me to get that?" Timothy yelled.

"Yeah, go ahead."

Cole slipped into the bathroom but not before hearing Timothy answer, "Cranton/Nightshade residence, Timothy speaking." Cynthia had been teaching him to answer their phone "professionally" when he was around. Cole smiled at the perfect effort.

A dialogue ensued while Cole peed, and he wondered if maybe Kenny had called. He didn't always have the opportunity. For Timothy's sake, Cole hoped it would be Kenny.

The open doorway into the guest room displayed a lived-in mess. Timothy had made himself at home. Books lay on the bed, along with his backpack. The clothes he wore to school were strewn half in and half out. Shin guards and soccer shoes rested where they had been flung upon entry.

"It's Josiah," Timothy said when Cole entered the kitchen. "He wants to know if you're pissed at him."

"Tell him yes."

"Did you hear that? He said yeah." Timothy giggled, then listened, smiling devilishly, and turned back to Cole. "Will you talk to him?" He still guarded the receiver with both hands.

Cole moaned loudly. "For God's sake, of course I'll talk to him." He held out his hand.

"Hello, Josiah."

"Hey, Cole, man. I'm so fucking sorry, man. Oh Jesus, I had no fucking idea this would happen. We had a photographer who somehow snapped a perfect picture of you arriving in a car. And, I said, 'Hey that's my brother.' And then Maryellen overheard me, and she's working on this story, and she says, 'Who's he?' So I tell her, and I fill her in a little about you. Then she says let's grab some dinner and you can tell me more. So we did and I'm thinking, shit, maybe this will get me the opportunity to do bigger features, you know? We go to her place for more background, and, well, um, we get in bed, and, well, we have sex, and I give her more background. Then, I find out she called you today and there's gonna be a big story about it tomorrow. And, oh, man, Cole, I felt like such a shit. I'm so sorry." In typical Josiah fashion, this was told without pause for a breath.

Cole wanted to be pissed. This was the type of shit the Bureau hated. But there was this thing about Josiah where he could be infuriating one moment and disarming the next. Josiah was in desperate straits because he knew he screwed up. It wasn't malicious. In fact, he would walk across miles of broken glass barefoot for Cole. It was just one of those Josiah things. Cole could, however, enjoy it a little.

"So, you were thinking exclusively with your dick."

A loud sigh on the other end of the phone. "Yeah."

Timothy's laughter pealed through the kitchen.

"I can't believe anyone would sleep with you for *this* story."

"Hey, that wasn't for the story. We'd done it before,"

Josiah said. "She finds me irresistibly cute. Anyway, I'm sorry. Have I gotten you into trouble?"

"They haven't seen the paper yet. I'll find out tomorrow." Cole suspected there'd be grousing and a chewing out, but after all, he hadn't been the one to screw up. "Don't worry, I'll survive. You, however, may get roughed up a little. Or get audited every year for a decade. Or maybe get your car towed a lot."

Timothy produced another round of giggles.

"That kid's laughing at me, isn't he?"

"Yeah, he is. By the way, how old is this Maryellen Otto?"

"A little older than me. Twenty-seven or twenty-eight, I guess." His voice brightened. "She seduced me. A much younger guy."

Cole snorted. "For God's sake, you're twenty-three."

"Exactly."

Behind Cole the stove timer went off. "All right, Josiah. You're forgiven. We have to eat now, so I've gotta go. I just have to figure out how to explain this to the boy here."

Timothy's mouth fell open. "That's insulting."

"I already told him. More or less," Josiah said, sounding sheepish.

Josiah's predisposition to talk without self-restraint knew no bounds. It was almost instinctual.

"That's not exactly the level of detail to share with a twelve-year-old."

"I'm thirteen, and that's even more insulting." Timothy continued to grin crazily.

"You didn't tell your mother, did you?"

If he had, Cole might expect a call from Flo.

Another crushing sigh. "I was thinking about it."

"Don't. For God's sake. She'll only call later worrying about me—and you for sleeping with older women."

"I wouldn't have told her that part, Cole. I'm not that much of a dope."

Cole snorted again. "Whatever, Josiah. Goodbye. I love you."

"Thanks, Cole. Love you too."

Munching on a piece of toast the following morning while waiting for Timothy to get out of bed, Cole watched the early news on the *Today* show. This wasn't his usual routine, but things changed, having a kid around.

He only partially listened to reports on President Carter's energy program. Then the news anchor shifted to a report of German commandos storming a Lufthansa airliner that had been hijacked by Palestinians to Somalia. The hijackers had been demanding the release of imprisoned German terrorists called the Red Army Faction. All passengers were rescued.

Hours later, another team of commandos representing multinational interests raided the hideouts of another secret terrorist group in a German town Cole had never heard of. The leader and his second-in-command died in the altercation.

The NBC reporter on assignment in Germany provided an on-camera summary. It sounded spotty, which meant the reporter didn't have a lot of information.

"Do you think that's Dad?"

Surprised, Cole turned around to see Timothy in the hall. He'd been watching the TV over Cole's shoulder. "Could be."

"Bullshit. You know it is. They said multinational."

"You're right. I bet he was involved. We'll never know, though."

"There he is!" Timothy's arm swung upward, index finger pointing to the TV screen.

Cole pivoted. Behind the reporter and far enough away from the camera to be blurry, a figure departed from the front door of an official-looking building and darted into a waiting vehicle. A casual observer who didn't know better would've dismissed and forgotten the person within a second. But to those who did know better, the figure was obviously Kenny. The posture, movements, and build all matched.

"I'll be damned," Cole said.

Timothy rubbed his nose. "Maybe that means he'll be home soon." Without waiting for a reply, he turned on his heels and returned to his room to finish getting dressed.

The headline for the bottom first-page article of the *Richmond Times-Dispatch* read "FBI Brings in Psychic Agent to Track Down Vampire Killer." Below these words was the photo of Cole arriving at Fort Concord—the one he vaguely recalled being taken.

"Oh shit."

Martin had pitched the paper onto Cole's desk.

"How'd they get this story?" Martin said.

"My brother inadvertently spilled the beans," Cole said.

"I thought he was one of those brand-new reporters who just did the TV listings or obituaries."

"He is. He just screwed up. Got a little too talky with his colleagues. Who's pissed?"

"Don't worry. I covered for you with the unit director. Lucky thing everybody likes you. Just don't talk to any journalists, especially this Otto woman."

"She called me yesterday. I hung up on her." Cole felt

defensive. He wondered, too, if Martin had been on the receiving end of some bureaucratic dressing down.

"Good. Keep doing that."

Cole had gotten off easy. While his abilities weren't a secret—as demonstrated by the open sharing with CIA researchers—there was an image to maintain. Better to keep material like this out of the press.

The *Times-Dispatch* story recounted the case involving Dr. Christopher Elmer from when Cole was twenty. It also focused on his experiences in Vietnam related to the warnings received from previously killed soldiers and civilians. In all cases, Cole was described as having saved lives through his abilities.

"You little devil." Cole sat back in his chair and smirked. Josiah had kept quiet about the gruesome events of Cole's childhood. That was impressive—at least for Josiah. There was some semblance of restraint. He'd have to call him back.

Unless his pillow talk with Maryellen Otto resulted in a string of articles.

4

Mapping the Fairchild Estate

April 1962

DURING HER TWO YEARS OF employment at the Fairchild estate, Edna Willow had grown to feel quite at home. With a massive two-story white house featuring a string of dormers and eye-catching red doors at both the front and back entrances, the estate provided not only a place to work but also a lifesaving sanctuary for her and her nine-year-old daughter, Paula.

Edna's husband, Clarence McClusky, had been a violent man when drunk—and he was drunk most of the time. With no money to her name, her options for escape were extremely limited. But the housekeeper, an old friend of Edna's mother, put in a good word for her with Mr. and Mrs. Fairchild when the position of cook came open. Mildred Johnson's recommendation wasn't just empty talk, either. Edna was an excellent cook who loved to prepare meals and never tired of the challenge regardless of whether she was making a quiet family dinner or a formal dinner for twenty.

When Mildred got her an in-person interview, she filled

Mrs. Fairchild in on Edna's situation. That meant Edna didn't feel the need to grovel and bring up her family life. Instead she could focus on her previous work in a swanky hotel restaurant, an establishment with which the Fairchilds were familiar.

While not the warmest of people—Mr. Fairchild was aloof, his wife a nervous woman—they were taken with her and offered her the job. The greatest perk was the free lodging for staff. Edna and Paula lived in one of the tenant houses. Mildred and her husband, John, who served as caretaker of the property, had the other. Clarence was now out of the picture. She'd divorced the son of a bitch and began using her maiden name, and he didn't dare show his face anywhere near the Fairchild property.

Two other employees worked there as well. The first was a driver who took Mr. Fairchild to his office in Washington DC or to the airport for his frequent business trips around the country and the world. Edna wasn't sure exactly what Mr. Fairchild did for a living, other than being some kind of fancy attorney whose clients were filthy rich and powerful.

The second employee, a nanny, resided in a small room on the second floor of the house near the boy's bedroom. Karen, the most recent nanny, had been there a month. She was the third they'd hired. The first left after eighteen months, and the second managed nearly three years.

"I'd think that young girls wouldn't last very long. They have their own lives blossoming ahead of them," Mildred said at one point. "But Mrs. Fairchild prefers younger nannies." She leaned closer to Edna. "Mr. Fairchild does too, if you catch my drift."

David, nearly five and quite the handful, kept poor Karen on her toes. His motor revved into high gear the moment he woke in the morning and stayed there until he was down at night. He scooted from one end of the house to the other in record time every day. Mildred was pleased as punch to see him so active after the extensive surgery he'd had when he was two.

"What was the surgery for?" Edna asked. It had taken place a month prior to her arrival.

"Growths on his belly," Mildred whispered. "Hideous things. I never saw anything like it in my life." She wouldn't say anything more.

᠅

"What do you think it's like to be a people lollipop?"

David sat at the sturdy wooden table in the kitchen eating his lunch. Edna had cleared a small spot for him by moving the canisters of flour and sugar to one side. The ham sandwich was disappearing at a rapid rate; he had a good appetite. Edna liked to see that.

Karen, the nanny, had an unspecified appointment and wouldn't be in until the afternoon. Minding the little one didn't bother Edna, though. Listening to a child's chatter warmed her heart, even with the wild stories that came out of David's mouth.

"A people lollipop? What's that?"

"I seen 'em before," David said through a mouthful of chewed ham and bread.

"My, that must've been a sight. I don't think I ever saw anything like that."

"I did when I was a grown-up."

Edna looked up from piecrust she was rolling out. Flour dotted her forearms, and a smudge whitened the tip of her nose. "When you were a grown-up? You silly boy. You're only four. You won't be a grown-up for a long time yet."

David shook his head and sipped some milk. After swallowing, he said, "Miss Edna. I'm talking about when I was a grown-up *before* I was a little boy."

Edna smiled at him. "Okay, sweetie, I get it."

He was so adamant and cute at the same time. His bushy brown hair flopped back and forth with every movement of his head. It added to the charm of his serious demeanor.

"Tell me what a people lollipop is."

David slurped the last of his milk. A white mustache remained, which he wiped with the back of his hand. "That's when the good guy puts his prisoners on top of a pole with a sharp point. The point goes right through the prisoner and he slides down the pole like melting ice cream." He put his plate and glass into the sink. Mrs. Fairchild required the nanny to teach her boy good manners.

Edna felt queasy. "Did Karen tell you about this?"

"Karen?" David looked surprised. "No way. She doesn't like bloody stories."

The piecrust was forgotten. "So where did you hear about it? It sounds awful."

"I told you. I saw it when I was an adult." Here David paused and placed an index finger on his lips. He looked skyward. "Or maybe I just learned about it then. I don't remember. I just sorta knew it."

Edna decided to let it go. Somewhere along the line David must've seen something horrible on TV.

While lost in thought, Edna didn't notice that the boy had sidled up to her. He gave her a hug. "It kinda scared me, though, because when I went to jail, I thought they were going to do that to me. They didn't, though." He embraced her again, and she reciprocated.

"That's good, honey," she said, perplexed.

"Uh huh, it was. I guess. Someone *did* come up behind me in the jail and put a wire around my neck and squeezed tight. That's how I died."

Three weeks later, Karen gave notice that she'd be leaving. Mrs. Fairchild got weepy when she heard the news; Mr. Fairchild said they needed to find someone to take over. They had a little time, as Karen said she could stay until Memorial Day.

One night after David went to bed, Karen joined Edna in the kitchen. Cleanup had taken a little longer than usual as Edna was preparing appetizers for an upcoming cocktail party.

"I thought I'd come down for some iced tea. Do you have any?"

"Of course, you know we always have some. Sweet or unsweet?"

"Full power for me," Karen said. She blew her blond bangs off her forehead.

Edna thought the girl was plain, but in a pretty kind of way. Her hair looked cute when it was up in a ponytail, but tonight she'd let it fall naturally.

"You look tired," Edna said as she wiped down the counter over the dishwasher.

"Boy, am I. Getting David down is always the biggest chore."

Karen had always been quiet around Edna. Maybe it was the age difference. She doubted Karen was any older than twenty or twenty-one. While always sweet and polite, Karen never went out of her way to be chummy. She wasn't standoffish, maybe just shy. Either way, her appearance in the kitchen was out of the ordinary.

"Yes, I bet he can be a handful."

Karen turned away from Edna, biting her lower lip.

"Has David ever said or done things that bothered you?"

Edna halted just for a second. But it was enough.

"He has, hasn't he?" Karen whispered.

"Well, um, yes. I mean, oh boy." Edna took a breath. "Yes, once he talked about a time when he was an adult."

"And he talked about people being impaled which he watched, while eating his dinner."

Edna gasped. "Not with that detail. Good heavens."

"What about prison?" The iced tea Edna had poured sat untouched on the table between them.

"Yes, he mentioned something…"

"Did he tell you he was sent there for biting people in the neck and cutting their necks?"

Edna was aghast. "Are you sure you heard him right?"

"I swear to God, Edna. When he said the part about cutting necks, he went like this." She ran her index finger swiftly across her neck. "It looked like he was mimicking a murder."

"Good lord. That I haven't seen."

"I didn't know what to think. I mean, he can be such a great kid. Funny and playful, but more and more of this stuff has been coming out." Karen's eye moistened with tears.

Edna reached for her hand and squeezed.

"A couple of weeks ago, he started coming into my room at night. I'd wake up and he'd be standing over me. Staring down. It was freaky. At first, I thought he was sleepwalking, but after a couple of times, I began to wonder." She lifted the tea to her lips and sipped. "Then three nights ago, I felt something in bed with me. I was petrified. For I second, I thought it was…well, never mind that. It turned out to be David.

He'd taken off his pajamas and was running his finger across my neck. I said, 'David, what are you doing?' And he goes, 'I'm not David. Let me cut you.' I got him back to his room and back in his pajamas. I said, 'Never do that again.' The whole time he had this grin on his face, and his eyes looked wild. It gave me the willies. And that scar from his surgery? I know this'll sound strange, but I swear it was moving like something was behind it.

"I was still shaking when I got back to my room. I mean, four-year-olds don't act this way. Where did he get these ideas? Since then, I've been locking the door to my room at night." While her eyes remained moist, her jaw looked set, as if she were preparing for a counterargument.

"That sounds frightening. I'm so sorry. Have you talked to the Fairchilds about this?"

A head shake. "I thought about it, but Mrs. Fairchild seems so fragile. So nervous, like she'd jump out of her skin if I surprised her. And the pills she takes. She's nice and all, but..."

This was true. The woman's case of nerves made her brittle, although she rallied if friends were around, especially if she had a cocktail in her hand. But David or Mr. Fairchild? No, she was shaky around her own family.

"And Mr. Fairchild?" Karen grunted. "Sometimes you have to stay beyond arm's reach of him. Anyway, that's when I decided I had to leave. Things were getting too strange."

The night before Memorial Day, Edna and her daughter went to work in the kitchen. Paula was helping her decorate cupcakes for a family picnic on the grounds—partly in celebration of the holiday but also as a goodbye party for Karen.

The girl had informed everyone that she'd decided to go back to college and wanted to spend time with her family before she left. Edna didn't have the heart to ask her if this was true.

Paula's job was spreading the vanilla frosting on the chocolate cupcakes and adorning them all with colored sprinkles. They jabbered back and forth about nonsense things as they set about their duties. The task almost done, Edna looked forward to cleaning up and heading to their little residence.

A brief shout cut through the gentle warmth of the evening, followed by a prolonged scream.

"What's that?" Paula spoke first.

"I don't know." Edna wiped her hands on a towel by her side and glanced out the open window. She bolted quickly from the room with Paula at her heels. Edna was about to tell Paula to stay in the kitchen when she almost ran into Mildred exiting the family room.

"Edna, you heard it too?"

"Gosh, yes, it sounded like... Oh my heavens!"

Both women had been racing toward the center hallway with a similar instinct to go up to the second floor. They never made it that far because Karen was stumbling down the stairs. She looked like she was in danger of pitching headfirst and tumbling the rest of the way. The only thing that kept her upright was her clasping onto the wrought-iron banister.

More troubling, her blouse was torn at the stomach, and a maroon stain expanded dramatically with each passing second.

"Karen!" Edna rushed over. Karen released her grip on the railing and collapsed into Edna's arms. The weight of the girl nearly sent Edna sprawling. The timely arrival of Mildred, who braced Edna as she staggered backward, kept them from toppling to the floor.

"David stabbed me. An accident, though." She glanced briefly at Edna.

Mildred set the girl down slowly so that she sat on the bottom stair. "What did you say?"

"An accident. I think." The last words were whispered in Edna's direction. Karen's left hand clasped Edna's upper arm and squeezed. "We were working on an art project. He ran to get the scissors. I told him no running. I followed him. He turned after picking them up. Too fast. He was holding them out in front as he fell into me."

"I didn't mean it!" David swayed at the top of the stairs, gritting his teeth. A pair of small scissors with a sharp tip remained in his hand. Blood smeared all the way to the pivot point. "It was an accident. Like she said."

Edna stared at the boy. Behind her, Paula said, "Gross" under her breath.

A trip to the emergency room was overruled. Mr. Fairchild, sparing no expense, arranged for a physician and a nurse to be dispatched to the house. They would arrive within thirty minutes—considerably less time than it would've taken to get an ambulance and proceed to the hospital. Edna and Mildred applied dressings in the meantime and tried to keep her comfortable. The two women kept exchanging glances.

"Should've gone to the hospital," Mildred mumbled.

"I think so," Edna said.

"Where's David now?" Karen said.

Edna and Mildred looked around. "Must be in his room," Edna said.

"Good."

"I'll go check on him. Put him to bed." Edna stood and left Mildred with the nanny.

David was in the bathroom trying to wash his hands. He stood on a small stool so he could reach the faucet. Splatters of pink soap decorated the vanity. It wasn't attractive.

"Looks like you can use some help."

"Yes, ma'am." Ever the gentleman. "My hands feel sticky."

After the bathroom routine, she helped him change into his pajamas and tossed his dirty clothes down the laundry chute. Edna doubted the boy would ever wear them again.

"It was an accident," David said after Edna pulled the sheet over him and kissed his forehead.

"I know." As she took a step toward the bedroom door, Edna noticed the scissors on his night table. She lifted them by a finger hole. "I think we should get rid of these, don't you?"

Edna didn't wait for him to reply.

The next morning, everyone said goodbye to Karen. The party had been canceled. Mrs. Fairchild said she was too nervous for it to continue. Fortunately, Karen's injury hadn't punctured any organs and required only stitches. Before Karen walked out the door to her car, Edna saw her talking with Mr. Fairchild in his home office. He wrote a check, which she accepted without hesitation.

℆

Mr. Fairchild decided that a change was in order. Specifically, he wanted a male to take charge of his son's development and introduce decidedly masculine activities. Through his professional grapevine, Mr. Fairchild settled on a young man named Scott Montrose.

Scott, a rising junior in high school, came from a well-established Virginia family. A varsity soccer player near the top of his class, he was pursuing his Eagle Scout badge and had a steady girlfriend—all of which suggested stability and maturity.

Still, Edna was skeptical. Men weren't typically the most reliable of the species, and this was doubly true for young men.

Much to her surprise, Scott won her over at the start. Expecting a brash demeanor, she instead encountered a polite and soft-spoken young man who developed an instant rapport with David. They were outside playing within moments of meeting each other, and they rarely came inside except to grab something to eat.

The Fairchild estate sat on over three hundred acres, and the house had a setup that Edna had found highly unusual when she arrived. The part of the house that faced the tree-lined drive actually served as the back. The drive took cars on a sweeping loop that circled to the rear where a courtyard and formal entrance were located. Two perpendicular wings extending from either end of the house framed the courtyard. Together the three sections of the structure resembled a letter *U* with three equal sides.

While the views from all angles were breathtaking, the one from the courtyard area was the best. Facing northwest, the vista featured rolling hills backed by the Appalachian chain. An extensive lawn lay to the left while woods encroached the property almost immediately on the right. This expanse served as the playground for David and Scott's activities.

They used the broad lawn area as a soccer field. David didn't know the game (the sport was slowly gaining in popularity, Edna learned), but Scott brought along a ball and some plastic cones to serve as the goal. David took to it immediately. Edna couldn't tell whether it was the game itself or Scott's enthusiasm and praise for David's efforts that did the trick, but even Mr. Fairchild noticed. New soccer balls for kids David's age, shin guards, and shoes materialized. So, much to Scott's delight, did two netted goals, which added more realism to the play (not to mention eliminating the need to retrieve the ball after scoring).

Then there were the woods. What better source of exploration could there be for two boys—Edna always thought of them as "the boys"—to enjoy. Different adventures awaited them each day. A search for fossils or arrowheads, an exploration of snakes or frogs in their natural habitat, a quest for bullets fired from Civil War muskets, or any other exploits that occurred to Scott.

A few days before the Fourth of July, the boys came into the kitchen for lunch. They were about fifteen minutes late, and Edna had sandwiches already prepared.

"Sorry, lost track of time," Scott said, not meeting her eyes.

Edna's heart melted. "That's okay, dear. Looks like you were having fun."

Both boys had beads of sweat on their faces. Their shirts and shorts also looked damp. Thankfully, Edna was downwind.

"Scott liked the covered bridge," David said. He reached for his sandwich.

"Uh-huh, young man. Have you washed your hands?"

"Darn." David skipped to the bathroom.

Scott grimaced and rose from his seat. He'd forgotten too.

Sounds of water splashing and Scott's voice reminding David to use soap issued from the small powder room around the corner from the kitchen.

"Isn't that bridge darling," Edna said when they returned to table.

"Yes, ma'am," Scott said. "It surprised me."

Edna had been charmed when she first saw the bridge. Mildred mentioned it one day in passing, and Edna asked Mildred's husband, John, to take her and Paula there. A hiking path led through the woods not far from the courtyard area. Once in the woods, it forked off in two different directions. Veering left took them to a covered bridge over a stream. Without the bridge, hikers would've had to turn back or get their feet wet.

"He wanted something unique for the trail," John explained, referring to Fairchild.

It was small scale, meant for individual hikers and not vehicles. Still, it was a marvel, charming in every sense of the word. The broadside of the bridge was painted red. Gray asphalt shingles covered the roof, which offered shelter in a surprise rain shower.

"A little beyond the bridge, there's a level area among the trees that would be a great spot for a clubhouse," Scott said. "Could we build something, do you think?"

"Yeah, that'd be neat," David said.

"You'll have to ask Mr. Fairchild about that," Edna said. She couldn't imagine why not. Neither he nor his wife used the trail much anymore, if at all. And the activity would take them the rest of the summer.

"David wouldn't be much help," Edna said. "You'd be doing all the work."

"I can help," David said, protesting.

"No problem. I'm not talking about a house or anything."

Sebastian Fairchild never did anything slipshod. The covered bridge was a dead giveaway. After approving the clubhouse, Mr. Fairchild worked with John, to get the right tools and the right lumber. He even had a plan drawn up. This was well beyond what Scott had in mind, Edna could tell. But he was game.

John, being the longtime maintenance man of the estate, knew a thing or two about construction. He oversaw the project and did a chunk of the work. Scott was not about to be outdone, though. He made extensive contributions and worked overtime when David wasn't around. Most importantly, he worked one-on-one with David to teach him how to use tools safely.

"That kid knows his stuff," John said, joining Edna and Mildred for a coffee break one morning in early August.

"He's good with David, isn't he," Edna said. "Give credit when it's due. Bringing in someone like that instead of a nanny was a good idea."

"I'll say. He shows a lot of patience," Mildred said.

"And they talk constantly," John said. "Scott takes everything that comes out of that kid's mouth in stride."

The unveiling came a week later. Edna, Paula, John, and Mildred joined the boys for the hike into the woods. Edna was astonished to find that the clubhouse looked like a miniature cabin. Inside was a single room with two glass windows that opened on hinges. The ceilings were beamed, and the wooden floor felt level and solid. Two adults in sleeping bags could lie there comfortably.

"This is amazing!" Paula said. "I can't believe you guys did this."

"Why not?" Scott said, laughing. He seemed pleased.

"I don't know. It's just so good."

"It is," Edna said. She walked around the room, swinging a window open as she went.

"Beautiful. Wait till your parents see this," Mildred said.

"I know. Won't they be happy?" David shifted his body from one foot to the other.

The clubhouse became a focal point for the remainder of the summer. Paula joined the boys periodically, but her interest waned with time.

"David talks weird for a little kid." She never explained what she meant to Edna.

℘

"Can I talk to you, Mrs. Willow?" Scott stood in the doorway of the kitchen. He was done for the day, as David had accompanied his parents to some high-roller outdoor soiree at the home of a DC lobbyist. While spouses and children were invited, Edna didn't doubt that some wheeler-dealer business would go on.

She hoped Mrs. Fairchild would manage. The poor soul had to take an extra Miltown tranquilizer before leaving. David seemed excited about the prospect of a new place to explore, though.

"Of course. Come on in." Edna was just cleaning up and looking forward to an early night at home with Paula.

Scott sat at the table and rubbed his lips. Edna pulled out a chair opposite him and waited. He scratched his head and mussed his sun-bleached blond hair in the process.

Edna offered her most disarming smile. "Something wrong, Scott?"

"Not wrong." He cleared his throat. "I mean, I wanted to ask you something. About David."

She waited.

"Has he ever talked to you about a past life?"

"Past life?" Edna played for time, realizing where Scott was going.

"Yeah. Past life. Like he remembers a life before this one."
He sighed. "Like reincarnation?"

Edna found herself nodding. Right away, the boy visibly relaxed. His shoulders eased, and he slumped a little in his chair.

"Yes, he has mentioned something like that in the past."

"It's only been recently with me. Like a week or so. I couldn't believe what I was hearing." Now that he had begun talking, Scott's words rushed out like a speeding train. "He started talking about a person named Glow. Weird name, don't you think? She was his wife, and they had been sent to jail. They were in jail because they took people and...and...did things to them. He told me, 'We fucking killed them all.' Excuse my language, but that's what David said. He and his wife, Glow. Then he did this." David made a cutting motion with his finger on his neck. "I guess that meant their throats were cut. And then he was killed in jail—"

"Choked, with a wire," Edna said.

Scott bolted upright. "Yeah, that's it. So he did tell you."

"Not all this. You got a lot more of the story than I did." Edna thought of Karen's experiences and almost told Scott about them but decided against it.

"He told the same story almost every day, just about. There'd be minor alterations, but...it was really messed up. And I never used any swear words with him at all. Or talked about killing. Never."

"I believe you, Scott. Don't worry."

"I'd hate for Mr. and Mrs. Fairchild to think that I was such a jackass that I'd talk like that in front of a little kid."

"They don't. They're very happy with your work here this summer. David's had the best time with you. They'll hate to see you leave when school starts."

"There's something more, though. I wanted to tell Mr.

Fairchild, but he's hardly ever around. And I wouldn't want to bother him if he wouldn't be interested."

"Interested in what?"

The boy smiled nervously and shifted to his side to pull a piece of paper out of his pocket. "My girlfriend—her mother is a secretary in the Center for Perceptual Insights at UVA. They study all this stuff related to ESP and mind reading. She works in an office called Reincarnation Sciences. That's their real name. They study reincarnation. Past lives. They're doctors and psychiatrists and scientists. Really."

Scott passed the piece of paper to Edna.

"What David was saying sounds like reincarnation to me. How would a little kid know all this if it wasn't true? Unless his parents told him, which I can't imagine."

Edna looked at the paper. A woman's name, phone number, and office address were listed. "You're thinking maybe Mr. and Mrs. Fairchild would be interested in taking David to see these researchers."

With the idea spoken aloud, Scott seemed hesitant. He nodded almost imperceptibly after multiple seconds had passed. "Maybe. I mean, maybe it could help. He's got to be confused, right?"

Edna nodded. That certainly was true.

"I'm not stupid, though. Mr. Fairchild is an important man. He may not be interested in checking this out. It could be embarrassing for him."

"That's a wise thought on your part. Have you mentioned this to Mildred or John?"

"No, ma'am, you're the first one. You were just sitting here, and I got up enough nerve right now."

She smiled. "I tell you what. Let me run this by Mildred and see what she thinks. And we'll go from there."

Scott exhaled loudly. "Gee, thanks, Mrs. Willow. Oh, and I wanted to make sure you know that I didn't mention any names. They think it's some neighbor kid. I kept everything confidential."

"Good boy. You used your head on that one. I'll let you know what happens."

"Oh boy, that's . . . that may be a little too far out there to bring up," Mildred said. "I think he'd pooh-pooh it."

"And maybe get angry," Edna said. "He doesn't cotton to any foolishness as he sees it."

So they said nothing and hoped things would settle down.

It was a day later that Edna, from the window over the sink, gaped in terror as she saw John helping Scott to the passenger side of John's truck. Scott's T-shirt had been removed, and when he twisted to lean into the seat, a gash that sliced from his shoulder to his hip became visible. She ran from the house at the same time as Mildred, both shouting, "What happened?"

"An accident," John said over his shoulder.

Edna drew closer. Blood was seeping unmercifully from Scott's wound. Scott held his shirt, bunched into a ball, and pressed it into a section of the injury, absorbing a fraction of the blood. More dripped down his sides and arm. There were splotches all over the front of his shorts.

"An accident with a screwdriver," Scott hissed as he swung into the car.

"Time to get you to a doctor, son." John shut the door. "I'll be AWOL for a while."

"We'll hold down the fort," Mildred said.

John trotted to the driver's side and looked back at them

before entering. "Who the hell is Glow?" Without waiting for a reply, he started the car and drove off.

"That looks like some accident." Mildred said, her eyes still on her husband's retreating pickup.

Edna's focus was elsewhere. She spotted David standing at the edge of the woods, looking sheepish. He had been watching the scene unfold and now looked at the ground at his feet, occasionally glancing upward.

Edna was at his side without even realizing she had moved. Mildred followed close behind. Splashes of Scott's blood dotted David's shirt and shorts. He held a screwdriver in his hand. The tool was slick with blood.

Kneeling in front of David, Edna asked, "What happened, honey?"

"I climbed up on the roof of the clubhouse. I wanted to surprise Scott and fix a loose shingle."

"Oh dear."

"When he saw me, he got mad. He said, 'David, get the hell off the roof before you fall.' I got scared and slipped. He caught me before I hit the ground, but the screwdriver cut him when he did. Like this." He made a slashing motion across his own chest. "There was a lot of blood."

"Well, let's get you inside and cleaned up. That had to be very scary. But Scott will be just fine, you'll see." Mildred led David toward the house.

Edna remained behind. On impulse, she started walking the hiking trail. It wasn't long before she reached the clubhouse. The structure and setting maintained its adventurous appeal. A perfect spot for young minds to explore everything under the sun. Inside the clubhouse, there were picture books, including one opened to a page on salamanders, as well as water pistols, a grungy balsa wood airplane that had seen more than its share of crash landings, and a soccer ball. A child-sized tool chest sat opened in the corner. Nothing inside looked amiss, although clearly a screwdriver was missing.

Outside, Edna didn't spot any blood splatters, although the house had been painted red, so maybe they would've been tough to see.

Then she examined the roof.

None of the shingles were loose or damaged. They looked as brand-spanking new as they did a month ago when the structure was built.

Scott didn't return to work for the Fairchild family. Edna never saw him again.

The school year began shortly thereafter. A month hadn't gone by when Mrs. Fairchild received a call from David's kindergarten teacher. He'd been talking about a previous life where he'd been married and went to jail. At first she didn't worry about it. After all, kids had imaginations. But the content of his stories, which the teacher wouldn't go into over the phone, was disturbing. Other parents had caught wind of them from their children and were becoming alarmed. Maybe they should talk with David or take him to a doctor. And, by the way, there were researchers at UVA who studied kids reporting past lives. She'd read about it somewhere.

The only reason Edna heard about the call was that Mr. Fairchild was consulting in Washington DC again. Beside herself, Mrs. Fairchild needed someone to confide in. Edna and Mildred proved to be helpful listeners, and they related their experiences along with Scott's. Mrs. Fairchild was flabbergasted but relieved that they didn't think she was out of her mind. When Edna gave her the contact information of the research office provided by Scott, Mrs. Fairchild made a dramatic decision.

"Let's talk to them. I'll fill my husband in later."

After some discussion, Mrs. Fairchild felt that she shouldn't accompany David to UVA. Someone might recognize her (although Edna couldn't imagine who). Could Edna or Mildred take David and report back to her? They could use a fake surname. Maybe they both could go. Mildred could be the grandmother while Edna played the mother.

Mrs. Fairchild needed another Miltown.

The whole charade seemed doomed to fail. Edna could anticipate all kinds of things going wrong. But they agreed and set an appointment with the reincarnation researchers.

"Can I have pencils?" David skipped into the kitchen.

"Of course, sweetheart," Edna said.

Mildred, who'd been talking to Edna as she prepared dinner, reached over to a glass jar with six or seven pencils on a small telephone table in the corner. "How many, David?"

"Four, please. And sharpened. Long, too."

"My, are you working hard?" Edna dug into the refrigerator for chutney, mayonnaise, and diced celery. The family dinner was curried chicken salad, a favorite of Mrs. Fairchild's.

"Yes, ma'am." David grabbed the pencils from Mildred's extended hand and tore from the room.

"Walk!" Mildred called after him.

"Okay." The boy's voice was already receding.

The young psychiatrist involved with the reincarnation research had talked with both Edna and Mildred after the UVA group finished interviewing David. Edna didn't think they successfully fooled the man into believing they were

David's mother and grandmother, but he didn't bat an eye. The debriefing he offered to them was shocking.

"David is reporting a past life of someone who was in prison. For murder and maybe multiple murders," the doctor said. "He talked about sadistic forms of killing in graphic detail."

Well, that revelation brought the proceedings to a grinding halt. Edna and Mildred drove back to the Fairchild estate and summarized their experience at UVA with Mrs. Fairchild.

Surprisingly, Mrs. Fairchild didn't break down into shambles. Edna couldn't help thinking that she may have had some hint long before now that something was awry with David. Mildred agreed.

But David could not continue meeting with this group at UVA, Mrs. Fairchild realized. Mr. Fairchild wouldn't be pleased—at all—if word were to get out. Edna called the researchers immediately and declined any further participation.

Edna couldn't help second-guessing their course of action as she chopped the chicken. Mildred disagreed, said it was for the best that David stopped going. When it came close to dinnertime, Mildred took her leave and Edna went to find David.

She called his name a few times while walking down the path toward the woods. When he didn't answer, Edna knew he was likely at his clubhouse. Blowing hair off her forehead, Edna prepared for the hike.

The trail used by the boys over the summer was now well-worn. Imprints of sneakers in dirt led the way through the trees. Edna watched closely for poison ivy and spider webs. The shade took the edge off the heat, but the closeness of the bush added to the cloying humidity. Gnats dive-bombed her face; repeated hand-waving failed to dispatch them.

The covered bridge was a delight as always. Mr. Fairchild had outdone himself, planning for its construction. The wooden floor barely registered her footfalls.

The red clubhouse came into view.

"David?" Edna walked closer.

"Inside." David's little-boy squeak was muffled by the walls.

"Can I come in?" She reached for the door.

At that moment, the door opened and David hopped out.

"Is it dinnertime?"

"Yes, dear. I've been calling."

"Yippee." David burst into a sprint down the path toward the house.

Edna started to say, "Wait," but gave up. He was a bundle of energy. As she turned to head back, Edna hesitated. What had the boy had been doing inside? David had bounded right back into whatever play activities struck his fancy when they returned from Charlottesville. Had the interview with the UVA researchers upset him at all? It certainly didn't seem like it.

Edna opened the door. The hinges made the tiniest screech. The inside was hot and smelled of perspiration. Faint tracks of mud dotted the floor. A few comic books rested on a wooden bench.

What caught her attention was a shoebox in the center of the floor, filled three-quarters of the way with dirt. The four pencils were buried halfway, eraser side down. The points were covered with a glossy red substance, and sinewy strings hung glistening down the shafts.

Four field mice had been impaled, one on each pencil.

Flies buzzed around the massacre. Despite her disgust, Edna continued to stare. She couldn't help noticing that the mice were gradually sliding down the pencils, leaving a trail of slime in their wake.

5

Unsettling Revelations

October 1977

THE SKETCH ARTIST'S FINAL PRODUCT looked like a movie vampire, complete with shading on the lips and chin. *In case it's facial hair*, the artist said.

Cole hadn't gotten his hopes up. Simon hadn't seen the person's face clearly and the results showed—the drawing was so vague and general it could fit almost anyone. Still, police canvassed the neighborhood behind the school, the staff at Michie Tavern, and anyone connected with the three victims. There were no hits.

The fiber people were still combing over Zachary's clothes, so nothing to go by other than a single brown hair. A long strand with a bit of a wave to it. No fingerprints across the board, suggesting the use of gloves. There was no semen, either, meaning the guy could've used a condom or taken care of business elsewhere. Or he didn't have a sexual motive. The two young women showed no evidence of vaginal tearing. A preliminary report from the coroner on Zachary didn't show obvious anal penetration.

Serial killers tended to stick to their preferred victim type. Here was one who went both ways. Could there be two different killers? A team?

Cole rubbed his face and returned his attention to the soccer game. He'd promised to attend and didn't grumble about making the ninety-mile trek to Charlottesville yet again. Timothy jabbered the entire way, thrilled to have his own personal fan base present.

Cole stood along the sidelines with the parents of Timothy's teammates. There was no score, as both teams played decent defense. The parents had seen Cole a few times over the years at previous games and knew him well enough to chat or at least give a quick hello. Today, though, there were furtive glances in his direction and heads leaning close together to share whispered comments.

They must've read the newspapers. The *Richmond Times-Dispatch* article had been picked up by other papers, including the Fredericksburg local. Now all the parents knew him as the psychic FBI agent.

There was no option for him but to nod in return and make himself look as normal as he'd always seemed in the past.

As Cole strolled up and down the sideline to follow the action, he caught dribs and drabs of conversations. Most were mundane and short-lived, but he picked up an occasional interesting fact. One from two moms had to do with how nice it was for UVA students to volunteer as assistant coaches and refs for kids' soccer games in Charlottesville. They drew him into the chat.

"I think they earn credit for physical education and maybe a certificate," Jenny Something said to him and Leslie Something. "Our teams have to rely on parents exclusively."

Cole looked to the sidelines of Timothy's team and saw two dads running along parallel with the ball, yelling instructions. The Charlottesville team had a head coach who was also likely a dad. He too shouted instructions to his players. His assistant, a college student, was more subdued. He leaned toward a group of players on the sideline and drew diagrams on a clipboard. The young coach's long hair kept flopping forward, and he had to swipe it back repeatedly.

"Yeah, I wouldn't have minded that opportunity," Cole said, just to participate in the conversation.

"When did you graduate?" Leslie said.

"A little over three years ago."

"I bet you didn't expect you'd be attending kids' soccer games at twenty-five."

Cole grimaced but passed it off as a smile. "Twenty-seven, actually."

"Oh, I see. You took off some time before going back to school," Leslie said. Jenny blanched at her side.

"Sort of. I was in Vietnam."

Jenny looked at the ground.

"Oh," Leslie said.

And that was the end of that conversation.

Cole returned his attention to the game as the other team scored the first goal. Everyone in his immediate area groaned but followed with shouts of encouragement.

Had the killer known his victims? Must have, at least to some degree. Getting them to these out-of-the-way locations took some trust. There was always the chance that he overpowered them and carried them there, but something said they were at least familiar to him.

Cole frowned. Nothing meshed. Two victims were in high school, one was in college. Two were female, one

was male. The male may have been homosexual. All three
stabbed with a combat knife with a six-inch blade: a slash
along the neck. The bite to the neck adjacent to, if not on
top of, the slash.

That had to be messy.

Simon's vampire had blood on its mouth and chest. It
certainly fit.

"You're Agent Nightshade, right?"

Cole's ruminations were interrupted by the college kid
who served as assistant coach for the other team. He had left
his post and traversed the perimeter of the field.

"Yes."

"Sorry to bother you, but those official guys over there
asked for you." He pointed to two men in ties, clearly out of
place, standing between the opposing team and the parking
lot.

"Shoot. I was hoping to avoid work today."

The kid smiled and shrugged. He jogged in the direction
of his team.

"I can't believe this," Cole said to Jenny and Leslie.
"Excuse me."

They chuckled politely, clearly storing this up for future
retellings.

Following the route taken by the assistant coach, Cole
approached the two visitors. Up close, he recognized one of
them as Dr. Rudyard, the researcher with Vector Labs.

"Dr. Rudyard. I'm surprised to see you here."

"Sorry, Cole. This is highly irregular, I realize. But I was
hoping you'd join us at my lab."

Cole looked at the unfamiliar man standing slightly
behind Rudyard. "I'm here to watch my nephew's game."

"Yes, I know. Under normal situations, I wouldn't intrude,

but something's come up that qualifies as urgent. I think you'd want to see this." Rudyard looked out of his league. He was a scientist, after all. A PhD in God knows what.

"What is it?"

"Something that involves your participation in our research the other day and the case you're currently investigating."

"We'll see that Augustine's son gets back to your place safely," said the second guy, whose face was all angles and shadows.

"Who're you?" Cole said.

"Oh, this is Jake Chesney. He's with us," Rudyard said.

"Us meaning CIA, I'm assuming?"

Chesney inclined his head.

Cole sighed. Of course, they'd know about Kenny and Timothy.

"All right. Let me go back and see if I can have one of the parents take him back. You sound and look scary." This latter sentence was directed toward Chesney. The man didn't smile, which confirmed Cole's assessment.

A group of parents were chatting in a huddle as Cole returned. Kids milled around looking unhappy. Cole surmised they had lost by the measly score of one to nothing.

Timothy approached him. "Something happen?" He looked anxious.

Cole realized immediately that he was thinking about Kenny.

"No, nothing serious. These guys need me to come and look at some evidence." This sounded accurate enough to not be lying.

"It's not about Dad?"

"No, honest."

Timothy looked relieved. "About that case, then? The murders?"

Cole never knew how much kids picked up on things, but he figured he should be honest. "Yeah. Exactly."

"Cole, we just decided to take the kids out for pizza and then have a sleepover at our house tonight. We can take Timothy now if that makes things easier for you," Leslie said. She and Jenny and their husbands had approached.

"Would you like that?" Cole said to Timothy.

The kid practically leaped with joy. "Yeah!"

"Thanks, so much. That'd be really helpful. I've got to check this out."

Cole felt immensely better. At least he wasn't leaving Timothy in the hands of some CIA operative or stranding him alone at the house until Cynthia came home. He gathered Timothy to the side.

"Listen, buddy. I feel awful about this."

"No problem."

"I know. You roll with the punches pretty well. But criminals never stick to regular business hours."

"It's okay, Uncle Cole. You came to the game. I think that's great."

He hugged Timothy, which embarrassed him to no end as evidenced by the quick escape.

"Catch the bastard," one of the dads said as Cole turned to leave. The young assistant coach from the other team happened to be passing by and reinforced that sentiment with a nod of his head.

Cole drove to Rudyard's office on the UVA campus. A few students were roaming around inside the building as he entered. Graduate assistants, probably. They had to be associated with the other offices in the building since the CIA wouldn't hire students for their programs. But then again, Cole didn't know that for sure.

Agent Chesney was nowhere to be seen. Rudyard waited in the lobby, accompanied by a different man Cole didn't know.

"Agent Nightshade." Rudyard advanced with an extended hand. "I'd like to introduce you to Dr. Tucker Adamson. He's the director of the Study of Reincarnation Sciences."

Cole shook Dr. Adamson's hand and noticed that his ID badge had an MD after his name. "Doctor," Cole said.

Dr. Adamson nodded with a smile. "Pleasure." Unlike Rudyard, Adamson was wiry thin with the easy movements of a long-distance runner. He looked younger than Rudyard as well, maybe mid- to late thirties. Close-cropped hair suggested ex-military.

"Let's go up to our offices." Rudyard swept his hand toward an elevator bay down the hall.

Cole recalled from his previous visit that the two offices were adjacent to each another on the second floor. He would've taken the stairs, as would've Adamson, most likely, but he followed Rudyard down the hall.

"Dr. Rudyard, I must admit to being intrigued."

"Yes, this does seem awfully cloak-and-dagger, I'm afraid. But your office said you were in town, and this seemed important to your case."

Cole didn't recall mentioning that he'd be at Timothy's game, but he must've somewhere along the way.

They stepped off the elevator. Cole was surprised to see them headed toward a door etched with the words *Study of Reincarnation Sciences.*

Unlike whoever dealt with such things at the spartan Vector Labs interior, the reincarnation researchers had gone all out with decoration. The waiting room had plush furniture in primary colors, shelves with books and magazines, and—most surprisingly—a huge selection of toys that would make a kindergarten classroom look barren.

"All of our research participants and patients are children between the ages of three and eight," Dr. Adamson said when Cole stopped to take in the setting.

A short jaunt through the waiting room doors and down a hallway led them through an open door to a spacious and well-furnished office. Adamson's desk was long enough to land fighter jets, and his chair resembled a rolling throne. To the left was a separate sitting area with a cluster of nicely padded chairs around a small table. In yet a third section, there were tiny chairs and a table for little kids to play or draw.

"Please sit." Adamson motioned toward the four chairs surrounding a coffee table. Rudyard led the way, and Cole sat while watching Adamson move purposefully to his desk and retrieve a recorder that had been positioned to one side. Adamson placed the audio recorder in the center of the coffee table and lifted the knees of his trousers before sitting.

"We're going to be skipping across a number of different events which, taken together, seem to connect your remote-viewing ability, our reincarnation research, and the mass murderer you're currently searching for. Our efforts probably generate more questions than answers, but we couldn't keep this from you."

"Okay. I'm still curious. What do you have?"

Rudyard took over. "It might make more sense if we report on this chronologically. If you recall the protocol for the remote-viewing experiment, a research assistant of mine—a UVA student—served as the "sender." This sender was positioned at a location that had been blindly and randomly chosen from a number of potential locations held by a third party. I didn't know the location, although I knew it was one of seven possible places, and the third party—an attorney—didn't know the location chosen. Only the student serving as the sender knew. At the start of the experiment, she got into place and began sending messages to you."

"Right. And I drew whatever impressions came to mind. I used sheet after sheet of paper, if I recall." Cole tried to push these two guys along.

"Sorry to rehash this, but it's important," Rudyard said.

Cole extended a hand for him to continue.

"You narrated while drawing and described a forest or woods, a dark box or similar kind of shape, and a tunnel. You also mentioned shadows, possibly of people. Ring a bell?"

"Yes."

"Okay, when I compared your account with the sender's location, I was excited. She was located at the Tomb of the Unknown Soldier."

Cole sat back and crossed his legs. That wasn't what he recalled seeing and said so.

"Still, though," Rudyard said. "You could see the connection—and keep in mind, the impression doesn't have to be an exact duplicate like a photograph. And you'd captured a thematically consistent impression. The box structure was a tomb, maybe? There are trees nearby. The tunnel a possible connection between life and death? The shadow or shadows maybe souls migrating?"

"Man, that doesn't really fit. I can see how you'd interpret it. But aren't you trying to force my reports to fit your hypothesis? I mean, I've been to the Tomb of the Unknown

Soldier. That wasn't what I was seeing. Mine was darker. More unsettling."

Cole's thoughts spun toward Timothy. "In fact, if you recall, I talked about seeing my nephew and a bag of potato chips."

"Yes, I remember. That would be the Augustine boy."

"Correct. Turns out he was sitting on our front porch when I got home that day. Timothy was pissed about being dumped there. If anything, I got the strongest impression from him. Or it was just a wild coincidence."

Adamson leaned forward. "Well, that account certainly adds to the mystery. Should I take over, Bruce?"

"Sounds like the perfect time," Rudyard said.

"Bruce came to me rather concerned after evaluating your remote viewing session *and* reading the article about you from the Richmond paper. If you haven't noticed, this entire building is dedicated to research into the realm of para-psychology. We're kind of the bastard stepchild of the fields of psychology and psychiatry. And we're tolerated by the medical school. In this setting, you'll find empirical studies being conducted on telepathy, psychokinesis, remote viewing, and out-of-body experiences. Bruce helped me with some of the research when I assumed directorship of the reincarnation projects."

Rudyard nodded his assent.

"He brought me the tape of your session. Immediately, I heard exactly the same thing that piqued his curiosity. Your words mimicked something we both recalled hearing from one of our reincarnation research participants."

"I'm sorry. You lost me."

"Let me step back for a second. There are times when a young child spontaneously begins chatting about a life before their current one. Usually, the parents don't pay much mind. You know, kids have wild imaginations and their stories are frequently attributed to that. But these accounts are often very specific. Kids talk about their marriages, their own children, other family members. All of this before their current life. Before too long, it becomes spooky, and the parents are more than a little unnerved. They quiz each other about whether the other said anything like this to their child. Typically no one has, and neither have extended family like grandparents, aunts, and uncles. After consulting with the pediatrician or a clergy member, or hearing about our work through the media, or even word of mouth, parents make an appointment with us. They're concerned about the mental health of their child."

"How old are these kids?"

"Young. This typically happens during the preschool years. Three or four. After the kids are eight or nine, the recollection of these details disappears."

"Why?"

"Well, regular age-appropriate school experiences, along with the development of individual identities that are swiftly reinforced by the here-and-now parents, siblings, friends, and extended family. The early memories of a past life fade and disappear. Nothing much is reported beyond that age unless under unusual circumstances."

Cole ran his hand through his hair. "Okay. Go on."

"Here, maybe it's best if we allow you to listen first to what we're talking about," Adamson said. "I want to play this entire tape for you. You'll find it interesting. I have a transcript for you to follow." Out of a folder appeared multiple pages stapled together. "This exchange is between one of our examiners, identified as 'E' on the transcript, and a four-year-old—almost five-year-old—boy. He's labeled as 'S' for subject."

Cole would've preferred to hear a summary of the tape before listening to it, but he acquiesced to Adamson's recounting method.

The compact cassette tape was already cued in the recorder. Adamson pressed Play.

E: How are you today.
S: Good.
E: That's nice. Do you know why we're talking today?
S: Uh-huh.
E: Can you tell me what that is?
S: We're going to talk about my other life.
E: Yes, that's right.

Adamson paused the recorder. "This isn't the first time the examiner and the child had met. She'd chatted with him earlier in the playroom and worked on establishing rapport. While the examiner never told him what to say, she did mention that she would talk to him about his previous life— or whatever word or phrase the child used to describe his experiences. This is standardized across all of our interviews."

E. Before we do that, can you tell me about where you live now?
S. I live in a big house. It has a red door.
E. Wow. A red door.
S. Mm-hmm. My bedroom is on the second floor. You go up the stairs and it's right there.
E. What's in your bedroom?
S. My toys and books and my bed.

E. Where do you parents sleep?

S. On the first floor. Although sometimes Mommy is on the second floor if she's sick or I'm sick.

E. What do you like to do for fun?

S. Go outside, play soccer, and go in the woods.

E. Do you have woods nearby?

S. Uh-huh. I go out the red door by the driveway and go right on the path to the woods.

E. What's in the woods?

S. Trees, silly. And a path. You walk on the path and you come to a stream. I can't go near the stream because I might drown. There's a bridge, though. A big, big bridge that has a roof on it. It's colored red, too. Just like our door.

E. I bet it's pretty.

S. Yeah. And cool. You can cross the water without getting drowned.

E. Can you keep going on the path?

S. Yes! You keep going and then you see my house.

E. Your house?

S. My clubhouse. Me and Scott built it.

E. Wow. Is Scott your friend?

S. Yes. But he's kinda like a babysitter, too. He's way older.

E. How much older?

S. A big kid like a teenager. And John the handyman helped too.

E. Can people fit inside? Adults and kids?

S. Yes, they can. All grown-ups and kids can fit. And you know what?

E. What?

S. It's red too.

E. Now that's cool.

S. Yep. Scott's gone away though.

E. He has? I'm sorry.

S. I think it's because I stabbed him.

[Lengthy pause.]

E. You stabbed him?

S. I think Dash made me do it.

E. Dash?

S. That's me. Or it was Glow.

E. Wait. I'm confused. Who's Glow?

S. My wife.

E. Oh, okay. You're talking about your other life. Before this one.

S. Yeah. They got in trouble.

E. In trouble? Tell me about that.

S. Dash cut up people with a knife.

E. Oh.

S. Uh-huh. Yep. He tells me in my head. I remember it.

E. That must be scary.

S. Nah. He liked it. Girls and boys. He cut them from here to here. [Indicated neck.] And he bit them there. A whole bunch of them.

[Lengthy pause.]

E. You saw this?

S. In my head.

E. What did Glow do?

S. She liked to watch. She gave Dash ideas. Do you know the lollipop people?

E. No. I never heard of them.

S. Dash told me in my head. They were on top of a big stick. Like a big pole. They'd be on top and

slide down. Dash read about it in a book and said
the man who did it liked to watch.

E. Did the lollipop people have fun?

S. No. I don't think so. The pole was sticking in them.
They were bleeding.

[Lengthy pause.]

E. Tell about how Dash and Glow got in trouble.

S. They got put in jail.

E. Where? Do you know?

S. No. They weren't together. Dash got kilt. Somebody
came up behind him and squeezed his neck until
he died. I died. The other me. Then I was floating,
and I woke up as me. This me.

Adamson poked a button and turned off the recorder. "The interviewer was just a first-year grad student. Twenty-four years old. She'd never heard anything like this and didn't think to ask for pertinent information. Number of victims. Names." He shrugged.

Cole's thoughts were racing. "How often do you get stories like this?"

"Kids reporting a previous life as a murderer? Not ever. This was the one and only," Adamson said.

"When was this interview conducted?"

"Nineteen sixty-two."

"Do you ever try to corroborate the memories? They could just be stories." Cole looked from Adamson to Rudyard.

"That's a critical part of all parapsychological research. We try to corroborate everything. Incorporate experimental controls. In the case of reincarnation research, we interview parents or other adults to see if maybe the kid could've overheard family lore being discussed. Or maybe picked it up from a TV show." Adamson clasped his hands on his lap. "Those things happen. If there's any inkling of contamination, we become skeptical of the account."

"Also, there's a strong effort to get identifying information from the child," Rudyard said. "Their name from a previous life. Family names from that life. Where they lived. The town or street name."

"And did you get that information in this case?"

The researchers exchanged a glance. Adamson answered. "No, the family decided to drop out of the research. They have a right to do that."

"So you never got the name of the—hell, what do you call it—the name of the reincarnated soul?"

"Who the child was purporting to be?"

"Yeah."

"No, we didn't follow up after the family withdrew," Adamson said. "We assumed Dash was the name, but never checked up on it. And in anticipation of your next question, none of us recognized the name from the news. None of us are true-crime fanatics. Please keep in mind that we only revisited this case over the past few days when the various connections came to light."

"Can you tell me who the subject was? Where he lived?"

Adamson shook his head. "We destroy contact information at a family's request. In this case, they made that request."

"What about the interview? Can they request for that to be destroyed?"

"Yes. But they didn't."

Cole stood and paced. "So, you don't have a name."

"Okay," Rudyard said with a sigh. "Now this gets complicated. We no longer have the name of the child or the form where we compiled the demographics. We did, however, keep the signed consent form. Although the signature is rather illegible."

"A parent signed it, though, right?"

"Yes. Two women accompanied the child. The mother was maybe around forty. She signed the form. The other was in her sixties. His grandmother, we presumed."

"How old would this kid be now?"

"He would've been four or five then. So, around nineteen."

Cole returned to his seat. "Okay. Besides the general similarity to the recent murders as reported in the paper, what made you recall this interview from fifteen years ago? Granted, it sounds disturbing coming from the mouth of a little kid, but..."

Adamson moved to the edge of his seat. "A couple of reasons. First, what the boy reported was unusual, to say the least."

"Second," Rudyard said, "the number of kids who come to us isn't huge. You'd be surprised what researchers can remember about specific cases. And"—Rudyard reached into his jacket pocket and pulled out another cassette tape—"you, Cole, tied it together for us."

"What do you mean?" Cole smiled uncertainly.

Rudyard smiled briefly in reply. "This is a tape of your remote-viewing session from last week. I consulted with Dr. Adamson after you left and, well, why don't I just play the sections of interest. That'll be easier than explaining it."

Adamson had a sheet of paper with numbers that served as locations for the sections of tape he was interested in. He pressed Play, and the recording hissed. The vocals had a slight metallic echo.

"Quiet...path...red door...dash...dash what?"

Scratching noises. Scribbling. Pencil on paper.

"Dash . . . dash . . . and glow."

Adamson pushed the Stop button. "One more sequence." He pushed Fast-Forward, watched the counter intently, and stopped. He pushed Play.

No words initially. No pencil scratching.

"Potato chips. That can't be right."

More silence. Then: "My nephew. Although he's really not my nephew."

Scratching noises resumed.

"Oh, oh, oh. God. Red door. Remember red door. Woods. Dark. Straight. Straight. Back to the tunnel. Flat flooring with sides and a roof. A covered bridge. Red. A red bridge. Dash, he says. Dash, what? Glow, glow. Glow what? Trees, trees, and more trees. The box. No, a square. A room. Red. The outside is red. Red shack. Red shack. Beyond. Oh God. Sharp, sharp. No, no. Stabbed. I . . . stabbed."

Adamson punched the Stop button with his index finger.

Cole felt heat rising in up his torso to his head.

"We weren't overreacting by contacting you, were we?" Rudyard said.

"Jesus. No." Cole reached for the cassette recorder and stared at it as if the act of holding it would make what he'd just heard seem real. "I remember you saying I was actively drawing for an hour. I don't remember that sense of urgency. I felt panic just hearing that voice. My voice."

Rudyard took the recorder from Cole's hands. "There's an intertwined sense of telepathy going on here. We have you with your presence and your history working on a case that sounds awfully like the reminiscences of one of our research participants—a four- or five-year-old—from nearly fifteen years ago. Our research subject described murders committed by him during his previous life. And to close the circle, you described, we think, the property of the little boy as he described it all those years ago. The red door, bridge, and clubhouse. Except you were in a state of panic, it seemed."

The remainder of the meeting involved Cole gathering facts on whatever the researchers could remember about the case, including possible locations of the family home and contact information of the student research assistant.

The consent form had already been retrieved and given to Cole. "The signature here. Looks like 'Ellen' or 'Elena' for the first name. The last name? I'm guessing 'M' and a small 'c' and an uppercase 'C.' But the rest, it's just a scribble."

"That's how it looks to me," Adamson said.

The child's name was easier to read—because it was written in block letters by the child. First name only: David. "We can check birth records from nineteen years ago. Take or leave a year. Maybe we'll get lucky and there are only a few Davids born with a last name starting with 'McC.'"

"Still, I bet there's a lot of them. David's a popular name," Adamson said. "Sorry we didn't have a complete record."

"It's a start. Who knows where it'll lead to? In the meantime, I'll track down Dash and Glow, if those are real names." Cole stood to leave.

"Not to throw cold water on your search, but the murderer—Dash—if he is real, then he's dead," Rudyard said. "I'm not sure what you'd get from finding out who he is."

"And again, if real, he would've died before nineteen fifty-eight at the latest." Adamson said.

"Why?" Cole said. "Oh, wait. Reincarnation."

"Right. Typically, the person's death is close in time to the birth of the subject. That's not a given, mind you. The act of impaling that our boy described had been a form of execution for centuries. One of the more famous practitioners was the ruler of fifteenth-century Romania, Vlad Dracula. He wasn't actually a vampire, of course, but people now associate him with the fictional character. The connection's already been made in the press."

"Yeah. The vampire of Charlottesville. I noticed."

"We think that Dash was fascinated with this history and maybe torture in general. His interest was passed along to our research participant. That's how the boy learned about impaling."

♋

Decidedly paranormal leads sat uneasily with the federal hierarchy. They could be pursued, but patience wasn't limitless. Fortunately for Cole, his partner and immediate supervisor was more than willing to explore such opportunities.

"This means finding the kid, if he's still out there," Martin said over the phone. "Or finding the mom. That would involve deciphering the signature, though. We can give that to the writing lab people."

"I can't imagine they'd see anything beyond the scribble. Going over birth records might be better."

A pause. "Okay. Still we'll let them have a look."

"What about this killer? Dash? Assuming that's him. I'd like to check his records and see if there's anything to be gleaned from them. Does he ring a bell?"

"Not off the top of my head," Martin said. "But I'll get somebody on it pronto."

"Any new connections found among the victims?"

"Zero still. Different schools, different age groups, different interests. They didn't appear to know one another, at least in what's been found so far."

Cole arrived home Saturday evening to find Cynthia already there.

"Timothy called to say that they made it back to Fredericksburg and that he's staying the night at Ricky's house. You knew that, he said."

"Yeah," Cole said, slipping off his jacket. He hugged Cynthia and kissed her deeply. "Well, I didn't know it was Ricky's house. The plans were fluid. I do know that the night is ours. The bedroom awaits."

Cynthia smiled and rested her head on Cole's shoulder. "My God, a free moment for us and you only think of one thing."

"And what's wrong with that?" Cole lifted her face and kissed her. "C'mon. I'm powerless in the face of your beauty. Weak in the knees and all that."

Cynthia had told him that sex seemed different when he was consumed by a case. He'd focus his gaze on the wall as if watching some image visible only to him. At times, she said, it was like he didn't even need her to be present. Not wanting her to feel like he was taking her for granted, he worked hard at remaining conscious of her needs and moods when he felt in danger of being distracted. He didn't think he was successful this time, however.

"I'm sorry," he said when he finished. His body was damp with a sheen of sweat.

Her arms still embraced him. "Yes," she said in his ear. "I could tell. Intense sex under stress. I'm not complaining, but you need to remember that I'm there with you. Sometimes I wonder if you forget."

Cole sighed and lowered his forehead to hers. "Honest, I don't. It's just..." He shifted to her side and snuggled. "You're my lifeline. My anchor to sanity."

"That's a lot of pressure." She squeezed him tighter.

"Oh, God. I don't mean to add more."

"We both leave stressful lives, Cole. We, you and me, need to keep that in mind for each other. So, what happened today?"

Cole kissed her cheek. "I was called away from the game. Right before it ended."

"I kind of figured something odd happened. Do you want to talk about it?"

"Yeah, but not now. I hate bringing those people into our bed with us."

Cynthia leaned close to him and pecked his lips. "Good. I haven't eaten all day and I'm starving."

"Aw shit, you should've said something."

Cynthia just looked at him. "Give me a break. With you, the choice between food and sex is never in doubt."

They showered and went to the kitchen to cook dinner. While they ate, Cynthia talked about her day in the emergency room. Another multicar wreck on the highway. One serious injury and a score of minor ones but no fatalities, thank goodness. Then there was a heart attack, a couple of kids needing stitches, ear infections, and a few early flu cases. Generally, not a bad day. Saturday night—which she didn't have to work that evening, thank God—brought the serious stuff: gunshots, knifings, drug overdoses.

Cole described his day and didn't downplay the weirdness of it. Cynthia had been with him long enough for her to read between the lines. She'd tell if he was minimizing something.

"I bet you didn't see that coming."

"No. Pretty funny for a guy who's supposedly telepathic, isn't it?"

"Do you even believe in reincarnation?" Cynthia pushed

her empty plate away and twirled her water glass in her hand. She had declined a glass of wine—which didn't stop Cole from having one.

"I'd never even thought about it, let alone considered whether it's real. I suppose no, I don't. But people do, I guess."

"There's a certain amount of irony here," Cynthia said around a smile.

"What?"

"A psychic who's a skeptic."

"Yeah, I guess. It's just that you hear a lot of bullshit. You know, frauds, fakers, scam artists. They should work in amusement parks. But I know I'm legitimate."

"That argument won't get you much support from your peers."

"Which? Psychics or federal agents?"

"I was thinking psychics." Cynthia took a sip of water.

"Yeah, well. I only trust what reality I can see with my own eyes. That includes telepathy."

Cynthia rubbed the small of her back. "Did you notice that the relationship only goes two ways in this trio you're grappling with?"

"What do you mean?"

"Well, you and the kid share the same images of the red house, bridge, and, what, a door? And the kid talks about memories of his previous life as this killer. You and the killer don't have a connection."

Cole pondered this and looked straight into Cynthia's face.

"What?" she said.

"Shit. That might not be true. I dreamt I was being stabbed. In the neck. My throat cut, to be more precise."

"God, Cole. My worst nightmare lately is about being

close to graduation and realizing I'd forgotten to take a required history class."

Cynthia extended her hand across the table. Cole reached for her in return. Cynthia's eyes watered slightly.

"I'm scared for you."

The words were whispered, and Cole had to revisit them in his mind. "Scared for me?"

A nod of her head and a squeeze of his hand.

"I carry a gun now. That's more than I used to be able to carry."

She sighed. "That's not what I mean. Or it's not all of it. I worry about the overwhelming...impact of all this on you."

Cole considered her words. "You know this is par for the course for my life. This shit would happen to me regardless of what I do for a living."

"I know, and we've been through this. I knew what I was getting into—all the way from sixth grade." She smiled. "I worry about the toll on you, including the physical toll. You always get hurt."

Cole stood and moved behind her chair. He leaned over and hugged her tightly. "Funny, I worry more about the toll on you, being a doctor and all. The shitty hours, the pressure."

Reaching up, Cynthia stroked his face, gently rubbing the stubble on his cheek. "Don't change on me. Please. I need you as you are."

"I will always be exactly as I am. Even as an old man. What brought all of this on?" He shifted position and leaned his butt against the table.

Her expression was strange. Could someone be scared and happy at the same time?

"What?" Cole brought his face closer.

Her eyes welled again. "I'm pregnant."

The words needed two seconds of processing. "What? Holy shit." After another second, he knelt and threw his arms around her. "That's fantastic."

"You're not worried?"

"No," Cole said. "Why would I be worried?"

"We've got our careers. We have to juggle so much. Babysitters, schedules, you name it. Things are going to change."

"We've got time. We can figure it out. Your folks will have ideas. So will Flo. Hell, when we're both busy we can pawn the baby off on Kenny. He owes us."

"A professional killer as babysitter? No way."

"What? He's a federal agent."

"As if that makes a difference." Cynthia squeezed him again. "We need to get married."

"Well, I've been asking."

That part was true. They were technically engaged, but Cynthia's education and training had garnered most of her attention. Cole, meanwhile, had been wrapped up in his own world. They never got around to planning a wedding.

"My parents will be relieved."

"What? That you're pregnant or that we're finally getting married?"

She swatted him playfully. "Oh, stop."

"C'mon. It's not like it wasn't in the eventual plans. They knew that."

"What do you say to something small and informal? Back home in a month or so. You know, just immediate family and close friends."

"That'll work. No hoopla is fine with me."

"God, I've got to work this into my schedule now. You too."

"Yeah. We'll postpone all murders at the office."

The next day felt like a whirlwind.

Kenny called. He would arrive home in a day or two. Timothy, far from fresh after a sleepover at his friend's house, was over the moon with the news. Still, after the excitement died down, he fell asleep on the guest bed working on some homework. Cole wrote a note for Timothy to remind him that he'd be in the office for a few hours. He couldn't count on him remembering and didn't want him alarmed if he woke up in an empty house. Cynthia had already left for her shift at the hospital, so the house was quiet as he pulled away. A few cars he didn't recognize were parked on the street. Someone must've been having a get-together.

Cole couldn't get his mind around the idea of becoming a father. And there was a wedding to think about. Not wanting to become overwhelmed, they decided to wait until Timothy was out of the house before weighing alternatives. Meanwhile, they weren't going to tell a soul.

Various agents involved with multiple cases occupied the BSU as he arrived. He noticed Martin in his office and stuck his head in.

"Happy Sunday."

Martin grunted. "I may have something for you later."

"Looking forward to it."

Cole started in with the Virginia birth records of 1958. Wondering how many Davids had been born with a last name beginning with *McC*, he was surprised to find that there weren't any. He tried 1957 and 1959. Still none.

Neighboring states came next. He stopped after West Virginia and rubbed his eyes. A stress headache was brewing.

He found one David McCarthy born in Maryland in 1958. Sadly, he'd succumbed to leukemia in 1970.

"What are the odds," he said to Martin, who entered his office without knocking.

"Odds for what?"

"I'm striking out on David M-c-C born in 1958."

"If you weren't looking for him, there'd be tons. That's the way life works. I've got something for you to check." Martin tossed two files on his desk.

"What are these?" Cole lifted the files and opened the top one.

"The records of Dashiell Grymes and Gloria Seely. Charming couple." Martin sat and tented his fingers before his face.

"So there was a Dash."

"Mm-hm. And Gloria was Glo, spelled G-L-O. The Grymes family was quite the upper crust back in the day, may still be for all I know. They're from Texas. They didn't take kindly to one of their own going on a murder spree with a mere commoner. She was blamed, of course, for leading the young man astray."

"How young?"

"They were eighteen and nineteen when their reign of terror began."

"How come we never heard of these guys?"

"Because it happened in the mid-fifties and the events were geographically spread out—at least by the standards of the time."

"Okay. Give me the short version."

"Over a six-month span, murdered eleven people. The twelfth survived—a fifteen-year-old girl who was disfigured for life. She was able to identify the attackers. Victims were all young, between thirteen and twenty-one. Females and males. Stabbed—slashed, really—throats cut. A bite to the neck, sometimes a chunk taken out. Body parts taken as trophies. There might've been some ritual associated with those. Some were found in a pot on a stove. This Dash guy was killed in prison within a month of his incarceration. Garroted. All sound familiar?"

Cole reached for Dash's file. "Well, shit."

"What?"

Clipped to the first page was an arrest photo. Dash had dark, slicked-back hair and a scraggly beard. "Fuck. I've seen this guy."

"He's dead." Then recognition spread across his face. "He's appeared to you, you mean."

Cole nodded. "Yeah, it was sudden. Right before my eyes while I was in that stupid tree at the military school. Startled me and I fell."

Martin shook his head. "I shouldn't be surprised. Anything helpful?"

"No, but I've seen him a couple of times."

"Well, we know our current killer isn't Dash. Let's explore these files, though. Christ, I can't imagine being in your head, partner." Martin took a few steps toward the door. "Oh, by the way. Gloria is still alive and in prison."

"Where?"

"Right here. How's that for coincidence? The Virginia Correctional Center for Women. In Goochland."

Cole exhaled. "I need to go see her."

6

Early Rituals

Summer 1971

DAVID'S AWARENESS OF DASH HAD come on quickly, although he didn't entirely understand what was going on. The first inklings started maybe when he was around three. There'd be a feeling...a word...an image.

Dash.

A girl in sunglasses with a scarf around her head.

I'm Dash.

The girl's laugh.

A book with big words.

Racing along the highway with no one else around but the girl. In a car with no roof.

Dash became more organized in his mind when he was four, when Karen was his nanny.

She's pretty, Dash said.

I like her.

I do, too. Do you think she's pretty?

David guessed so. *How do you know?*

If you like to look at her. And if you like to be around her. Do you?

Yes. She's nice. Her skin is pretty.

And her smile.

Uh-huh. And her smile.

I like the way her neck looks, Dash said.

David thought so too.

We should touch her neck when she isn't looking.

Okay. When?

At night when she's asleep.

Okay.

Let's do it now. She's asleep.

David sat up in bed. *We must be quiet.*

Take your pajamas off.

Why?

You'll be more comfortable.

Later:

Climb on her bed.

Okay

See her neck? Touch it.

Okay.

Do you like how it feels?

Yes, I do.

I thought you would. You and me. We're the same.

They were. David knew that now.

Imagine your scissors on her neck instead of your finger.

Oh. She might get cut.

Do you like how it feels?

Yes.

Karen woke up, though, and she was angry. She didn't like what was going on. David was confused because he thought she'd like it too.

It's wasn't long after that when Dash gave him another idea.

Hey, David. Your scissors are bright and shiny.

Yes, and sharp too. I have to be careful.

I know. If you run with them, you can get hurt. Or hurt someone else.

Uh-huh. That's what Karen said.

That's why she keeps saying, "Walk, David."

I know.

Remember how good it felt to imagine the scissors on Karen's pretty skin?

Yes, she's pretty. And the scissors are shiny.

You're going to need them soon. She'll want help cutting your art project.

Oh.

Do you know what to do? It'll be an accident, right? Run for the scissors and run back.

"David, can you get your scissors for me, please?"

"Yes!"

David ran, snatched them, and ran back. Somebody tripped him just as Karen yelled, "Walk!"

There was a lot of blood. Scary, too. But exciting.

Karen was upset and she never came back, which was sad.

On the other hand, David made a new friend in Dash. Someone he could talk to anytime.

And talk they did.

Dash was in the background when Scott came to play.

Wow. I never played soccer. It's fun!

Yes, it is. I get to kick, kick, kick.

He treats you very nice.

Uh-huh.

And he wants to build a clubhouse?

Yes!

That's wonderful. Let's do it.

Yes! Yes! I hope Dad says okay.

He's such a meanie sometimes.

I know. But he said yes!

Holy shit, kiddo!

Yeah! Holy shit!

The clubhouse is amazing.

Yes, we can play.

We can. And do secret things there.

What kind of secret things?

Well, let's think about it for a while.

Okay.

Later:

Scott is such a big and strong guy.

Yes, he is.

You can be strong like him.

You think so?

Think so? I know so.

How?

By cutting him. Like Karen.

Cutting him? Won't that hurt?

Nah. He's a big, strong boy.

How, then? I don't want to hurt him real bad.

No, we're just talking a scratch.

I don't have my scissors here.

But you have the screwdriver. Remember?

Oh yeah.

Well, climb on the roof and jump on him. Stab him by the neck on the way down.

Oh. Okay. I'll try.

Well, that was a mess. Scott was taken to the doctor and he never came back.

David was sad, but happy too. It felt good to do what Dash said.

His interest in human sacrifice and torture also blossomed around this time. Dash showed him the lollipop people. He had a vision of people sitting on top of long poles. Just sitting. But if he thought about it at all, he realized they couldn't stay up there. They'd have to start sliding down. The top of the pole was a point. And the point would slowly stick the people as they slid. Then the point would poke out near the head.

It was gross. But neat to look at. He tried to make it work with the field mice, but it wasn't all that exciting. People were heavier, and you needed a much longer pole.

That's why it's not realistic.

Dash was right. He'd never see it work with people.

But with a knife or scissors. Or a screwdriver? Zip-a-dee-doo-dah.

Zip-a-dee-doo-dah? What?

Yes, kiddo. Like, ta-da. When you see something cool.

Hmm. That's weird.

Well, someday you'll understand.

When he was around ten, he saw a picture of what'd he'd called the "lollipop people" in a book.

Impaling. A form of execution.

This was the torture method of choice by the historical figure Vlad Dracula.

Holy shit, Dash. Is this the same Dracula as the movie monster?

The prince from those long-ago days, the Impaler? He was real. The vampire was named after him.

Oh. But still. You like both, right?

Excellent observation. I can't impale anyone like that. But I can stab them. And I like necks, don't you?

Yes.

Of course you do. Slice and bite. That's my motto.

Slice and bite. Sounds funny.

And exciting.

Yes, exciting. David had to wait for his boner to go down before he stood up from his seat in the library when he finished with the book.

Sometime during the summer of 1972, David was first introduced to Gloria, Dash's wife.

Just call me Glo. Nice to formally meet you, David.

Nice to meet you, Glo.

The thing was, David had sensed that someone else was around. She wasn't a separate person, though. She somehow came from within Dash.

That's right. She's in my memory. The gal might still be alive. Maybe you can meet her someday. She'd be older now, but let me show you what she looked like when we were together.

An image. The girl David had seen a few times riding in a convertible with the wind blowing her kerchief. That was Glo. Pretty with a nice smile. David got butterflies in his stomach when she smiled.

An endearing facet of her personality was her sense of humor. She'd laugh at herself when she did something wrong or said something stupid. Glo reacted the same to Dash, although this sometimes pissed him off and he would lash out. Like the time he tripped over a dead body.

"Goddamn, Dash," she said, laughing. "Don't be such an oaf."

"Fuck you, Glo. I'm trying. She ain't light, you know. I'd like to see you lift her."

Dash couldn't take a joke, but Glo always shrugged things off.

The real prize was the sex part.

David learned about everything and remembered everything. After all, he was Dash and Dash had the memories.

He first saw Glo naked. Up close too.

What do you think? Do you like what you see?

David did. He couldn't imagine her as an old lady.

He kissed parts of her body he'd thought he'd never see, let alone kiss. At night in bed, he and Dash would have sex with Glo. All different positions and sometimes more than once.

You're good at this. Someday you'll do it for real.

Wasn't this real? Of course it was, but it wasn't *his* memory.

Nonetheless, it was nothing short of amazing. Sometimes his underwear and his sheets were still wet and sticky in the morning.

You're a good pupil. We'll be training you.

This was from Glo, which pleased David to no end.

An interesting development involved the surgical scar on his belly. It began twitching when Glo was around. By the time he was fourteen in 1972, it happened every time she appeared to him or talked to him.

The twitching felt like a flutter of his skin—a tic that kept a muscle firing. David could sit for the longest time watching the scar and surrounding skin jump. Sometimes he had to take his shirt off because the contact made the sensation intense. While it wasn't unpleasant, it felt weird.

❧

David loved libraries. While the local one in town would do, the main library at UVA was amazing. Accumulating memories and random thoughts from Dash—and through him, Glo—prompted his excursions. He had to learn more.

The overall theme from Dash's memories was accumulating power through sacrifice. Human sacrifice, to be exact. This was not the kind of thing a kid could casually ask his parents or teachers about, and interrogating Dash yielded as many questions as answers. While Dash knew something about strange cults and rituals—and Glo chimed in about her own favorites—he didn't present the information in an organized fashion. It was as if he couldn't keep things straight in his mind.

God, you're dumb, David said to Dash.

Fuck you, kid. These are my memories. And I'll have you know I'm self-taught.

Here was the gist of Dash's instruction.

There are many gods. This thought popped into David's head when he was around twelve, maybe thirteen. Glo kept reinforcing it with her own thoughts on the subject.

You see, a hell of a lot more gods than the one god you learned about from Christian fairy tales.

Not that David had been taught that much.

There're gods for the sun, night, sorcery, spirits, vegetation, and so on.

The gods have sacrificed themselves for humans. That's what's kept us alive and flourishing. They nourish us. Keep crops going, shit like that.

We need to return the honor. Show our dedication. Our commitment.

David listened attentively to these musings, filing them away for future library investigations.

How do we do that? David wondered.

Well, through blood sacrifices, kiddo.

What kind of sacrifices?

Animal and human of course. Human is best.

Hmm. But that's murder.

That it is. So, you must be careful to avoid capture. People wouldn't understand.

You've done it.

You bet. Sure as shit. And this is the cool part: as a result of my efforts, I've been elevated to deity status.

Wait. If you're a god, then that makes me a son of god.

Not so fast, David. I earned my elevation. You've got to earn yours.

So, what did you earn?

I, kiddo, am all powerful. I could wander among people completely invisible. I could sell my dope and not be seen by a cop. I could sacrifice without being caught. I was meant for great things.

But you were *caught.*

Rub salt in the wound, why don't you. Yeah, we were caught. A small oversight that did not take away from my overall achievements.

I need to learn more about this.

What do you think I've been teaching you?

But I need to learn more. How else can I learn?

Shit, I don't know. I learned from studying the ancient ones.

Don't hold back, man. Who are they?

The Aztecs.

You shoulda said so in the first place.

Now David had a frame of reference. Trips to the library began filling in the huge gaps in his knowledge.

❧

David sat at a small desk along the wall of the UVA library. Paula, who'd planned to meet up with a friend who went to the university, had given him a ride. A senior in high school, Paula was trying to decide between UVA and William and Mary, although she was leaning toward the latter.

Because the distance to UVA was too far for a bike ride, David always had to rely on others for a lift. Sometimes Edna could do it if she needed to run to the grocery store, or John if he had a chore. Once in a blue moon, his father would take him if he had work in Charlottesville. Mom was a lost cause, perpetually strung out on her valium. Mother's Little Helper. David imagined she'd overdose someday.

With no way of knowing when the next the trip would be, David had to be prepared and use his time wisely. Typically he'd have an hour, tops.

On the desk before him lay a huge book on Aztec history. Carrying the sucker almost gave him a hernia. He also had two bound anthropology journals, one from 1971 and the other from 1968. An unfolded sheet of paper from his pocket contained journal citations. He'd taught himself how to read the citations and locate specific articles.

The massive textbook contained multiple chapters on all the Aztec gods and a whole separate chapter on human sacrifice. Dash was right (*of course I was*) about human sacrifice being a regular part of society: specific forms for specific gods, seasonal festivals, atonements.

David scanned a section about specific gods.

There! That one. One of my favorites. We honored him a lot with our rituals.

David peered at it more closely. He saw Tezcatlipoca and attempted to sound out the name under his breath.

Yeah, I could never pronounce it either. I just called him Tez-cat.

Tez-cat. That was cool.

See, he's the god of sorcery. If he wants to, he can save your life. Or not. You can never predict him. A definite I'll-do-what-I-fucking-like attitude. Seriously.

David had to find out more.

Tez-cat was the god of war and played off both sides. He'd work them into a frenzy, man, to set off the wars. That meant more sacrifices for the other gods. The Aztecs would sacrifice a young guy on an altar on top of a pyramid to him. That's who I get my power from.

A vision of blood spurting and cascading from Scott's chest caught David by surprise. He had conducted his own sacrifices to Tez-cat in the past.

Yep, you sure have. Scott was a good one. Turn the page, man. Let's check out more.

Thumbing through the pages, David perused scores of additional gods.

Mixcoatl

Mixy's cool. You get to dress up like a hunter. Glo liked that part.

Tlaloc.

God of rain. He got off on child sacrifices—their hearts were ripped out. That's what we did too. Especially good luck if the kids cry on the way to their death. You'll remember someday.

Huitzilopochtli.

Can't say this one either. But Huey's a biggie, Dave. God of the sun. Huge. His victims were painted blue, placed on an altar, and had their hearts cut out.

David took a moment to imagine the scene.

We worshipped all of these, and others too, kid. Important for your growth to know and adore them. They make us powerful. We're transformed along the way. Is that fucking cool or what?

David still couldn't remember how he (or they) conducted the sacrifices. *What's involved, exactly?*

It'd blow your mind to see it all at once. You'll get it in stages. Remember those small exercises when you were four? The cutting? Well, those were your first lessons. Setting you up for something bigger.

A little frustrating, but also a relief. David wasn't sure he could imagine cutting out someone's heart.

He spent a lot of time reading up on rituals. There were the Aztecs, of course, and then he went on to the Mayans. He came across some kind of Cuban voodoo, but he struggled to understand those guys, and they only did animal sacrifices. The human offerings were more graphic and exciting.

Somewhere along the line, David got the idea all on his own—no prompting from Dash. He'd practice his own ritual.

Not on anything alive. He'd learned from his two accidental stabbings that people don't look kindly on that.

When you take the big step into the majors, kid, one thing to keep in mind. Don't get caught.

Yes, Dash.

Twenty yards beyond his clubhouse, there was an elevated area that would serve nicely as a miniature altar. A flat slate rock jutted out horizontally about a foot off the ground, and a berm of earth extended beyond that about another foot. The flat rock was maybe three feet long and a foot wide.

Now, something to practice on. A model of sorts. Hmm.

Think about who you've worshipped around the house. This was Glo. David's scar twitched a few times.

He couldn't think of anyone.

Bullshit, kiddo. Who do you jerk off to the most in your fantasies? Dash said.

Around here?

Then it dawned on him.

Oh, Paula.

A two-person chorus of *yes.*

But she's left for college.

Paula had decided on William and Mary. Edna was so proud of her.

I'm not saying to sacrifice her, Dash said. *What kinds of things are representative of her? Right here on the grounds?*

In her house?

Sure, why not?

David thought. She must have pictures. Items of clothing.

Yep. Now you're thinking.

Truth be told, David had spied on Paula a lot before she graduated high school last year. He knew her comings and goings. During the summer, she'd lie out in the sun near Edna's house wearing a bikini that left little to the imagination, though David did his best to imagine it anyway. Sometimes she'd have a girlfriend over, which was all the better. Sometimes a boy would join her, and that would piss off David because he had to be more careful.

Paula owned a Polaroid camera, which she frequently kept with her. David watched her snapping shots of friends and posing for the photos her friends took of her.

She had to have tons of pictures in her bedroom. In fact, David knew she did because he'd spied in her windows some nights. While Paula pulled her shades, there often was a sliver of space to peek around. He noticed where she placed photos—inside a shoebox that rested on a shelf.

There you go, Glo practically squealed.

A symbolic item for a sacrifice as reported in the books.

A good one, too, David thought. After all, he wouldn't ever want to actually sacrifice Paula. She had always been nice to him.

Who knows, you might find something else over there too. Dash was always thinking.

The following day, David approached Edna's house. He strolled casually so as not to arouse suspicion, taking a circuitous route to avoid walking past the kitchen window where Edna might see him.

The limbs of trees hung listlessly, leaves drooping. The lawn, scorched to a lifeless beige in the late-August sun, was unresponsive to his sneakers. Fluffs of dried grass and dust ballooned around his shins. Once behind the house, David trotted to Paula's window. The shade was pulled down like it always was.

He tried the window. It was locked.

Shit.

Try the front door, dopey. Edna doesn't lock it, does she?

Dash had a point.

He took up his stroll again, trying to look natural. At the door, David decided to knock, just in case. He could say he thought he saw someone in there. Yeah, that would work.

No one answered, of course. He tried the door.

Ta-da! See?

It opened and he slipped inside.

The layout was small and unimaginative. A kitchen with a small dining area, living room, bathroom, and two bedrooms. Still, it was appealing. David was used to a huge expanse of living space. Something like this for himself would be kind of cool. Like an enlarged version of his clubhouse.

He made a beeline for Paula's bedroom. The shelf with the shoebox came immediately into view. David sat on the floor with the box in front of him. There weren't as many pictures as he would've expected. Maybe she cleared some out or filed older ones away. Possibly in a scrapbook. He glanced around the room and didn't see one. Damn. But there were probably enough in the box for him to choose from.

Right away, he came across an ideal shot: Paula from the waist up, sitting on a beach by what looked like a lake, though David didn't recognize it. She wore a blue bikini. Her belly was flat with an eye-catching contour. David could almost see the peach fuzz around her belly button. Her wavy brown hair was given even more life by a steady breeze.

In another picture—David guessed it was from prom—Paula stood next to her boyfriend, looking gorgeous in a purple gown. The boyfriend ruined the picture, but David could cut him out easily enough. He stuffed both pictures into his left pocket and straightened out the remaining pile in the shoebox. He returned the box to the exact spot on the shelf where it had rested.

David scanned the room. Was there anything else he could use? Books lined the other shelves, but nothing jumped out at him. A cardboard box from a grocery store sat in a corner where toys were jammed to nearly overflowing—dolls and stuffed animals for the most part. Other than that, Paula had left the room in spartan condition.

Dash wasn't finished yet, though.

I see something.

What?

The box. Take a look.

David stared carefully. He wasn't seeing what Dash saw. Wait. Two naked legs extended from the pile. He pulled on the legs, and out came a Barbie doll. She had wild and knotted brown hair with a dress pulled up to her armpits.

See what I mean?

David chuckled. *Yeah, I do.*

He pawed through the box and came across a baby doll. This had possibilities, too.

Certainly does.

He yanked the clothes off both dolls and tossed them into the box. He thought about a few other items he could use. Completing another sweep of Paula's room, he found what he was looking for.

Time to roll.

David was at the edge of the woods before realizing he'd taken a course close to the back of the house. If Edna looked out a window at the wrong moment, she might've seen him running by, carrying two dolls.

Not much you can do about it now. Even if she saw, she may not have given it a moment's thought. Kids run around outside when it's summer.

Glo could be reassuring when she put her mind to it.

David flew through the small covered bridge. The sounds of his footfalls on the wooden boards startled a few birds from the opening on the far side. Trees towered above his path, seemingly reaching out to one another to keep him safe in the shade. His sneakers pounded out dust from the dried dirt, but not as much as the lawn in the bright sunlight.

Slowing to a trot, David eased past the clubhouse and headed to his proclaimed sacrificial altar. Twenty steps beyond, he remembered that he needed his pocketknife, which was inside the structure.

Oops, shit. He ground to a halt, turned on his heels, and

sprinted back. The inside was hotter than hell, like an oven. He grabbed his knife and tore back to his altar.

The pictures came out first. David gave the bikini photo the place of honor—smack dab in the middle, leaning upright against the dirt wall perpendicular to the rock slab. Next came the prom picture. David used his knife to remove the jerky boyfriend. Then he took out a spool of yarn and a red magic marker. Lastly, came the dolls, which he had placed on the ground to remove the contents of his pockets. Barbie was positioned on the left, the baby on the right.

David stood and admired his setup. No doubt about it, the whole thing looked juvenile. Still, he was pleased with his selections and creativity. Especially for something done on short notice.

Not bad, kid.

The woods were quiet. Maybe all the life-forms were taking a break from the heat. The canopy of leaves above appeared to be the only thing alive. No bees or flies. No birds or squirrels.

David smiled. His belly scar twitched.

He shed his clothes and tossed them to the side. He knelt on his haunches before the altar.

The ritual began.

Dinner was prepared, and Edna finished plating the cold salads for the Fairchilds. She was looking forward to scooting home for a relaxing evening after she cleaned up. The prospect of an evening off was welcome. She'd been distracted over losing Paula. That was how she thought of Paula's departure to college, losing her.

Her attitude had improved over the past day or two,

though. This was a natural stage of her daughter's life. It was always going to happen, so she might as well be happy. And she was, too. Edna had actually begun contemplating next steps in her life. She was young still, not even fifty. New adventures awaited her now that she didn't have a child living with her. Maybe travel, maybe as-yet-unidentified activities. Paula had even teased her about dating.

"No, I'm way beyond that, honey."

"No, Mom, you're not. You look great," Paula said.

"For someone my age."

"Actually, I was going to say you look great for someone who doesn't look a day over sixty." Paula stuck out her tongue.

The idea of dating again was scary, but other types of socializing could be in the offing. Mildred and John had retired and moved to Virginia Beach. They'd invited Edna to visit. Well, maybe now she could.

Edna's musings were interrupted by the sight of David running past the window and toward the woods.

Glo's comment in David's head was prescient—to a point. Edna didn't take that much notice initially. Seconds later, however, she realized he had been carrying dolls, which struck her as odd. David didn't play with dolls, nor did he own any.

So where did they come from?

The only dolls on the premises were stored in the box of old toys that Paula still kept in her bedroom. Which meant he'd snuck in there. But why? What would he want with dolls? It was likely some stupid boy thing, but the idea of David snooping in her house was more than a little disturbing.

Edna stored the salads in the refrigerator. The family wouldn't eat for an hour. Time to take a little hike to her house and check things out.

The unlocked door opened easily. A quick survey of the living room showed nothing amiss. The kitchen was as she'd left it. A peek into her bedroom didn't raise any concerns. Paula's room also looked untouched at first glance.

Edna sighed. Could she be wrong about David? God, she hoped so.

As she turned to leave, her gaze traveled over the shoebox of photos.

They were in a different order. At least the one on top had changed.

Normally this wasn't the kind of thing Edna would notice. But she'd been missing her daughter. Upon dusting the room after Paula left for school, Edna noticed the shoebox and looked through the photos. They were fun shots of Paula with her buddies. The top one had been her and her best friend, Janet. She was sure of it.

Now there was a picture of the lake.

Edna walked over to the box that contained the toys. The clothes for the two dolls, one of them a Barbie—she could tell—had been removed and tossed on the top.

Edna felt queasy. What was David doing in Paula's room? She needed to find out.

The Fairchild estate had always felt safe to her. Obtaining her position had allowed her to escape the clutches of her ex-husband and provide a peaceful setting in which to raise Paula. The friendship of Mildred and John was also an added benefit. Mr. Fairchild was generous—he paid her a good salary and had even helped her with investments. Mrs. Fairchild was kind despite her fragility.

Edna felt exposed walking on the lawn. The woods looked ominous, as if something loomed in the shadows. She'd never experienced this before, and she didn't like it. David had his moments, sure, but she'd never felt threatened by the boy. He was only fourteen. He wasn't capable of… of…

Of what?

The stabbing incidents certainly weren't characteristic of him anymore. Those were the accidental acts of an immature child.

The trees provided immediate relief from the glaring sun. Late afternoon was always the hottest time of day; but the shade offered a one-degree drop in temperature, maybe two.

The path had been vigorously beaten down by David's constant marches to and from his clubhouse and the woods beyond. The beauty of the woods remained the same, although the scorching weather had produced more drooping vegetation. Hidden animals scurried under the brush. Edna imagined squirrels and chipmunks darting around to get away from her.

As she passed through the covered bridge, Edna considered calling for David, but something stopped her. The sense of unease hadn't lessened its grip. She didn't like that. She should be able to trust the boy.

Up ahead, the red clubhouse poked its way out of the bushes. Another option before her was to sneak a peek inside, though she hadn't gone in alone since the day she found the field mice impaled on upraised pencils. The thought of skirting the clubhouse was appealing, but not logical. David could be inside.

Edna took a breath and held it. She clasped the door with a shaking hand and yanked forcefully. The door swung more easily than she remembered, and she almost fell backward. The interior was cluttered but unoccupied. Comics, paperbacks, a pair of binoculars, and sports equipment were scattered around. She swung the door closed softly.

Hands on her hips, Edna scanned the immediate area. She noted where the path continued around the clubhouse and deeper into the woods. Call David's name or not? She decided not to and chastised herself a second later.

The bushes and shrubs grew denser. Insects buzzed close to her face. Edna could feel a layer of sweat breaking out all over her body. She'd need a shower later to get comfortable again.

Ahead, a series of objects appeared on a rock jutting from an elevated berm. Edna knew what they were, but she couldn't allow herself to acknowledge it.

The Barbie doll had been decapitated. The legs were tied together with yarn. The arms were similarly tied and forced behind the doll's back. The head balanced on a small rock. Blood had been drawn with a red magic marker. It streamed down the rock and across the Barbie's breast. The baby doll was propped against the wall of earth behind the rock. Its chest had been slit open from neck to groin. Blood splatter had been added to this opening.

Two pictures of Paula completed the display. They were covered with blobs of a white, viscous liquid. Edna lifted the photo of Paula in the bikini. The substance slid thickly down the photo and touched the edge of Edna's thumb. It was warm.

Edna paused, wondering. When she finally realized what it was, she dropped the photo, an *ack* sound involuntarily escaping her lips. She wiped the semen on a patch of ground-cover and turned abruptly to flee.

Edna nearly rammed into David, who stood behind her.

She gasped and stepped back.

David's eyes narrowed. After a heartbeat, his head tilted as if observing an unusual specimen. All the while his hands held his pocketknife at chest level. Fingers worked furiously, unfolding and then folding the master blade to the handle. A faint snapping noise of the blade drowned out every other sound in the woods.

Edna swallowed.

"Hi, Edna. Must be close to dinnertime," David said.

Edna shifted slightly to ease her departure. She wanted to keep some distance between them as she turned to leave. "Mm-hmm. Yes, that's right. I came to get you," she stammered.

David smiled, but his expression remained distant. "You know what, Edna?" He stood stock-still. "Boo."

David's arm flashed outward.

Edna had stepped to her right at that moment. Startled by the sudden move, she raised her left arm upward and caught the point of the blade from David's knife in the heel of her hand. The blade sliced awkwardly and continued forward, inserting briefly at the underside of her forearm.

David pulled his arm back rapidly. "Jesus, Edna, why did you walk into it? I was only joking."

Edna gawked at her hand and arm. Nothing happened for an instant. Then blood poured dramatically. With a gasp, Edna turned and fled.

"Edna!"

His voice continued to call after her. Frantic images of him chasing her flooded her mind.

Oh my God. Oh my God.

She ran as best she could, but she was almost fifty! No way could she outrun a child his age. Her chest tightened. Each panting breath seared her throat which, in turn, threated to close. A coppery taste flooded her mouth.

She felt as though she were running in quicksand. She

could imagine unseen hands clasping her ankles to trip her and then hold her for David's approach.

Why did she come out here? Dear God, what would happen to Paula?

Pounding sneakers advanced. How long before a hand reached out to her shoulder and brought her down like a lion did to its prey on the savannah?

The covered bridge approached, and the shadows of the interior filled her with panic. Had he somehow sprinted past her? Was he waiting inside to ambush her? But no, the shade disappeared in the blink of an eye.

Almost to the house. Almost.

There, she saw it, coming closer. Her gasping breath turned into squeals as she neared. Oh God, please let someone be home.

Just yards away, she passed Mr. Fairchild's parked car. The red door was yanked open before her. For an instant she saw David... but it was Mr. Fairchild.

"Edna? Jesus Christ, what happened?"

She stumbled, fell, and slid along the pavement.

"Edna, Edna?" He was yelling now. He lifted her, and she collapsed into his arms. Blood smeared on the man's dress shirt. "What the hell?"

She tried to talk, but the wheezing gasps prevented it. Only squeals emerged.

"Come on. Inside."

As they staggered through the doorframe, Edna glanced behind her.

David was nowhere to be seen.

&

For the next two days, David spent most of his time in

his room, seething. No outbursts, those were bullshit. But he paced and banged his head (softly) against the wall.

You've got to use your head, kid. Stabbing the lady was dumb.

It was an accident.

Well, maybe, maybe not. Be honest.

Truth was, David didn't know. He wanted to scare her, yeah. Maybe mess her up a tiny bit. But hurt her? No. Well, not really.

That's a little better. You gotta start being honest with us. With yourself. That's the way to control, man.

Control? God, what're you talking about?

Knowing yourself is self-control. It keeps you on your toes. Helps with foresight so you think ahead.

How should I have thought ahead?

Easy. Your trophies of Paula were good choices. But damn, kid, you don't leave the evidence around. Have a plan to clean the fucking shit up. Especially your creamy tadpoles on the girl's picture. I mean, jeez. People will think you're a psycho or something.

When David emerged from his room, he was shocked to see a small van parked outside Edna's residence. Two guys were packing up things from the house.

"Edna's leaving?"

Mom's eyes were red-rimmed. She didn't look at him. "Yes. She felt she couldn't stay given what you did."

"I like Edna. What happened was an accident." David *did* like Edna. He truly hated to see her leave.

"Oh, David. Your father will explain things to you." She moved away and walked outside.

Edna was by the van talking to Dad. They both nodded, and then she hugged him. Edna turned to his mom as she approached. They reached for one another. Both women were crying.

Well, shit. This didn't look good.

David had followed Edna to the house after the stabbing. When Dad appeared on the scene and helped her inside, David ducked behind some shrubs to stay out of sight. He waited for God knew how long, hoping Dad would be distracted with Edna.

No such luck.

His father rushed around the corner as he was climbing the stairs.

"David. What the hell?"

"I didn't mean it." He blurted the response without thinking.

"Jesus. Get upstairs. What a fucking mess."

When he said "fuck," he was *really* pissed.

It was probably ten minutes later when he realized he hadn't removed the sacrifice display. If Dad went out there, he was screwed even more.

Of course, Dad did.

After Mom and Edna stopped hugging, Edna walked toward the door.

Goddam, she was coming inside to see him.

"Goodbye, David." She kept a considerable distance from him.

"Edna, I..."

"Shh. I know." Her face crumpled a bit. "I will miss you." The last word was partially muffled by a catch in her throat.

"I'll miss you too." David looked down at his bare feet. He felt sad and angry at the same time. Footsteps retreated.

When David looked up, he saw Edna getting into her car.

Sometime later, his father entered his room.

"Your mother and I have decided a boarding school will be the best place for you."

"What?" David was too stunned to say anything more. He already had a private high school all lined up. It started next week.

"Things are getting out of hand. You leave in two days."

"Dad…"

"That's it. I pulled some strings and I got you in. A good school, too. Fort Concord Military Academy."

Dash popped into his head. *Man, you're totally fucked.*

7

Retrocognition Blues

October 1977

THE INTRODUCTION OF THE REINCARNATION element nagged at Cole. Supernatural leads or evidence were fine if *he* experienced them. On rare occasions he'd also believed in other people's abilities when those abilities resembled his own. But none of his otherworldly encounters had involved reincarnation, and that made him hesitant to accept its potential role in the case.

Now here he was, traveling to immerse himself in the three Charlottesville crime scenes and let the psychic evidence materialize via telepathy. His version of telepathy, that is. Something grounded in his reality. Like his sightings of Dash Grymes.

Or a young man with a beard who looked like Grymes.

That's not what you thought when you saw the picture in the file. You were positive it was Grymes.

Yeah, well.

So went his inner argument. Cole felt weird about adding reincarnation to the mix, even after he saw (may have seen) the guy who'd allegedly been reincarnated.

Cole conferred with Martin first thing in the morning about driving to visit the scenes. Martin gave his blessing for Cole to search around.

"By the way, I'm working on getting you into the prison to see that Glo woman."

"Thanks." Cole expected Martin to work his magic quickly.

He drove to Michie Tavern first. It wouldn't open for about an hour, but staff were already setting up for the midday meals. The fall season meant a lot of retired folks would visit and not families because school was in session. The weather remained pleasant and, with fall colors approaching peak, they could expect a good turnout.

The on-duty manager seemed nervous when Cole introduced himself.

"We're still reeling from it." The woman bit her lower lip. "But I don't know how much more we can help."

"Were you working that day?"

"No, I was off. Evelyn was running the show." She patted her well-secured hair.

"Anyone else here today that worked then?"

The manager looked around. "No, believe it or not. One of the girls quit shortly after...you know. She was petrified. We all were. The others on duty were college students who work weekends. They're at school today."

Cole thought as much. "Okay, just wanted to check and let you know that I'll be prowling around in the trees by the employee parking, near the scene. In case you get questions."

When he left the dining area, Cole couldn't help noticing the haunted expressions on the other staff. Murder did this to those who'd had even the most tangential relationship with the victim.

The area where employees parked was naturally the farthest from the tavern. Like a lot of Virginia, the surrounding landscape was wooded and attractive. Cole noticed some paths crisscrossing the trees and bushes. With the dropping leaves, shafts of sunlight illuminated the paths more than they would have just three or four weeks ago.

Cole stepped off the pavement and worked his way among the trees. His nose tickled with the smells of fall. Scents of pine and decaying leaves and possibly ragweed, which gave some people miserable allergic reactions. Then there was an aroma of dryness, like cotton sheets on a clothesline. The scent always transported him to his early childhood with his grandmother. His chest swelled with images of an inviting fire in her cabin keeping a chill out of the room.

The rush of emotion caught him off guard. With his eyes closed, Cole inhaled deeply and returned to the present. Overhead tree branches waved in the breeze, and a momentary display of sunlight warmed his face.

A girl's giggle caught his attention.

Patricia Loots, looking as old as she would ever get, was approaching in Cole's general direction. She'd changed out of the period-piece uniform worn by dining staff and into her street clothes, a sleeveless blouse and shorts. The clothes she wore when her body was found. The remnants of yellow crime-scene tape fluttered in the breeze about fifteen feet away.

Cole remained stationary. No matter how many times he'd been privy to such images, the initial sighting never lost its emotional impact.

Patricia's giggle eased into a warm smile.

So, she knew the killer. In fact, she seemed pleased to see him.

She paused and presented an exaggerated expression of surprise.

Cole watched for a sense of fear or shock, but neither came. If anything, she grinned more broadly.

So, not an attack by a stranger by any means.

She stepped beyond the line of trees and reached out her hands, still smiling. As was often the case, Cole couldn't see the killer directly. A shadow of a figure almost took solid physical form. This dissipated—but not before an arm completed a single rapid swiping motion.

Patricia looked stunned, then confused. All-out horror immediately followed. Her hands flew to her neck and she stumbled backward, falling on her backside. One hand instinctively reached behind her to brace for the fall. This allowed Cole a bird's-eye view of a massive gash on her neck. Blood rocketed from the wound. She looked at her killer, and Cole thought she was going to ask why he'd done this. But her eyes dimmed instead, and she slumped to her back.

Cole stepped forward as an oval mark appeared on Patricia's neck. The oval turned red and bunched together as if squeezed by an invisible force. The perimeter burst, and lifted chunks of skin wiggled from side to side before snapping back into place.

That was the bite.

Her right hand severed from her wrist.

Then the entire display dissolved into fragments until the nightmare was gone and the charming fall day returned.

"Jesus. That was vivid."

A couple of things were clear. This guy hadn't messed around here. No tormenting. Instant death. And no fumbling with the body, sexual or otherwise. Patricia had landed about four feet from the pavement of the parking lot, so he did take chances. Anybody could've waltzed right in and witnessed the entire thing. Maybe that's why he didn't waste any time.

Cole traced his steps back to the car. The interior had gotten hot sitting in the sun. He opened the door, leaned against the side, and waited for the air to circulate.

Nothing surprised him anymore. Still, the number of people with diseased minds walking around haunted him.

Cole drove to the second crime scene at Pen Park on the north side of Charlottesville. Nadine Rudy's body had been found in a wooded area along a hiking trail. Somehow, the killer was able to entice his victims into the woods.

Cole found the location easily enough. The hike wasn't too far, and the shade made the trek comfortable. He received an occasional odd look—his jacket and tie certainly looked out of place in these surroundings.

Nadine's body had been discovered about fifteen feet off the trail. Cole stepped over some underbrush and circled the location. Unlike earlier, Cole didn't see, hear, or feel anything. He circled one more time and scanned farther into the woods as he went. Still nothing.

He sighed, feeling both frustrated and relieved. Returning to the trail, he noted a shower of yellow and orange leaves shaken loose by the breeze working through the branches. Birds flew from tree to tree and sang gaily.

When Cole stepped onto the path, he spotted Dash Grymes spying on him from about thirty yards away. His posture was rigid, shoulders raised and fists clenched. Grymes's head tilted downward as he glared menacingly through hooded brows.

The figure couldn't do anything to him. Cole knew that. Yet when it broke into a charge toward him, Cole flinched. For a second, he expected to be rammed at full speed and hurtled to the ground. Dash's figure vanished, however, when he'd cut the distance between them in half. Cole felt only a mild swoosh of air accompanied by the brief scent of decay.

Well, this was interesting. Dash seemed to be threatening him—or at least trying to frighten him. More important, though, was the fact that he'd appeared at all. Dash wasn't directly involved with this particular crime.

Unless, of course, Cole bought the reincarnation explanation.

More grist for the investigative mill.

Fort Concord Military Academy was east of the city. Cole had arrived from the opposite direction during his first trip, and he passed the entrance without realizing. Grumbling to himself, he turned around and drove to the administration building. Robert Lee was away from the office for the day. That was a pleasant surprise. Cole informed the next in command of his intention to review the scene and the woods behind the athletic fields. He turned down the offer for a guide, explaining that he remembered the way.

"I'm the guy who fell out of the tree."

"That's right," number two in command replied.

The secretary overhearing the exchange nodded vigorously. "I remember that. I hope you're feeling better."

"Yes, ma'am, I am. And I won't be climbing any trees today."

Cole walked between the various athletic fields. One of them was being used by what looked like a gym class. Everywhere else was quiet. No one seemed to be curious or concerned about his stroll.

He stopped at the infamous tree. Cole glanced upward and found the branch he'd stood on. He marveled at how far he had fallen and how damn lucky he'd been not to break any bones.

The immediate section of woods had been scoured for physical evidence, so he didn't expect to spot anything further. Instead, he waited for the jolt of psychic evidence. Today had been jam-packed with experiences. He expected, and in fact welcomed, another from this place. But the same setting could produce something one day and not another. Maybe he was more receptive at certain times or in certain emotional states. Cole wished he knew.

Cole wandered farther along the path until he reached the county road behind the woods. This was where their suspect had evidently parked, or at least somewhere nearby. The homes down the road apiece looked quiet—which they probably were given the time of day. Adults worked. Kids attended school. These poor souls were likely spooked, too.

Cole retraced his steps to the infamous tree. He kneaded his temples while leaning against it. His head was starting to ache. It was probably from hunger—it dawned on him that he hadn't had anything to eat since breakfast. He shut his eyes and exhaled. God, he was tired all of a sudden. The tree provided support as he pushed off to stand.

A sensation of vertigo hit when Cole opened his eyes. Horizontal perspective shifted dramatically to a forty-five-degree angle, and Cole fell to his knees.

Shit.

He reached for the tree trunk and grasped it, stopping himself from collapsing on the ground.

"Whoa! What a fucking ride man." A voice outside his head.

The spinning slowed but didn't stop. Cole closed one eye and tried to focus. He willed the earth to stop wobbling.

It didn't, but he could make out Zachary Tillman approaching through the chaos.

Again, the view shifted. Hushed voices in greeting. A T-shirt dropped to the ground.

Another viewpoint shift and another T-shirt was pulled over Zachary's head and released. He couldn't tell where it landed.

The maniacal face of Dash Grymes appeared before his own, roaring with laughter. The laughter subsided to a cackle. Rancid spittle flew over Cole.

Gagging and choking noises. Grunting, the sound of a body collapsing. Wheezing. Silence. Then the panting of someone winded.

The vertigo subsided.

I wasn't meant to see what happened.

"That's right. Take it. For the offering."

Who the hell was that?

Cole pushed off the tree trunk in time to hear a *thwap* sound. There was another, and then a third.

"It's not easy, I know." Dash was talking to someone. Who?

Zachary had crumpled to the ground. An ax lay near his body. He'd been decapitated.

A figure sat cross-legged within reach. A male, in profile. Cole couldn't make out the facial features or the torso. But the killer's hands were distinct enough for him to observe.

The hands held Zachary's severed head.

"Glo wants to kiss him. You gotta honor her wishes. Don't fail us now."

The hands brought the head toward his face. He paused momentarily before resuming.

The figure kissed the head on the lips.

Cole felt ill. He swallowed back bile. It stayed down for barely a heartbeat.

His vision cleared moments later. Standing on shaky legs, Cole noticed that the knees of his trousers, especially the right one, had picked up a good deal of dirt.

"Of course." He brushed them off as best he could. God, he hoped he didn't look like a physical wreck like last time. At least he wasn't bleeding.

The secretary didn't comment on his appearance when he asked to use the phone. At least that worry could be laid to rest.

Somewhere along the way back to the administration building, Cole had decided he needed to talk to Dr. Adamson at Reincarnation Sciences. To Cole's utter amazement, the doctor answered his own phone. And would be happy to see Cole right away.

UVA students dodged and weaved their way around Cole with determined speed. Late-afternoon classes had likely been dismissed, and dinner was on the horizon. Cole's hunger pangs had resumed after his vertigo-induced nausea in the woods behind the military academy faded. He figured he could hold out on food until after he met with the reincarnation shrink, though. With Cynthia working this evening, he looked forward to choosing a fast-food option.

Cole bounded up the stairs to the second-floor research offices. The remote-viewing office across the hall was dark, so no telepathic-warfare research. The waiting area of the reincarnation science suite was deserted, but a middle-aged woman sat behind a desk with a sliding-glass window partially shut. Business hours were essentially over.

"Hi," Cole said to the woman. "I'm here to see Dr. Adamson."

Before she could answer, the psychiatrist called from the hallway. "Cole, come on in."

The receptionist nodded and smiled. She pointed in the direction of a door to the clinic and interview rooms.

Dr. Adamson extended his right hand to Cole while clapping Cole's shoulder with his left. "Good to see you. Come into my office."

The room had maintained its inviting look. Two or three sheets of paper lay on the desk—these appeared to be academic writings, not confidential patient reports. Nothing of any personal nature stuck out for Cole to observe.

"Thank you for seeing me on short notice." Cole sat in a chair on the other side of Adamson's desk.

"You mentioned that it involved the case you're working on. I figured it was urgent."

"It is. I don't want to take up too much of your time, but something has thrown a monkey wrench into this whole ordeal. I need to sort it out."

"All right."

"Before I start, I have to ask if you've heard about my personal history."

Adamson nodded slightly. "I'm assuming you're referring to your psychic abilities. I've heard some, but my understanding is that there's considerably more."

Cole sat back and laced his fingers in his lap. "There is, and I'd rather not go into details. But I can say this. My history with telepathy or whatever you want to call it goes back to when I was a kid. I remember seeing my mother when I was around eight. She died before my first birthday. Since then, I've seen people die tragically, usually due to murder or acts of war. Often, these visions served as warnings. I was able to identify threats to myself or others before they happened. My career trajectory, tracking down serial killers, is a by-product of this whole thing."

Cole paused to catch his breath. He'd been speaking with an intensity he hadn't intended.

"And somehow, there's something different about this case?" Adamson said.

Cole shifted to his left side and leaned his elbow on the armrest. He pursed his lips. "Yeah. I'm being bombarded by this reincarnation...whatever it is." He held out his hands, palm up.

"Bombarded?"

"Yes. On two different levels. First, I'm trying to reconcile my skepticism while being a firm believer in my own abilities."

"So, you don't trust anything unless you experience it yourself."

"You're a mind reader too?" Cole said.

Adamson chuckled. "Not at all. It makes logical sense. You're science driven. Evidence for something must be observed. Your work demands that. I suppose you folks can infer motive based on physical evidence, but the strength of your case depends on the evidence. Two little and charges won't stick."

Cole was impressed.

"I like to watch cop shows on TV," Adamson said. "What's the second level of bombardment?"

"I've received certain images related to this case—showing how victims died or what happened to their bodies. That's typical. Up until now, I've always see the victims, never the identity of the killer."

"And now?"

"I'm seeing *a* killer. The guy who committed the murders

in his previous life. I don't know if he's providing instruction or relishing the vibes. Maybe he's just providing memories to our perpetrator. I don't know."

Adamson nodded.

"Plus, I saw him near my house, which was alarming given that my nephew was visiting. My question is, how can this be happening? From a reincarnation standpoint, I mean."

Adamson tilted back in his chair and raised his feet to the desk, clasping his fingers behind his head. "Interesting." He gazed at the ceiling for a long time.

"I hope you've got more for me than that."

Adamson grunted. "So do I. Okay, I'm thinking. First, it seems like you've started giving credibility to the reincarnation theory."

Cole thought about this. "I must be because I've seen it firsthand."

"Or you think you have."

"C'mon, Doctor. Give me a break."

"Okay, you're not here for analysis. Let's look at this. If we accept the premise that the previous killer has entered the picture as a memory or an active soul in the life of your current murderer, there is a possible explanation. I should warn you that it's rather far out."

"More than what we've been talking about?"

"I'm afraid so. Typically, the former lives of our young child subjects—and those anecdotal reports of reincarnation—lose impact as the child ages."

"I remember you saying something like that before," Cole said.

"Yes. Kids tend to forget these memories by the time they're ten or twelve."

"That's what you've seen here?"

"Yes, in all cases from our research pool. But anecdotally, we've encountered cases where the previous life maintains consciousness within a child. A separate entity if you will."

"What happened in those cases?"

Adamson removed his feet from the desk and rolled closer on the chair. He propped his arms on the desk. "The outcome wasn't positive."

Cole sat quietly, waiting for Adamson to continue.

"The previous life has an agenda, usually. A score to settle."

"Like?"

"I'm familiar with one case, involving a political leader from a small city in India. He was assassinated on the street in broad daylight. No arrests were made. Twenty years later, a murderous rampage occurred in the community. A young man killed the assassins and many of their family. Twelve people, I think, in all. The young man who committed the murders claimed to be the former politician."

"How do you know this wasn't an urban legend or something?"

"Because I talked with the young man myself. A week after it happened. He was very convincing."

Cole loosened his tie. "Shoot. Why does this happen?"

"Here is where things push the boundary even more. There's a spiritual realm called the Akashic Records. It's a depository or container of all human thoughts, feelings, behaviors, social interactions, and so on. A collection of all human events from the past, present, and future. You, Cole, as a psychic, can tap into these records and 'see' the past. We call it retrocognition."

"Dr. Rudyard mentioned this. Retrocognition is when I see or sense how people died."

"People who see the future—have precognition—may also be tapping into the records. Don't dwell on this too much, by the way. There's no empirical evidence for it whatsoever."

Cole grunted. "Yeah, I don't need something else to stew about. But these records, what've they got to do with things?"

"My guess is that the man you've been seeing, the deceased individual who was the former life of your current suspect, has somehow maintained his active memories within the Akashic Records. Probably his emotional states, too. Unprocessed anger, maybe."

"He's alive in there."

Adamson shook his head. "Not in so many words. It's a spiritual realm. But his soul, for lack of a better word, has maintained a presence. And given that the records hold all human events from the past, present, and future, he can maintain his consciousness within your guy. They can freely come and go, together."

Cole stared at Adamson, weighing all of this. "If we play this out, what do we do?"

"About the soul in the records? Nothing as far as I can see. It's within a spiritual realm. The only thing you can do is catch your killer before he's influenced to kill again."

Kenny's car was parked in front of the house. Cole spotted it from the end of the block as he drove home. At the same time, Timothy rode his bike from the other direction. The kid must've been spacing out, because he was nearly on top of his dad's car when he swerved awkwardly. Cole grimaced, expecting him to slam into the car. But Timothy recovered and swerved around it, onto Cole's front lawn.

Cole slowed and watched Timothy jump from his bike, then pause as if he was deciding whether to remain aloof and pissed. Joy must've won out. He sprinted and launched into Kenny's arms as Kenny approached from the porch.

Cole pulled into the driveway.

Timothy was jabbering away about whatever exciting thing had happened recently. Kenny smiled and nodded; his left arm draped over his son's shoulders while his right hand brushed wayward strands of hair from Timothy's face. The gestures were tender, reminding Cole of the complex nature of his best friend.

"Well, Timothy, the old man returns."

"Yeah, like a bad penny." Timothy beamed.

Kenny was forgiven, at least for the near future.

Cole grinned at his friend. "Welcome home."

"Thanks."

Timothy ducked out of Kenny's arm. "I'll go get my stuff." He took off for the house.

"How was Europe?"

"Fine. You know I always like Madrid."

This was a running joke, a way for Kenny to indicate that the action was completed—whether successful or not was never clear. As far as Cole knew, Kenny had never been to Madrid.

"We saw you on TV," Cole said.

"Yeah, that wasn't supposed to be. Damn reporters." Kenny shrugged. "How'd he do?"

"Angry at first, then calmed down. I think he feels safe here."

"I know he does. I owe you big time, remember that."

"We will. You can babysit sometime." The last comment just slipped out.

"No problem." Thankfully, Kenny didn't catch it.

Timothy burst out the front door with a rolled-up bundle of clothes drooping under his arm. Schoolbooks were hoisted under the other arm while his backpack flopped on his back. A textbook fell from his grasp and tumbled down the steps. The front and back covers spread open, and the pages crumpled on the bottom stair.

"Oops." Timothy looked at the book, then his own full hands, and continued to the car. A distinct rip of a page carried over the distance.

"Yeah, oops. That's a school-owned book, right?"

"I'll tape it at home." The words were breathless.

They watched the car being loaded for a second before Kenny turned back to Cole. "I read about you in the paper. The *Post* picked up the Richmond article. Talk about unwanted media attention. How'd they get the story?"

Cole shook his head. Out of the corner of his eye, he saw Timothy return for the book. "From Josiah. The journalist is sleeping with him, and she got him talking."

Kenny laughed. "Oh, man. That kid. Did you ever meet her? Is she good looking?"

"I haven't, so I don't know."

Timothy ambled over to them after trying unsuccessfully to get his bike in the car.

Kenny chuckled. "God, Cole. You bring out the wildness in everybody. I'm so happy I know you."

"Yeah, and this'll probably get wilder. The whole thing is really strange."

"I wouldn't expect anything less." Kenny turned to Timothy. "Need help?"

"Yeah. The bike's caught on something. I got it in last time."

"Let's go take a look." Within seconds, Kenny saw the problem and shuffled things around. The bike slid easily into the car.

"Did Uncle Cole tell you about his stitches?"

Kenny turned back to Cole. "Now what did you do?"

"Nothing. Just a stupid move on my part."

"He fell out of a tree while looking for the murderer," Timothy said.

"I guess that means you didn't catch him, then."

"Sadly, no."

"I'm looking forward to that story, too."

Timothy jumped into the passenger seat while Kenny leaned into the driver's seat rather gingerly. So, an injury of sorts from the recent operation. Cole would never learn about it, so he wouldn't bother asking.

Kenny suddenly halted, backed out of the car, and squinted at Cole. A mischievous grin spread over his face.

"Babysitting. Should my lips be sealed?"

"Yes, for heaven's sake."

Kenny nodded, eased into the car, and drove off.

8

Absorption

December 1976

FORT CONCORD WAS SUPPOSED TO be punishment for David's wayward behavior. Irony of ironies, David thrived there. Discipline shaped him as it did all great people. He felt as though the deities of the universe were molding him, making him ever more powerful.

"Mr. Fairchild, excellent grasp of the command focus and strategy of battle."

"Your point is well taken regarding the European explorers and expansion of the New World."

"Not quite my cup of tea, but your exploration of autonomic nervous system arousal and torture habituation is interesting."

Overall, he wowed the shit out of the assholes who ran the school—and who would be writing his letters of recommendation for college.

Dash was there for the ride, too, cheering him on. The guy was not stingy with his running commentary.

Way to go, man.

Good response, no backing down this time.

Charge harder on that play. Don't mind the pain.

It was all rah-rah-rah.

Christmas vacation senior year was meant to be the break that ended all breaks. David hoped to go skiing once or twice and maybe get laid if he found a willing girl. Instead, he met Regina at a fellow cadet's house on the twenty-first of December. He spotted her right away. A black-haired beauty with dark eyes that smoldered with a sense of mystery. She licked her lips after taking a sip of a drink when she caught his eye across the granite-topped kitchen island.

She wants you, man, Dash said.

Go talk. Be your charming self, Glo added.

"Let me guess. Another hero in the making, a Fort Concord man." Her lips remained moist.

David's stomach scar tingled and twitched.

"Obvious, huh?" David replied. "David Fairchild." He extended his hand.

"Regina McKenzie."

She was dressed in tailored black pants and a white blouse. On any other girl it would've looked plain, but not Regina. She wore it like royalty.

"A pleasure. How do you know Raymond?"

"That's the host's name? He's your classmate?"

David nodded. "A senior like me. We play soccer, among other things."

"I don't know him at all. Which one is he?"

David pointed him out. "So, you're crashing the party?"

"My forte. Actually, my best friend is a friend of a friend of his twin sister." She strolled around the island toward him.

"Ah, yes. The friend of a friend of a friend of the twin angle. I like it." Another pleasant spasm.

She smiled warmly and rested her hand on his chest. It lingered for some time before her hand gently slid down his torso and stopped at his belt buckle. "So, what do you do besides play soccer?"

"Go to class, study hard, learn about warfare, engage in the conventional social relationships of a Virginia gentleman. You know, the usual."

She raised an eyebrow and took another sip of her drink. The liquid in the bottle of bourbon at her elbow was the same color as the liquid in her glass.

"There's my darker side, though. Espionage, human sacrifice. I dabble."

This made her smile. "My father warned me about boys like you."

"Did he? Well. He never met me." David stepped closer.

"I've got my slapjack ready, just in case."

This made David smile.

Thirty minutes later they found an empty bedroom upstairs and had sex for the first time.

"What exactly is a slapjack?" David said as he lounged with Regina on the stranger's bed, enjoying the daringness of the situation. Their faces were nearly touching. Regina turned and kissed his lips.

"A self-defense weapon."

"Seriously?"

"My father wants all his girls to be able to fight off attackers."

"Huh." David grinned. "Let's see it."

"I'm not joking. My father's a defense contractor. He knows a thing or two about fighting. He might make us carry a gun when we're older. He makes my mom."

Regina rolled over and reached for her pants. She pulled a leather strap out of the waistband. David hadn't noticed it before.

"I wear it inside on my hip. This part clips over the waist."

The slapjack was about nine inches long with a small clip on the end for the clasping. The shape was spoon-like and had pieces of leather sewn together. Inside the handle was something solid, yet flexible. The business end was wider than the handle and considerably heavier.

"There's—"

"Lead on the inside," Regina said, finishing his sentence. "Hold on to the handle and swing the weighted end. It's like a nightstick that cops use."

David tapped his head with the weight. "Wow, that would hurt."

"You could knock someone out cold if you hit them hard enough. Kill them if you hit too hard."

"I like it, it's the damnedest thing," David said. "I'm happy you decided not to use it on me."

The relationship lasted an intense seven days. Other than going skiing at Wintergreen one day and a movie one night, the rest of their time together was spent in bed. David had never imagined anything like this ever happening to him. She seemed insatiable.

Of all her extraordinary physical attributes, the most fascinating was a series of scars. Regina had a sequential pattern of parallel slices on the inside of her forearms.

"What're these?" David said during one of their respites.

"Ah. I need to feel pain. There's something about it that makes me feel alive."

"Really?" David said, aroused. "What about biting?"

Regina loved the idea. They added biting to their repertoire, not drawing blood but making marks on both of their necks, her hips, and the inside of his thigh.

"What's the story with your scar?"

"Oh, that. A growth was removed. I was a baby."

"It jerks a little when you're excited."

"Yeah, it's the strangest thing."

"I've got a present for you," Regina said.

"You didn't need to do that."

"It's nothing really." She handed him a narrow present wrapped in snowflake paper.

David opened it and found the slapjack. "Cool." He smiled.

"I knew you were intrigued when you first saw it."

"I was. But how will you fight off all the nasty boys?"

"I won't need it now that I have you."

On the day after Christmas, Regina came over for a visit and spent the night. His parents met her and thought she was wonderful (his mother gushed that word privately to him when Regina left to use the john). They didn't bat an eye when the couple excused themselves to go up to the bedroom.

Regina didn't appear to need sleep. David dozed off and on throughout the night, but Regina kept waking him up for another round. When he couldn't perform any more, David resorted to oral sex. Regina was fine with that.

When she left after lunch the next day, David called Raymond and provided a brief summary of the previous twenty-four hours.

"Man, you get all the luck."

"But shit. I couldn't function after a while. I'm all, like, chafed."

"Which one was she again?"

David described her. Raymond still had only a vague recollection of who she was.

David was to meet her parents on December twenty-eighth. Her father came to the door when he arrived to pick her up for an evening out. The weather was raw with a threat of cold rain. He zipped up his jacket after he rang the doorbell.

"You're David Fairchild," her father said when he opened the door.

"Yes, sir." David extended his hand.

The old guy could've been an administrator at Fort Concord. Short cropped hair, stern expression. He looked like he had no sense of humor or couldn't stand being around a teenager.

The man did not shake David's hand.

"I'm sorry to disappoint you, young man, but my daughter will not be seeing you anymore. She's not well, and the relationship isn't good for her."

"Not well? What's wrong?"

"Never you mind. Just go home. It's over."

David was stunned. "What do you mean it's over?"

The door swung toward him and would've latched shut if David hadn't blocked it at the last second. "I'd like to talk to her."

Yeah, there you go. The fucker. Dash had arrived.

"Young man, remove your hand."

He can't do this!

"No, sir. I want to talk to her. You can't do this."

The door swung open with such speed that David was caught off balance. Mr. McKenzie grabbed David by the front of his jacket and shoved.

"Don't you dare tell me what I can and cannot do on my property, you little shit. Get out of here. Now."

David backtracked to the driver's side of his car. "Fuck you, man." He realized he'd sealed his fate with those words but didn't care at the moment.

McKenzie glared at him but didn't utter a word. David drove home.

What the hell, man? What the hell?

David stormed around the interior of his bedroom in a full circle, punching whatever solid structure offered the opportunity. He managed multiple dents in the sheetrock. His old man was going to be pissed, but he didn't give a shit.

What the hell, man? He can't do that. He can't.

He tried calling, but the old fucker kept answering the phone. David slammed the receiver down each time.

Shit. Shit! He couldn't do this to him.

The next morning, he called and got Regina's mother, thank God. Despite being whiny on the line, she at least told him what the hell was going on.

"She's had mental problems in the past, David. Nervous breakdowns. We saw this one coming on but thought maybe the holidays would help. They didn't. Yesterday was especially bad. We had to hospitalize her."

While the old bitch didn't say it was *his* fault, she did say that their relationship wasn't "healthy." David wanted to say that the constant sex was more out of her need than his. Not that he didn't like it, but he would've been okay with other activities.

I mean, damn.

On January second, he received a letter from Regina. It had been postmarked in New York City.

I'm here in a nuthouse, as you've most likely heard. It's not the first time. They won't let me tell you where, but it's north of the Mason-Dixon line. Yankees do it better, I guess.

What a ride we had.

My last morning at home, I felt you on me and in me. You were so hot with fever that I was burned from my inside to my outside. Your marks were everywhere. I never had such welts. I devoured you and you were delicious. You're seated now on a throne . . . at the right hand of a minor god. That makes you a minor god as well.

David turned the notepaper over. There was nothing more. No signature, no nothing. The whole thing was messed up.

Also, what was this about a minor god? That couldn't be right. A major god is what she probably meant.

Two months later, Regina McKenzie slit both wrists while in the bathtub at home. She wasn't discovered until both she and the bathwater were cold. David didn't hear the news for another six months.

9

The One True Glo

October 1977

MARTIN BOUNDED INTO THE DEPARTMENT, smiling. He pointed a finger at Cole.

"Guess what?"

"I can't imagine."

"I got you permission to visit Gloria Seely at Virginia Correctional Center for Women. It's today. So, you're going to Goochland. You should feel privileged."

"You worked that out quick." Cole was already tossing paperwork aside. He'd need some time to collect his thoughts.

"It's a skill. Most people don't have it. I also spent some time talking to this old journalist in Texas. He covered the case back in the day. His name's Gillespie."

"Learn anything?"

Martin sat in a chair on the opposite side of Cole's desk.

"Yeah. This was the biggest scoop of his career, and it happened right before he retired. Gillespie was a little shaky on names and details when we chatted, but I gleaned some tidbits that went beyond the just-the-facts details of the formal reports."

"Okay…"

Martin thumbed through a pocket notebook. "Young Dashiell Grymes was a real head case. When he was ten, he stabbed not one but two playmates. One out of anger because the other kid wouldn't hand over a ball or something. The other was planned. Another kid numbed his side with an ice cube and allowed Grymes to stick him to see how far they could get the knife in. Luckily, in both cases, he used a small pocketknife. After stitches, the kids recovered. No charges due to Grymes's age and the Grymes money."

Martin ran his finger down the page. "An on-the-sly psychiatric assessment—needed to appease the legal crowd, most likely—suggested a simmering rage just below the surface in young Dash. Some stuff about feeling inferior in a power-grabbing family. Nothing came of this, however. No counseling as far as Gillespie could find. Not the first course of action in their neck of the woods.

"Let's see, what else. In no particular order, Grymes and some buddies tackled a Mexican kid their age and held him down. They branded him with a hot poker. This was Texas, after all. Post-puberty, Grymes was known to have sex with calves."

"What?"

"That's what the man said. It had to be a sight to behold. When he graduated to girls, there were rumors of a pregnancy or two, with or without abortions. He wasn't sure of the outcomes. Shit like this until he met Miss Seely. Gloria Seely had by all accounts a normal childhood. Good student, popular in high school, plans for college. That kind of thing."

"No criminal record?"

"None. Far from it, evidently. But when she and Dash Grymes got together, it was like a nuclear reaction."

That sounded like an understatement.

"Here's where Gillespie got a little vague. Evidently, these two became acquainted with or followed some combination of"—Martin checked his notes—"Cuban voodoo and Aztec religion. The latter involved human sacrifice."

"Human sacrifice," Cole said.

"That's what he reported."

"Hold on. That can't be an active religion, can it?"

Martin shrugged. "I'm not sure. Nor do I know anything about Cuban voodoo. Dash and Glo either read about it or made the rituals up as they went along. That last part came from Gillespie directly."

Cole's mind raced. "They mimicked the human sacrifices as they, what, understood them?"

"Yep. Apparently the Aztecs had a rich history of this kind of thing. A number of their gods required blood sacrifices in one form or another. While animals could be used, humans were considered more worthy."

The three recent deaths didn't look like sacrifices. Or did they?

"What was involved?"

"Well, the Aztecs had those pyramid temples in the jungle. You've seen the pictures. They'd bring up the sacrifice—usually a slave, or a child, or a volunteer—and slit the throat. They may have eaten parts of the sacrifice or drunk the person's blood. Hearts were yanked out of the offering's chest still beating. I'm not sure how."

"Shit, so the, um, slit throat feature is part of our killings now. And, oh jeez, the biting of the neck…"

"Exactly. And Dash and Gloria's rampage back in the fifties."

Cole rubbed his eyes and sighed.

"There's more. Dash went a few steps beyond the Aztecs. He took trophies, like our current guy does, and kept them hidden in various locations. He'd cut chunks off the trophies and put them in this cauldron and make a stew as another form of offering. This is where the Cuban voodoo comes in, according to Gillespie. From each victim came a different body part. They were trying to combine parts to make a full human."

"Why?"

"Somehow it would make them godlike. Dash was evidently obsessed with this. Gloria not so much. Anyway, they'd have special powers that enabled them to be successful in their criminal enterprise on earth—Dash sold dope on the side—and they'd be actual gods after they died. They thought they'd have more time to continue the rituals, but they got caught."

The chair was becoming uncomfortable, so Cole stood and leaned against the wall behind his desk. "I'm glad you didn't mention any interests in reincarnation on the part of those two."

"I know. That would've been too much."

Prison sounds were the same anywhere. A steady rhythm of jangling keys reverberated from all directions. Shouts from the prisoners, pitched higher than in a men's prison, ebbed and flowed with an irregular beat. The buzzers and clanging slams of barred steel doors jolted Cole's hearing.

"Bit young for an FBI agent, aren't ya?" The warden ushered Cole through maze-like hallways.

"How old do you have to be?" Cole kept his eyes forward, not giving the man the courtesy of a glance. There was an oiliness about him, slippery and hard to contain.

The warden, named Roberts, grunted. He swiped his sweaty brow and receding hairline with a stained handkerchief. "And a psychic, too. You read fortunes?" He snorted. "I read the papers, son."

"I'm surprised."

A final pat on the forehead and the cruddy-looking hanky vanished into his back pocket. "Just sayin'. I don't want some green rookie in here causing me any problems."

"Don't worry, Warden. I'm not and I won't."

"Hey baby, come give me some of you." A hoot from a darkened cell to their left.

Roberts grunted again as if the prisoner's comment proved his point.

"So, you think talking to Gloria is gonna help you with the vampire killer?" The warden chuckled.

Cole ignored the comment.

"She may be charming as hell; just don't let your guard down. She's a dirty old bitch, too. Some years ago—before my time here, just so you know—one of the guards took a liking to her. Wanted her to, you know, give him a blow job. She agreed, and no sooner had he slipped it in that she started chomping. Swallowed whole chunks. Took a couple of guards to pry her jaw open—but not wide enough, because she stripped his skin like a vegetable peeler as he pulled out. Weren't much of the old joystick left. Poor guy retired. Drunk himself to death two years later. Just sayin'."

Cole shrugged as they reached the final security door. "Sounds like he got what he deserved."

"Your weapon, please," a guard standing behind a barred window said. Cole surrendered his handgun along with his badge. "Thank you, sir."

The warden stood adjacent to him, looking pissed. "Don't fuck this up, kid." He turned abruptly and disappeared.

The security door slid open on a track, and Cole entered the fortified unit. Another guard, a black woman with arms more bulked than Cole's, escorted him to a side room for interrogations. Behind him the steel door slid closed, followed by a buzzer and a heavy bolt ramming home.

"I'll go get her. She'll need to stay restrained. Roberts is one of those good-ole boys who thinks he knows shit, but he's right about this bird. She'll kill you just as soon as look at you."

"Thanks. I'll stay on my toes." Cole smiled at her.

"Yeah, I guess you will. I can see it in you." She strolled back to the door as if she were in a community park. "I'll need to sit in, but I'll stay back. Name's Diane, by the way."

"I'm Cole."

"Cole. That fits you." She nodded and left.

Cole exhaled, allowing his poker face to slip almost imperceptibly.

Despite his career trajectory, Cole avoided setting foot in prisons when he could. They triggered memories of his early experiences in a state-run mental facility. Worse, the impressions of torturous encounters from souls who'd once walked the halls of the institution transformed into visible manifestations.

During his brief passage through this prison, Cole had seen a pale young woman—a girl really, maybe nineteen—

walk through the bars weeping. Her prison jumpsuit was torn raggedly at the shoulder. She bled from her neck. She disappeared as she walked beyond him and the warden.

Then there was the young black woman who swung at the end of a noose within her cell. Blood seeped down her legs from her crotch.

Another woman sat in a corner with one side of her face bashed in so violently that her eyeball on the other side bulged like a balloon.

After these three hauntings, Cole made a point of looking straight ahead for the remainder of his escort to minimize the chances of receiving additional images.

A key turned a lock in the secure door. Cole, who'd been sitting at a table in the otherwise barren room, stood. Diane pushed the door open and stepped aside to hold it ajar.

A tall woman entered. Cole knew she was in her early forties but would've been hard-pressed to guess her age without having read that information from her file. Her hair was a combination of blond and premature gray, with the gray clearly taking over. Her face didn't possess the wrinkle lines associated with frowning or squinting. A slight sheen on her cheeks, nose, and forehead suggested moist skin.

Gloria Seely paused when Cole stood to greet her. She smiled, and the edges of her eyes tilted upwards, creating a twinkling effect.

"My, a gentleman. You don't see that much anymore." Gloria resumed her walk to the table. The wrist restraints attached to her jumpsuit made pulling the chair from the table slightly awkward at first, but she managed without hesitating. Diane sat in a chair at the back corner of the room, cloaked in shadow.

"Miss Seely. My name is Agent Nightshade and I'm with the FBI. I'd like to talk with you."

A brief nod.

"I'm investigating a case and thought you might provide some help."

"The vampire of Charlottesville." A tight smile.

"Yes, ma'am. You're familiar with the case?"

"Familiar?" A chuckle. "Young man, I've been following the news. It's quite the hot topic right now."

Somehow, Gloria Seely reading the newspaper seemed more believable than Warden Roberts doing the same.

"Yes, the papers do like this kind of thing," Cole said.

She smiled again and leaned forward. "I adore the color of your eyes, Mr. Nightshade. They're the most attractive shade of violet. Almost like twilight in the mountains."

"Yes, ma'am. I've heard that very thing many times."

"Twilight Eyes. Maybe a future moniker for you."

Cole cleared his throat. "The case has certain similarities to—"

"Ours," Gloria said. "Yes, dear. That it does."

In the corner, Diane crossed her legs. The swoosh of her uniform fabric drifted toward the table.

"What similarities do you see?" Cole said.

"Come now, dear. We both know you're interested in Dashiell's work. He's back now, isn't he?"

"Somebody may be imitating him."

She gave him a side glance. "Now, now, Cole. May I call you Cole?"

Cole nodded, wondering where she learned his first name. Then he remembered the article.

"My Dash—some sense of humor he had. He called me

Glo. Quite the stitch. Anyway, he's back. I know that and you know that. Have you had the pleasure?"

"Can't say that I have." Cole kept his voice neutral.

"You're fibbing. I know you have. This is what he was working for."

"What's that?"

Gloria smirked. "You're such a hoot. But don't try my patience." She stared at him, and Cole maintained her gaze. "To come back. Godlike, if possible. Dash always played his cards close to his chest. Only I could see his hand."

Cole recalled something like this in the report. "Because you called the plays some of the time."

"Exactly. Different tastes, Dash and I had. Traditional, I suppose. I preferred the young men."

Someone hollered outside the room. Undecipherable words were followed by peals of laughter. Diane's head turned involuntarily in the direction of the door. When a muffled cry of "Shut up" sprang from a guard, Diane turned her attention back to the table. Gloria didn't seem to notice the outburst.

"How did you two start your killings?"

Gloria waved her fingers as if to brush his question away. "Tell me, Cole. Does he bite them first or slice their necks?"

"I'm not sure."

"What's your guess? Come on. Right off the top of your head."

Cole thought about it. "My guess, and it's only a guess, is that he'd prefer to cut their necks. Biting would be more exciting, but the victims would likely put up a fight. There's a risk that he won't be able to control the situation unless the victim is subdued. Blood's more likely to spew in his face that way, though I doubt he's squeamish."

An emphatic nod. "Exactly. You have a mind for this.

Now, you want to know how we began our enterprise. Boring, but typically procedural for your types."

Cole reached for the notepad in his jacket.

"Ah, yes, you'll need to write this down."

"Yes, Miss Seely. My memory is faulty." He tapped the side of his head.

She laughed heartily. "I bet you remember every detail of every trauma you've encountered."

That was an interesting line. Cole kept his hands busy with the notepad.

"Okay, let's see. I do remember we had finished high school. Not at the same one, you should know. He was sent to some snobby boarding school. The Grymes were money. Big money. An oil family. They had plans for Dash. Taking over his father's business, continuing the hand-over-fist money gathering. But Dash's personality was a problem. Not a rah-rah type of guy. Little interest in being the bronzed masculine hero with a dazzling smile and dynamic presence. He was a loner with odd interests... dark things that didn't fit the Grymes aura. Don't get me wrong, he loved the money and the opportunities it provided, but he had little interest in the civility of it. If you call Texas oil families civil. Not the same as you Virginia families and the civility that came along with tobacco, cotton, and slavery." Her smile positively gleamed.

"I wouldn't know. That's not my experience."

"You're not Tidewater? Northern Neck?"

Cole shook his head.

She sighed. "You're from the mountains? I should've known. You look rough-hewn, but in a good way."

Cole kept his face impassive.

Glo clucked her tongue. "Back to Dash. He liked dominating and torturing things *and* people. There is an art to doing this in a manner acceptable to Texans, especially among the oil families. But Dash's versions didn't fit that bill. Playmates receiving cuts from knives that happened to be in Dash's hand, that kind of thing. His antics were kept hush-hush for as long as possible. Then he became drawn to killing. He had ideas about how to make it work for him, but he couldn't harness them until I came along. Then, it was off to the races."

"How did you and he harness them?"

Gloria raised her restrained hands to her face. She kissed the tips of her fingers and blew in Cole's direction. When her hands returned to her lap, she sat up straight and gazed at Cole. Her lips puckered slightly, and then she grinned.

Cole stared back with interest, his gaze flickering only once when Diane crossed her leg in the back of the room.

"I have a feeling, you know, Mr. Cole. You've seen major influences."

"Seen what? You've lost me."

"Yessir, Agent Seer."

It required extensive effort to remain nonchalant. He reminded himself that she'd read the article from the Richmond paper.

"I'm still confused. Fill me in."

"Cole. You're disappointing me. Think dark, mysterious, Romanian prince. Sharp teeth. Who comes to mind?"

Cole's eyebrows rose. "Dracula?"

"That's right. Vlad the Impaler. The real Dracula. Dash said that author who wrote the book, Stoker, borrowed the name, so to speak. Dash was infatuated with his favorite form of torture. Loved the idea of people being impaled and sliding down the pole. Excited him to no end." Gloria smiled. "But you knew that already because Dash showed you himself."

Cole shook his head involuntarily. She was wrong about this.

"No? Well then, maybe it's coming indirectly from Dash through the new version of Dash."

Cole leaned forward and placed his elbows on the table. He clutched his pen and notepad. Diane watched with a wary expression, no doubt thinking he was too close to the prisoner. "What makes you so sure of all this?"

"Elementary, my dear Watson. Oh, I know my Sherlock Holmes. The prison library has the stories. It is obvious, though. Someone's imitating Dash and me. You're the psychic cop, so your mind already leans in the direction of the supernatural. You're thinking some kind of possession angle. That's all the rage these days. After all these years, I still remember my Dash and his sense of wonder about all things otherworldly. He felt he'd come back. Somehow."

Okay, she'd put two and two together. Smart. Brilliant, even.

"The other influences on him?"

She bowed her head slightly and batted her eyes. "You're going to make me say it? Okay, it was me. And the Aztecs. Those devils."

"You're one step ahead of me. Tell me more."

"Oh, Cole, you're such a tease."

Cole felt a rising impatience. "You were talking about how you started. And how you influenced him. And the Aztecs. How were they involved?"

"Oh, yes. How we started. Let's see." She glanced over his shoulder and tilted her head. An act to make it look like she was retrieving an ancient memory. "I remember seeing him at a party just after graduation. Tall boy. Striking jaw that suggested power. His eyes had an amber tint to them. Unusual in the same way yours are. We talked, drank some beer. Ended up making out in his car. Then having sex in his bed at his parents' mansion. All in one night. He liked to bite; so did I. Isn't that funny?"

"Did you both act together from the start?"

"Oh, no. Dash had already started. He drove to San Antonio to find just the right kind of girl. Saw her on the street. He was so charming. Got her in the car. They drove to the area's make-out point. He confessed to me that his first effort was sloppy. He wanted her out of the car so the upholstery wouldn't become stained. She objected and tried to run off. Very messy. She was dead before he could do anything. I needed to train him."

"Train him. How?"

"That's how the Aztecs got involved. Dash had a fascination with the culture and learned all about it. You know how kids can be infatuated with trucks or dinosaurs? For Dash, it was Aztec human sacrifices. He said it grew out of his interest in impaling people. Strange, right? Anyhow, he got me interested. I just had to read up on them. Went to a college library. Did it all just right."

Cole had heard more about Aztecs in the past few hours than he'd ever had in his life.

"Dash transformed over a few weeks. The killings took on a purpose."

"To become a god or something."

"Mm-hm. That's right. Those people had such rituals. Dash thought the body parts would be an appropriate offering to obtain power. If we gathered representative parts, we'd make an entire person."

"Which would make Dash, what, immortal?"

"Who knows? That was Dash's idea. I'm not sure I

believed it. But the ritualistic aspect of the whole thing was remarkable. Truly."

Cole doodled in his little notebook. "So, the process of finding victims—"

"Sacrifices." The interruption was firm.

"Okay, sacrifices. You had to make the killings look like a ritual. Be more...organized."

"You could say that. We started one facet at a time. For instance, we had to track down the right girl. Figure out how to talk to her. Plan things out. What did he want to do? You get the idea. He knew he couldn't impale someone like in his dreams, so a knife had to do. Then there was the overpowering part. A decent punch in the nose would typically disable anyone long enough."

"So, you rehearsed things with him at first."

"Heavens, Cole. Not at first. Each time. My Dash was always a bit impulsive. Besides, I was there. To help."

"You were present, then. For each killing?"

"Of course. I so enjoyed participating. Naturally, we couldn't just serve his needs. We went after boys, too. Young men. Men I found attractive."

"You actively participated with the males."

"Definitely. Early on they thought they were getting lucky. Big surprise for them at the end." An exaggerated sigh.

Cole leaned back and rubbed his chin. "Twelve in all. If I'm not mistaken, seven females and five males. Ages ranged from thirteen to twenty or so. Different body parts removed from each one."

"That's about right. It's been twenty years. Heck, you're probably more familiar with the details than I am."

Pushing his chair back a few inches, Cole crossed his legs. One knee rested on the table. He tapped it with his pen, thinking. Gloria continued to sit up straight as if at a formal engagement.

"What type of individual should I be looking for?"

"Ooh. I like that question. Almost flattering." Gloria edged back in her own chair. "For all of his creativity, Dash was insecure. He needed me and my guidance. Does that make sense to you, Cole?"

He nodded. "Yes, it does."

"Good. My direction was important because if left to his own devices, he'd get tangled in knots. Get in over his head, so to speak."

"You're saying there's more than one person involved now."

"No, that's what you're saying. And you could be right. But he could be following Dash's example. Which, if you follow the logic, means he'd be following my direction. All well and good if Dash's guidance is delivered accurately."

Cole squinted at her. "Dash is dead, though. And there's certainly no instruction manual."

"You're sure of that?" Gloria smiled and winked at him.

Diane stood in the back of the room. She pointed at her watch. Time was up. Cole uncrossed his legs and stood. "Gloria—may I call you Gloria?"

"Of course, Cole."

"Thank you for your time. I appreciate it."

"Always happy to oblige the FBI. You've been a gentleman."

Diane approached from behind Gloria. "I will take you back to your cell now. Agent, if you'd wait here for a moment."

The two women moved toward the door. Gloria shuffled due to the restraints. She turned as Diane reached for the security door.

"Oh, Cole. One more thing."

"Yes."

"There've been three murders so far. Correct?"

"Yes, ma'am."

"Oh, ever the gentleman. Two young women and a young man? He lost his head?"

Cole nodded.

"That's what I thought. Do you have children?"

"No."

"Hmm. Interesting. Still, you'll want to check out our fourth one."

Cole made a mental note to look at the case file.

"Have a good day, Cole."

Even though Warden Roberts was an asshole, he did provide a private office for Cole to make phone calls.

"This woman's a trip," Cole told Martin, relieved that his partner was available. "Dashiell Grymes was a disaffected rich kid, an heir from a big ranch family. Evidently a major disappointment to his parents. Into sadistic activities and other weird shit. He met his soul mate in Gloria—Glo—Seely. Dash sure sounded like a psychopath given his predilections, and he was impulsive. Had to be controlled by Glo."

"According to her," Martin said.

"Yeah, according to her. She'd read the *Richmond Times-Dispatch* article, so she knew enough about me to freak me out a little. I mean, she questioned the truthfulness of my comment about not having had contact with Dash. I had to work at maintaining my poker face. She overplayed her hand, though. She assumed I knew things that I had no idea about. Specifically, me knowing about a favorite fantasy of his—impaling others on poles. Like the real Dracula."

"Huh. There was a real Dracula who liked impaling people?

"Oh yeah. Also, Dash was into the paranormal, as in performing human sacrifices to an Aztec god in order to turn into one himself—or at least achieve immortality. She was comfortable with the idea that Dash had returned somehow. She hinted at possession. You know, by his evil spirit."

"Like *The Exorcist.*"

"Yeah. She said something about it being all the rage now. What's interesting is that she never mentioned reincarnation. That wasn't on her radar."

"But she knew enough bullshit to cast these murders in supernatural terms," Martin said. "Interesting."

"She also recommended that we look for an impulsive male. Someone who could make good use of order being imposed on him."

Martin snorted into the phone. "She up for the job?"

"I've got an idea. First, though, anything on the UVA research subject?"

"No, we're striking out."

"How about visitors recently? Any weird people come to see Glo?"

"Nothing there either. No visitors. She's kind of ancient history in the mass-murder world."

Cole shifted gears. "Here's my thought. Interested in hearing it?"

"Sure."

"Let me give an interview to my brother. We plant some details about us searching for someone who appears to be a copycat of these killers from the fifties. We also slip in a line about a reincarnation expert giving us a tip about someone thinking they might be one of the killers in their previous life. And that we're searching for the identity of this person."

"Oh, Jesus, Cole. We're going to get all the crazies calling in."

Cole had anticipated this reaction. Truth be told, he had the same concern. "I know, I know. But what else have we got?"

"Wait. Let me think. What's the angle? Something like we're not taking it seriously, but if someone thinks along these lines, maybe we ought to check them out just in case? Is that where you're going?"

"That's it. Couldn't agree with you more. I can get Josiah to work on the grammar."

Martin groaned. "I'm not excited about this. I tell you what. Go see your brother. In person. That'll give me time to run this idea past the higher-ups. Call me before you do anything. Read the article before it goes to press and make sure it reads according to our specifications."

"You got it." Cole was on the verge of hanging up when he remembered something else. "Hold it a sec. Who was the fourth victim of Dash and Glo?"

"Why?"

Cole described Glo's final comments as she was being escorted out.

"Hold on." Shuffling paper sounds reached the receiver. "Here." Martin paused, likely reading. "A kid, male. Thirteen. Shit. They did a real number on him. Cut out his fucking heart. Jesus. And whoa. This is disturbing. He was the son of the lead investigator."

"Goddamn." Cole's mind raced. "You don't have a kid old enough to fit the profile of the fourth victim, right?"

"No. Two girls. Oldest is six."

"Still, keep an eye out. We need to alert Charlottesville PD. Someone may have one that age."

"Dominici does, I'm pretty sure. I'll call him. You get to Richmond."

❧

Cole realized with a certain irony that he was undermining his own complaint of being treated as a parlor trick by going full-on spectacle with this story. But he'd do anything to catch a monster. At least this was how he justified it.

It all came down to upbringing. After being accepted by a folk healer—make that two folk healers if he threw Agnes into the mix—Flo, who treated him as normal regardless of the weird events he'd generate, and Cynthia, who fell in love with him, Cole usually felt comfortable in his own skin.

It was like being born blind or missing a limb. The support of others meant their afflictions were just a piece of them. Oh, there'd be aggravations and disappointments, but they handled them. At least that's how it looked to him.

So, he was a seer with all that implied. Cole knew nothing different. Sometimes he felt aggravated by the idea of being a parlor trick. Other times, he used it to his benefit.

With that in mind, he called Josiah.

"Josiah Trout."

Cole suppressed a snicker. Josiah sounded so grown up.

"Hey, I'm coming to see you. Should be there in an hour."

"Cole, what?" Josiah's tone was instantly excited and pleased.

"I need your help." Cole described the plan.

"Ha. This'll be cool."

"It hasn't been approved yet, so don't say anything to anybody before I call Martin back from your office."

"Okay. And it's my desk. I don't have an office."

Cole made it in fifty-five minutes. Finding a parking spot took an additional five minutes. His second spin around the block netted him an opening on East Franklin Street right near the front of the building.

Josiah met him in the lobby. "Hey, man." He looked sheepish.

Cole recognized the signs. "You told."

"I had to. This is bigger than me."

"Who's in on it?"

"Crime editor and Maryellen."

"Ah, Maryellen. Did you get any sex out of it?"

They approached the newsroom.

"Shut up, man," Josiah hissed. "We have a thing going."

Cole smiled, genuinely pleased for Josiah.

"A thing, huh?" He glanced at his brother. Josiah stood two inches higher than Cole. With dark, long, wavy hair that bounced with each step, he was disarmingly good-looking. His success with young women—and girls, if you counted high school—was legendary, at least as Josiah presented it. Cole didn't doubt the tales. For the past decade it seemed like Josiah always had a girl on his arm. Flo worried nonstop for years that there'd be an unplanned grandchild springing out of Josiah's relationships. But so far, so good. It was a humorous quirk of fate that Cole would be the one to bring truth to that worry.

Josiah led him to a desk crammed into a corner. A scuffed baseball sat on a small plastic holder, obviously memorabilia from Josiah's baseball-playing days. In his junior year at VCU,

Josiah had been hit by a pitch in the face. His cheekbone was fractured and his jaw dislocated. While his eye escaped major damage, the bruising was horrifying to look at. Josiah joked about being New River's version of Tony Conigliaro. The injury essentially ended his college baseball career, but Josiah confided to Cole that he would've hung up his glove anyway. He wasn't major league material and wouldn't want to risk scrambling his brain any more than it already was. Besides, he'd been shifting his dreams toward writing and journalism.

Josiah swiped a notepad from the cluttered desktop and escorted Cole to a conference room. Along the way, Cole noted other cluttered desks, some occupied by reporters typing or on the phone. Cups of coffee adorned all surfaces while ashtrays with smoldering cigarette butts sat on about half.

Inside the conference room, an overweight middle-aged guy and a young woman stood from their chairs at a table strewn with paper and legal pads. These were covered with typewritten words or illegible handwritten notes. The walls of the room were glass. Beyond, the reporters ignored them.

"This is Cole Nightshade," Josiah said to the others. "Cole, this is Roman Harris and Maryellen Otto."

They shook hands all around. Maryellen stared at him intently as if trying to see inside his brain. She followed her probe with a wide grin. She was cute, with strawberry blond hair and the remnants of childhood freckles on her face. Her eyes were a light green. When she smiled, whatever hard edges she had—and there weren't many—disappeared. Maryellen Otto probably could disarm someone easily in an interview. The editor, Harris, was balding with a significant paunch. A sprinkle of stains, probably coffee, dotted his tie.

Harris spoke first as they sat around the table. "You want

us to do a puff piece on reincarnation bullshit and a murder case." His bass voice commandeered the room.

Cole took a breath. "We're trying to gather some leads in the murder of two high school students and a college student. You call that puff? What kind of paper is this?"

Josiah's jaw dropped, and a noise escaped his throat that sounded like a croak. Even Maryellen gaped for a moment before she turned and snarled at the editor.

"For chrissake, Roman. We're looking at an exclusive here. Let's talk about this."

Josiah's head nodded shakily. He really was low person on the totem pole. Cole eased back.

"Look. This was an idea on my part. We've little to go on, and this bastard has killed three times in a month. Ghastly stuff. You obviously have the general idea from Josiah, and I want to see if we can play this out. If not, just say so. Even if you're comfortable with it, I'll need to call my partner to see if we have an okay from our section chief."

Maryellen Otto answered for the publication. "I think this is something we can work on. I've even composed a preliminary draft—with Josiah, of course—for us to work with."

So, somewhere along the line, someone had already given Maryellen the go-ahead. Harris was just engaging in a brief pissing contest.

The draft wasn't bad. In fact, Cole couldn't think of a way to improve it. They'd captured the gist of what Cole had described to Josiah in a condensed journalistic manner: The recent murders showed some similarity (Cole liked the "some") to a series of murders from the 1950s committed by Dash Grymes and Gloria Seely. Without the gory details, the story mentioned the number of killings and basic patterns. The FBI had received an anonymous tip about a person who claimed to be Grymes in a prior life—and who knew important facts about the case. This unknown individual was now a person of interest, and anyone who knew of someone boasting of his connection to Grymes was asked to contact the FBI. While the FBI wasn't commenting on the reincarnation angle, they were following all leads. In the final paragraph, a source connected to Reincarnation Sciences at UVA described how young children between the ages of three and eight are prime for spontaneously reporting memories of former selves. The article ended with a note that the person of interest may have reported their memories of Dash as a young child.

"What do you think?" Josiah leaned forward with his elbows on the table, his lips pushed together.

"I like it. I'm wondering…"

"What?" Josiah leaned closer.

"We wanted to capture the idea that you were investigating any and all leads," Maryellen interjected. "That this reincarnated-person tip fell into your lap, and you were intrigued because they knew more than they should've. The copycat angle is hinted at, and while reincarnation scientists were consulted for the story, they didn't report the tip. While we can't guarantee it, this may cut down on some of the crazies calling in."

"I get it. I think it works. But I've got to call my supervisor and partner before we go any further."

Maryellen strode along the length of the conference table. She reached behind Cole, grabbed a telephone on a table perched against a wall, and sat it next to Cole. The phone line and receiver cord were tangled, and she took a few seconds to unwrap them.

"Reporters aren't the neatest people," she said.

"Yeah, I noticed that walking in."

Cole punched in Martin's number on the push-button desk phone and summarized the previous fifteen minutes.

"Read it to me."

Cole did.

"We've got the okay, but our asses are on the line if this fucks up. So let's get it right. Is there anything else you'd like to see in there?"

"Actually, yeah." Cole looked around the table. "I was wondering about some information about the suspect. Young. White male. Late teens or early twenties."

Josiah started jotting down notes.

"You've got that from the research transcript," Martin said through the earpiece of the phone. "What if that's just coincidence and it's not our boy? We could go with late teens or twenties. Take out 'early.'"

"I can live with that." Cole turned to Josiah. "Take out 'early' and just say 'twenties.'"

"How about suburban or rural upbringing?" Cole said into the phone.

"To get at the images of the woods. Hmm. Sure, that's innocuous enough. What about biting?"

"No. I think that would be a disaster. Kids bite all the time. Talk about getting a lot of calls, plus all the angry ex-lovers with kinky sex experiences." Cole couldn't help glancing at Maryellen and then Josiah.

"That gives me an idea, though," Martin said. "We need to look at emergency room reports on human bites over the last couple of years. Oh, by the way, Walter Dominici does have a kid that age. Or close to it. I guess he's a little older. They're not going to let him out of their sight for the foreseeable future."

Cole wondered if Gloria Seely somehow already knew that the Charlottesville detective had a kid the age as their fourth victim. The notion chilled him.

"So, are we good to go?" Cole said.

"Shit, yeah. We're good. Run it."

Cole hung up the receiver. "Run it."

After some quick revisions, the draft was given to a copy-editor.

"Cole, how do you know the guy who was supposedly reincarnated didn't just know about the case?" Josiah said.

"As a five-year-old? I wouldn't think so."

"Maybe not then, but now. He could've read the book," Maryellen said.

"Or saw the movie," Josiah added.

"Hold it. What? There was a book *and* a movie?"

"*Wrath of a Minor God*. Straight to paperback, sold in supermarkets and drugstores. It's a highly fictionalized account. The movie was definitely low-budget. Sort of like the movie that came out last year, *The Town that Dreaded Sundown*, about the Texarkana murders in 1946."

Cole shook his head, completely unaware of any of these things. He lifted the receiver of the phone and dialed Martin again. "There was a book and a movie based on the Dash and Gloria case."

"You're kidding."

"No. *Wrath of a Minor God* is the name. It's a fictionalized account, evidently."

"Well, damn. We'll check for libraries who might've carried it and who checked it out. Likewise, we'll see if it played anywhere remotely near here."

"It's probably one of those D-grade movies done for shock value," Cole said.

"Yeah, but Charlottesville is a college town. They probably have that kind of thing playing all the time. I'll check."

Cole hung up and rubbed his temples. "I had no idea it was a movie." He turned to Josiah. "Thanks for the clue."

Cole stood, and Maryellen stood with him. "We'd like something in return for our assistance, Agent Nightshade."

"Such as?" Although he guessed what was coming.

"An exclusive on this case."

"Sure, that can be arranged. Josiah would be involved, I'm assuming." This was a condition Cole had already considered.

Josiah appeared to gulp involuntarily. Maryellen ruled sections of this newsroom. The editor, Harris, had long been pushed aside.

Maryellen smiled and nodded. She seemed to have anticipated this as well. "Of course. Otto and Trout. Has a nice ring."

"Like Woodward and Bernstein," Cole agreed.

Back at Josiah's desk, Cole patted his brother on the back. "Thanks, man. I hope something comes out of this."

"Are you kidding? People eat up shit like this. We'll get calls and so will you. How useful they are is another story."

"We'll just have to wait and see. On another note, I'm guessing you took my advice and didn't tell Flo about the other thing. If you had, she would've called me."

Josiah made a zipping motion across his lips.

Cole laughed. "As if that ever stopped you."

The phone rang at Josiah's desk.

"I'll let you go. You've got work to do." Cole turned and walked across the newsroom while Josiah answered. He was maybe ten steps from the door when Josiah called, "Cole!"

Josiah held the receiver in the air. "For you."

Confused, he returned to the desk. "Cole Nightshade."

"Get your ass back to Charlottesville," Martin said. "Dominici's kid goes to a park to play his guitar while waiting for some girl. He told his dad that there's been some guy watching him the past few times."

"The kid just now brought this up?"

"Yeah. He'd figured the guy was just weird and didn't think anything of it. Until his dad talked to him. They're setting up a sting operation this afternoon."

"That was quick. And Dominici's using his own kid as bait?"

"He's a little older than I thought. Fifteen. And he's game. The place will be under surveillance. We'll be there. If you can make it."

Cole checked his watch. He could be there in the nick of time.

10

David and All the Others

October 1977

THE SCAR ON DAVID'S BELLY was twitching wildly. His T-shirt rubbed against the scar, aggravating it further. Shifting position, which he'd been doing for the past thirty minutes, didn't help. The shirt only settled back and touched the area, predictably triggering another twitch. Slipping the shirt off would help, but he was sitting in the middle of his English class.

The meaning of the sensation was clear. Dash was waking up and trying to fit into his skin. And when Dash came on the scene to make himself comfortable in David's body, Glo was sure to follow.

The professor droned on about *Jude the Obscure*, a boring book about the stupidest character ever. Between the lecture and the pending arrival of Dash, David couldn't wait to get the hell out of this room.

You know what I want this time, don't you?

Like magic, Glo was present and accounted for. No Dash yet, but he'd arrive sooner or later. When he did, she'd be nagging Dash to satisfy her urges—which meant she'd be nagging David, too. Not that this bothered him; he relished their moments together. It was just that he had trouble thinking of anything else until the deed was done.

Such was the life of an executor of the will of the dead.

The final ten minutes of class felt like ten hours. No one talked except the professor, who looked irritated that no one else was having orgasms over Thomas Hardy's writing. When the minute hand finally landed on its mark, the students issued a collective sigh as they pushed out of chairs and streamed out the door.

"Mr. Fairchild? A word?"

Oh, shit. David hoisted his backpack and moved to the front. "Yes, Professor?"

"You were having trouble sitting still. It was distracting. Are you okay?"

"Sorry. You're right. I couldn't get comfortable. Stomach cramps." It sounded convincing.

The dickwad just stared at him, then exhaled noisily through his nose. "Well, then. I won't take it personally. Carry on."

David was dismissed. He turned and walked from the room, all the while imagining what it would look like if an ice pick were rammed under the guy's chin.

"Hi, David." Tiffany Massey linked her arm through his. "Was that the most boring class ever?"

"No shit. I thought I'd die before I got out of there."

They walked down the hallway for a few steps without talking. A guy coming the other way nodded to Tiffany, who smiled in return.

"Are you doing all right?" she asked out of the blue.

David smirked. "Yeah. Hell, man. You're the second person to ask me that in, like, the last thirty seconds."

"Professor Hellior asked you? I wouldn't think he'd notice anything."

"Yeah. He thought I was insulting him or something. I'm just feeling weird. In my gut. It happens. I'm not contagious."

Tiffany nodded as if this made sense. "Okay. It seemed like you were tense or something."

David had known Tiffany through a friend in high school. Not well, but enough to say hi. They became much better acquainted after starting at UVA two months ago. He looked forward to sleeping with her before the semester was over. At least that was the goal.

"I don't think so. I mean, not any more than usual."

She squeezed his arm. "You up for going to the library?"

David smiled as warmly as he could. "Any other time, I would, but I'm feeling a little out of it."

For a brief second, he considered inviting her back to his room. Sex could be awesome when Dash made an appearance. At the same time, Dash could also make things messy, and he didn't want that. At least not at this juncture. Besides, another job awaited.

Tiffany made an exaggerated pout, then smiled. She was into him, that was for sure.

"That's fine. Maybe next time."

David bowed slightly. "My pleasure. You can count on it."

Back in his dorm room, David tossed his stuff onto his desk and locked the door. His roommate had gone home for a family emergency, so he had the place to himself.

The twitching kicked into in high gear as he stripped

off his shirt and flopped on the bed. He breathed softly and placed his hand over the scar. It jiggled under his palm.

There you go. Maybe we can all eat dinner together.

Whatever, Glo.

She's a lovely girl, that Tiffany. A future lay and slash, maybe?

David ignored her.

Suit yourself.

The sense of Glo's presence changed. From a nebulous voice in his head, she gradually coalesced into a nearly physical substance. It landed under the scar on his stomach and pulsed visibly like a runaway nervous tic. He lifted his hand and ran the tip of his index finger over the scar. The scar throbbed in return. Never failed.

The clock on his roommate's desk said eleven. He placed his hands behind his head and stared at the ceiling. Too soon for lunch, and he couldn't concentrate on homework. And there was no kiddy soccer practice this afternoon.

What to do?

Dash and Glo would have a plan.

The chatter from Dash and Glo over the summer had been more of a low murmur. Every now and again he'd hear above-a-whisper chants of *get ready* or *your time is coming* or *prepare for reverence* or *prepare for the offering.* Strangely bizarre if they caught him off-guard, but usually he had a sense of who was saying these things and what they meant.

With the start of college in the fall, Dash and Glo were revving themselves up and revving him up. And that, kids, would set the world alight.

Take the essence of those sacrificed and offer them up.

Their sacrifice enriches the gods above. Gives them more power. And with each body you acquire, you become more like them.

You gradually become godlike. That's what I'm training you for. Me and Glo. To carry on our work so we can achieve greatness. You and us.

The first jolt to his system came when he ran into Nadine Rudy during freshman orientation. She was a sophomore, a year older, and she had a job at UVA that involved helping the incoming freshmen. David had met her at the Christmas party, a friend of Regina. Nadine was the person who broke the awful news.

"I'm so sorry about Regina," Nadine had said. Her eyes watered. "I miss her."

"What about her?" David said. His face must have registered his confusion, because Nadine's expression blanched.

"Oh, God. David. You must've…maybe you didn't… Oh." Tears spilled over.

A sinking feeling in his stomach. "What, Nadine? What're you saying? Is she okay?"

"Oh my God. I hate to be the one to tell you."

She was the one, though, who filled him in about Regina's suicide.

David's legs trembled beneath him. Feeling unsteady and lightheaded, his arms shot out in front of him and landed on Nadine's shoulders. She must've thought he was going to fall; her hands secured his upper arms. The sense of disequilibrium ebbed quickly, but his stomach began a revolting churn. He breathed deeply and slowly to mask the inner turmoil.

"Shit. Jesus."

Nadine hugged him, and the pressure offered a sense of grounding. He could stand without falling to his knees.

"Goddamn. I had no idea. We hadn't talked since…we stopped seeing each other."

"Do you want to go somewhere and talk?" Nadine looked worried.

"Um. I think I need to get my head on straight first. Maybe later."

The real reason he couldn't talk was the abrupt appearance and subsequent uprising of Dash and Glo—and the freaking twitching scar.

It's time, David my boy. Let's get ready to rumble!

Nice girl, David. She'd do wonderfully in a ceremonial sense.

Shit, Glo, not now.

Of course. Further down the line, though. Let's keep her in mind.

The urges to *get the show on the road* became explosive. The low-level voltage zinging through his body (starting at his surgical scar) ran unceasingly.

Get psyched for the ritual, kiddo.

A nice young woman, honey. That's how Dash started.

Yeah, I made a few mistakes with my first one. We'll help you to avoid those.

The incessant chatter was confusing until he saw the girl. All the pressure within him released with a burst of relief. But seeing her was one thing, performing the ritual was something else. Within minutes of recognizing her fitness for the task at hand, the pressure buildup resumed.

It was a warm, toasty Saturday morning. The first game of the season would start within minutes. David was a new acting assistant coach for a bunch of eighth graders. The job was fun, and he felt like he was channeling Scott with the kids.

Patricia Loots caught his eye. She had come to the game to watch her little brother. This wasn't the first time David had seen her. One day at practice, a week before the first game, she'd introduced herself to him—as did a number of other family members. David nodded in return but didn't make a big deal of it. He didn't want anyone to notice or suspect something between them.

Throughout the game, however, David couldn't help glancing in her direction from time to time. He couldn't do it frequently; after all, he was helping coach the game. But Dash prompted him every so often (*check her out now, she might be looking*). His sidelong peeking probably only had a forty percent hit rate, but it was enough.

David received a smile with each meeting of their eyes.

After the game, David carried some equipment to his car. Patricia just so happened to have parked next to him. She was waiting outside her car. Her warm smile disarmed him.

"I work at Michie Tavern and I gotta go to work now. Do you know where that is?"

"I've been there." David tossed a duffel bag full of soccer balls into the trunk.

"Want to meet me when I get off later?"

"Sure." He offered a charming smile.

They made the arrangements and she drove off. David looked around. No one had noticed a thing. If they did, he would have a story ready.

Well, it looks like we're all set, Mr. David.

Yeah, Dash. You're just noticing?

Atta boy.

Hell, man, we've been preparing for this.

True, true.

And they had been. The key was efficiency and quickness. No trying to get it perfect like Dash had done did his first time. Overthinking messed shit up. Get her out of any kind of open space. Slice quickly with the knife and take the hand.

Whoa, kid. You got the knife?

Yeah. You were there when I took it.

David's father had these two swords above the mantle in the den. He referred to them as falchions. Below them was an automatic switchblade knife. It had been sitting up there as long as David could remember.

Why not? David doubted his father would ever miss the damn thing. Dash was thrilled.

I remember. Just keeping tabs. Now, be early, take the ax, and hide it. Then with a swing or two of that baby we'll have the offering. And you're on easy street. What else?

No talking, or if I must, keep it short and sweet.

Glo wouldn't be denied her contributions to their plan.

How are you going to coax her over to your hiding spot?

Don't worry. I'll think of something.

No, sorry. That will not do. You boys don't have the brains to think on your feet in difficult situations. Have a plan.

Okay, Glo. What should we do?

What would impress a girl? Hmm? How about a bouquet of flowers?

That's nuts.

Is it? How else are you going to get her out of sight? Say, "Hey, baby, come here"?

Okay, okay. I'll get the flowers.

Entice her with them. After you're done, remember to bring them with you. Don't leave them lying around.

Right. David thought he was ready.

Don't forget to bite.

David laughed.

Dash, you are such a card, Glo said.

The entire operation went like clockwork, if David thought so himself. He wasn't nervous or anything. He left the scene with the ax, Patricia's hand, and the flowers—which were thrown into a trash bin ten miles away. His clothes, a T-shirt and gym shorts, were kind of a mess, so he stopped at home for a quick visit. He rinsed the clothes off in the shower while he washed. They then went into the washer with some other laundry that he'd conveniently brought home. Patricia's hand, minus the pinky finger, which he'd chopped off seconds before, was wrapped in newsprint and placed at the bottom of a deep freezer under some frozen meat that hadn't been looked at in months. He knew it was safe—the staff wouldn't bother checking beyond what they needed on top of the meat pile. Finally, before he got comfortable, he walked to his ritual area beyond the clubhouse. David had an old pot he'd pilfered from the kitchen about a month ago. No one noticed it was missing. Inside the pot were tiny portions of other sacrifices—all from insignificant forest animals. The smell was rank, and maggots and flies danced over the surface. The finger was tossed inside the pot. His cauldron served as a forerunner of bigger sacrifices to come. Something to keep the gods appeased.

Neither of his parents came to meet him upon his arrival. Dad was likely gone somewhere. Mom too, unless she was floating in a peaceful Valium haze. He decided to relax at home, have one of his father's beers, and wait for his laundry to finish washing and drying.

Then David packed up his laundry and drove back to UVA. Not a soul noticed his coming and going.

Yup, the first one was a killer. We learned from our mistakes, didn't we?

David sighed, sat up, and swung his legs off the side of the bed. Dash was taking credit, but that was understandable. *Yes, we did.*

With elbows on his knees, David rested his face in his hands. A peek through his fingers showed eleven twenty on the clock.

Nadine was also an easy sacrifice. Did he want to talk, she had asked? Yeah, but I need to get away from campus. How about a run in Pen Park? She agreed and off they went. They talked about coaching soccer. Nadine was an assistant coach of a ten-year-old girls' team. After a few hundred yards, they went quiet.

At one stretch where there was absolutely no one around, Dash made his move.

Now, kiddo, into the trees.

David slowed a step behind Nadine, grabbed her, yanked her off-balance into the woods, removed his blade from his pocket, sliced once (it wasn't enough), then again—both times from behind so most of the spurting blood missed him. The whole thing took ten seconds, maybe fifteen. Nadine never made a peep. David took a quick bite.

Just take a finger. You don't have your ax.

Good idea.

He scampered away among the trees. It was hours before her body was found.

David's nervous energy escalated. Glo was gaining strength to make her move, since she had dibs on the next blood offering. Oh, man. It wasn't fair that she got it twice in a row.

Hi, sweetie. Hey, stop pouting. Zachary fit into the scheme of things pretty nicely.

Give it a rest.

Glo had set her sights on Zachary back in high school. David hadn't known Zachary was gay until that night senior year, around April first. Zachary, a junior, was struggling in a math course that David sailed through with ease the year before. David was good at that shit and responded to kids who asked for his help.

The fateful evening in question, David was sitting up in bed finishing some reading. It was late, he was dressed only in his boxers, and he was ready to turn off his light when he heard a knock at the door. David opened it and found Zachary standing there with that anguished look his classmates got when they didn't understand trig or calculus. They sat on the bed side by side while David explained the problem.

At that moment, Glo sprang to life.

He's a good-looking boy, sweetie. Let's get to know him.

David ignored her. He was getting tired. Unfortunately, his scar began to twitch and jump.

"Holy shit, man," Zachary said.

"Yeah. That happens."

Another spasm.

"Does that hurt?"

"No, just feels strange."

"Can I feel it?"

David couldn't respond right away.

Oh, let him.

Zachary had his palm over the scar already. Another tic. Zachary smiled, then slid his hand down David's belly and past the waistband of his boxers.

David stood up abruptly in his dorm room at UVA and shook his head to rid his mind of the memory. He didn't want to revisit it.

Why not? I enjoyed these moments. Glo seemed breathless.

Dash came to his rescue. *Because maybe he didn't enjoy them.*

Oh, come on, Dash. How else would we have gotten that kid to meet David in the woods late at night?

Dash groaned at the same time as David. *Nevertheless, maybe he didn't like doing those things with another guy.*

That's right, David thought.

Sure seemed like he did.

Shut up, Glo.

David paced around his dorm room. He remembered that night. Calling Zachary earlier to arrange the meeting in the woods behind Fort Concord. Parking on the near-empty street away from the path. Carrying the ax by his side. Walking in darkness to the tree (*let's meet by that big tree*), hiding the ax nearby, climbing the tree to get a view, making the carving while perched on the limb, then climbing down when Zachary appeared.

Poor Zachary never knew what hit him. The bite was kind of gnarly and gristly, but David managed.

He hacked off the head and dragged the body out of the woods and propped it up on the stone wall. Glo wanted one last kiss with the head. The taste wasn't as bad as David thought it would be.

David made it back to the edge of the woods when he heard a sound behind him.

The kid had appeared from nowhere. Shit, what should he do?

Kill him.

See, this is why you need a woman's perspective. Scare the crap out of him. He won't remember any particulars. Just this creepy guy with blood all over his face and chest.

David growled, soft at first and then louder. He took two steps forward. The kid bolted faster than he'd appeared.

David took the ax and head and returned to the car.

They repeated the routine a third time. Go home, clean up, place the offering (minus a small piece) in the freezer wrapped in newspaper, place the small piece (a bitten off chunk of lips) into the pot at the altar area. He spent the night and a good part of the next day studying before returning to school.

Dash had suggested that the gods would protect him.

They did for us back then. They make you practically invisible.

It was true. He'd told his parents that he'd likely come home that night and part of the next day because he needed some quiet to study. His roommate planned on having a girl over, so he needed to scram. They accepted his explanation without question.

See? Invisible.

It was showtime. Nearly noon, and David had to get something to eat. After that, he needed to get into position to conduct his observation. Today was just reconnaissance. Get a lay of the land, so to speak. Tomorrow would be the big deal.

A younger kid for the sacrifice. An offspring of a cop on the case. His case.

One thing for sure, David knew he wasn't going to do anything sick to this kid.

Listen to you, Glo snarled in his head. *Here we are, preparing for the next sacrifice—which involves ripping out a beating heart. And you're thinking about impaling him. I know you are. But you aren't going to satisfy my desires. Where are your priorities?*

Shut up. There's no way I'm doing anything like that.

Listen to the kid, Glo. Nothing perverted.

Glo stormed out in a huff.

11

Things Go South

October 1977

"HOW DOES CYNTHIA KEEP UP with you?" Martin said. They sat in a nondescript gray sedan one hundred yards from Rives Park, close enough to watch the Dominici kid enter and sit on a bench.

"It's the other way around. How do I keep up with her? She hardly gets any sleep and she's on call day after day. What a stupid training model."

"I don't know how you two do it. You've got to be like ships passing in the night. Missing that human contact would drive me crazy. Linda likes to be home with the girls."

"I don't know. It works for us. We're not dependent on each other. Not that you and Linda are. I mean, we both get lost in our own little worlds. Neither of us gets bent out of shape about it." Cole tilted his head. "Why are you asking?"

Martin snorted. "Linda's worried about you. Me, I'd be freaked out if my wife was a psychic. You two can thrive on the odd, that's for sure."

"Shit. Tell Linda I'm fine. I've lived my whole life this way. It's normal for me."

Cole had hauled ass out of Richmond and made it to the stakeout location with twenty minutes to spare. Charlottesville PD was good. Plainclothes cops were scattered around the park, but they blended well. A jogger going by, a young woman sitting on a far bench gently rocking a stroller, a maintenance crew raking leaves...any could be police. Dominici was nearby somewhere, probably a nervous wreck using his kid as bait.

"Would you let your kid volunteer for this?" Cole said.

"Shit, I don't know. The place is surrounded. I think the risk is low. The kid was evidently jazzed about doing it. Although now he looks like he'd jump ten feet into the air if anyone said boo to him."

Dominici's son was almost sixteen. Cole thought he looked confident, strumming his guitar, but he glanced around occasionally. "Let's hope our guy doesn't pick up on that. If it is our guy. I sure hope the girlfriend doesn't show."

"She's been told to stay away. The kid'll have a good story for when he talks to her next."

Jimmy Dominici's physical description of the suspect didn't match the drawing of their vampire. Then again, nothing probably would. Cole scanned the horizon and saw nothing out of the ordinary. There was a squawk over the radio followed by a reply that Cole didn't catch.

Cole exhaled and waited.

Finding the place was easy. David had been to this park before, but it had been a while. After he paused and thought about it, the location came back to him. From that point, the travel was smooth as silk.

He parked and took in the grounds before him. The windshield was a marked by dried waterdrops and bug splats, but not extensively. The marks could even serve as camouflage, so he didn't let them bother him.

David opened a textbook on his lap and leaned it against the steering wheel. If anyone noticed him, they'd think, Here's this college guy studying. What a good kid. He raised his eyes and scanned rapidly across his field of vision.

It took longer than he expected, but eventually he found the kid. David made a point of looking in his rearview mirror to run his fingers through his hair. This permitted a search of the rest of the park. Nobody suspicious, so he could sit here for a few more minutes before taking his stroll.

The textbook was boring as hell, and concentration was impossible given the circumstances. David ended up reading the same passage over and over. No sooner would he get to the bottom of the page than it dawned on him that he hadn't attended to a single word.

Shit. He checked his watch. He'd been here ten minutes. Good enough. This was just a scouting expedition, after all. Funny how Dash wasn't running his mouth off at the moment.

You're doing fine. I don't want to mess you up.

Ha. There he was. *Okay, let's take a walk.*

Might as well.

David tossed the textbook on the passenger seat and opened his car door. He stepped outside and stretched his legs.

ᵹ

"He's coming," a whispered voice said over the radio. It belonged to Dominici's son. Cole heard a guitar chord for a second.

Cole sat up straight. "Do you see him?"

"Not yet," Martin said.

More radio jabber.

"That might be him." Martin nodded to the right.

A young man, probably in his twenties, shuffled over. His gait was off somehow.

"Strange walk," Cole said.

"I'm guessing cerebral palsy, but I'm no expert."

"He's looking straight at me," the kid said.

David kept his eyes on his prey but tried not to make it obvious. He made a point to look beyond at the horizon and then over at the opposite side of the park. Nothing to see here but a guy taking a break from his studying.

The kid was doing his thing, oblivious to his presence.

You're invisible, remember?

Yep.

"Almost here."

"We're watching, Jimmy. Keep playing."

The guy with the awkward gait was within feet of Jimmy Dominici When he reached the bench, he literally fell onto it next to the kid.

"Jesus," Martin said. He reached for the driver's side door handle but didn't engage it. Cole did the same with the passenger door.

The radio blasted. "Hey, what're you doing? Stop."

"Damn, the kid's freaking out," Martin said.

A chorus of commands on the radio. Cole and Martin jumped out and sprinted in the direction of the melee. Jimmy Dominici was yanking and pulling away from the suspect, but the man had a firm grasp on his windbreaker. The guy yelled something, but Cole couldn't make out the words. Before the two of them arrived on the scene, three plainclothes officers jumped into the struggle. Dominici was a second behind.

The situation was under control by the time Cole and Martin closed the final twenty yards.

Yes. Identity confirmed.

That's our boy, right? Dash asked.

That's him. David scanned the kids doing drills on the soccer field. The kid with the long blond hair. Nightshade's son. He remembered him from the game a few weeks ago. Nightshade's story had been in the paper that same day, and David made the connection on the spot.

Cool beans.

Dash had stupid sayings, that was for sure.

"I suppose that could've been worse." Martin ran his hand through his short-cropped hair, his face strained with frustration. "For a brief second, I thought we might be able to end this."

"Yeah. But I knew it was wrong as soon as I saw the guy walk up," Cole said, leaning against a jungle gym. They stood a number of paces to the side in the children's play area to let the locals handle things.

"Yeah. Me too."

The "weird guy" Jimmy Dominici had spotted over the past few days was Wallace Pageant, a thirty-one-year-old disabled man who lived in a neighboring group home. He worked at a supermarket stacking the shelves and walked by the park on his way home. He enjoyed Jimmy's guitar playing and would stop to sit and listen.

Today Wallace had wanted to tell Jimmy how much he liked his music but tripped over the lip of a slightly uneven sidewalk panel. Jimmy had the living shit scared out of him while Wallace was shaken up by the rapidly descending police force. The Charlottesville PD was not exactly gentle in their handing of Wallace in those first few moments. Fortunately, Officer Dominici quickly read the situation and calmed everybody down.

Jimmy Dominici stood awkwardly behind his father, who was trying to console both Wallace and a social worker from the group home. The kid had a hangdog expression.

"Time to restore some self-confidence," Cole said to Martin.

He walked over to Jimmy and introduced himself. "You did fine today. It's not easy to keep cool in a threatening situation like that."

The kid shrugged. "Except it wasn't threatening. Just some poor disabled guy. Not an evil killer. I feel like such a shit."

"Still, you did the right thing. You felt uncomfortable and you trusted that feeling. You'd feel worse if it were the guy and you never spoke up."

Jimmy nodded. "Thanks."

Cole clapped him on the back and rejoined Martin.

David hunched down in his car as soccer practice broke up. Nightshade's kid chatted with some of his teammates before they headed for home. Most, including his target, hopped on their bikes while a handful slipped into cars driven by parents.

David resisted the urge to pursue at high speed. He didn't want to look like a predator. He waited a good fifteen seconds before starting the car and slowly driving off.

As he exited the park, David wondered which way the kid would go. Ahead there were two possibilities, and hot damn, Nightshade picked the best one. David turned right onto a street that the kid had turned seconds before.

A little-used service road was in the works to become a major thoroughfare in a new residential development. No plots had been identified—at least to the novice eye—and no foundations had been built. It was just a street with turnoffs and a few signs indicating "Future Site of Chesapeake Park Homes." Up ahead, David saw the retreating figure of the kid scooting along on his bike.

Within seconds, David figured out exactly how to carry this off.

And that would involve bringing the kid back to his sacrificial altar in the woods.

12

Everything Comes Around Again

October 1977

"It's soccer." Cole burst into the office suite with the announcement.

"What?" Martin stood in his open doorway. A new agent and their secretary looked up from the files on the conference table at the same time.

"It occurred to me while I was driving in. I mean, it just hit me. Soccer. The connection between the victims. Here, look."

Cole strode over to a six-by-four display board with tacked-on crime-scene photos and handwritten notes. He pointed to the first victim. "Patricia had spent the early part of the day at her little brother's soccer game."

Another step. "Nadine played soccer and coached a girls' soccer team."

He leaned toward the far edge of the board, "Zachary played soccer at Fort Concord."

Cole looked around the suite. They stared back.

"C'mon. This is the only connection," Cole said. To his ears it sounded like pleading.

"It is," Martin said. "Unfortunately, nobody's jumped out as a suspect that connects them all—even through soccer."

"So, let's check."

Cole entered his office. Martin popped in right behind. "Your article is out. The reincarnation connection." He handed the Charlottesville paper to Cole. They had reprinted it from the *Richmond Times-Dispatch*.

"Did you read it?"

"Yeah, it's not as bad as I'd feared."

Cole smiled. "So we dodged a bullet. No one's pissed off at us?"

"Don't get too cocky. The day is still young. Anyway, take a look. I'll start looking into soccer connections."

Martin was right. The article was nicely written and expressed the sentiments he had talked about with Josiah and Maryellen. It didn't come off wild and bizarre like a supermarket tabloid story. Just matter-of-fact. He placed the paper to the side and began the search for potential soccer-related leads.

Cole started with the military school. The secretary for pupil services was helpful and gave him the names of all kids who were currently on the soccer team. As an afterthought, he also asked her for the names of soccer players who'd graduated over the past three years. The woman would need to get back to him about those.

Martin was still working on names of UVA students who had any connection to soccer. It was one hell of a list. He had the students actually on the soccer team. But there were also kids who played high school soccer and loved the sport but weren't playing in college.

"That's going to take a while," Martin said when Cole peeked into his office. Martin's phone was tucked between his head and shoulder. "A few students are assistant coaches in the community. They do this for credit, evidently. I'm waiting for that list."

Cole nodded in reply. He remembered something about that from a discussion at Timothy's soccer game a few weeks ago. He turned and nearly ran into their secretary.

"Cole, these women would like to talk to you about the newspaper article in the paper. They drove up from Richmond."

Two women stood near the door of the conference area. One was young, maybe mid-twenties, and looked pregnant. The other was an older version of the first, in her fifties. She clutched a purse close to her heart.

"Sure," Cole said. He approached the women. "My name is Cole Nightshade. How can I help you?"

"We have information for you. Can we talk somewhere?" the younger woman said.

Cole directed them to his office.

The older woman sat in a chair that Cole held out for her. The younger woman seated herself.

"My name is Paula Sutton. This is my mother, Edna Willow."

Cole shook hands with both. The name Edna struck a chord within his chest. He sat behind his desk.

"My mother saw the story in the Richmond paper this morning and called me. I read it and suggested we come to see you."

"I didn't want to bother you in case, you know, it wasn't important," Edna said, her voice tight. "It's just that what was written..." She shook her head.

"We know, or knew, someone who took part in reincarnation research at UVA about fifteen years ago," Paula said. "This kid talked about being a murderer in his previous life."

Edna sighed. "But he was such a little boy at the time. I can't imagine."

"Mom. He stabbed two babysitters before he was five. Then he beheaded my dolls and masturbated on pictures of me. On an altar in the woods."

"I know. I know."

"And then he stabbed you."

"He said it was an accident. He was a confused adolescent at the time."

"She left the job with the family after that last one," Paula said to Cole.

Cole needed to slow this down. "Let me go back over all of this with you in order. So I can get the complete picture."

"Okay." Paula sat back in her chair and arched her back slightly to shift position. Cole hoped she wasn't too uncomfortable.

A thought popped into his mind. He opened his desk drawer, pulled out one of the case files, and quickly found the reincarnation evidence. "This is your signature, correct?" He showed Edna the signed consent form used for the research study. "Edna, M-c-C-something."

"Oh." Edna's hand leapt to her mouth as if she'd burped loudly. "So, you know about this?"

"Mom, they're the FBI."

Cole smiled. "Yes, and none of us could read your signature. The researchers at UVA had no other records. We've been looking for a David McC-something for days now who would've been born nineteen years ago. Couldn't find one that fit the bill."

"That's because his name is David Fairchild," Paula said.

"McClusky is my married name. I went back to Willow after my divorce. I used McClusky on that form."

"It was a covert operation," Paula said to Cole, deadpan.

Edna Willow explained how she'd landed a job at the Fairchild estate as their cook. Throughout her eleven years' employment, the Fairchilds treated her wonderfully, giving her a generous salary and a place to live on the property.

"Their son, David, was adorable," Edna said.

"Mom, for Pete's sake, he was a creepy little kid. He talked weird, stabbed people, and impaled small animals."

"Let's talk about that," Cole said.

Edna related a number of incidents that, despite her vague descriptions, sounded gruesome. Her account of bringing David to UVA for the reincarnation interview dovetailed with the rendition presented by Doctors Adamson and Rudyard at UVA.

"Do you remember the names of the nanny and babysitter?"

Both women shook their heads. "Only first names. Karen and Scott. They were lovely young people," Edna said.

"Her characterization of them is accurate, unlike David."

"I've always wondered what happened to them," Edna said softly.

"The other thing you should be aware of," Paula interjected, "is that Mr. Fairchild wanted to keep all of this quiet. When everyone left because of David, they were paid well to keep their mouths shut."

Edna nodded. "Very generous. I felt guilty. But a huge help financially."

"You've not seen the family or David since you left?"

"No. I thought it best to stay away."

"I had just left for college, and I never came back. Mom moved to Virginia Beach. Mr. and Mrs. Fairchild were nice, but strange."

"In what way?"

"Mr. Fairchild had an important job. He was gone frequently. Mrs. Fairchild struggled with her nerves. She took tranquilizers. A lot. She was anxious about everything," Edna said.

"Including her son?"

Edna looked to the ceiling. "I wouldn't say that. She wasn't afraid of him. Instead it was like she was afraid for him. Or worried about him."

"Do you think she sensed something?"

"Yes. But she felt powerless to act, I think."

Cole stroked his lips, considering the wealth of information. "Do you happen to know where David is now?"

Both shook their heads. "We lost touch over the years," Edna said.

The phone rang. It was his third line, a number only a certain few had.

"Pardon me. My secret line." Cole kept it light.

"Would you like us to leave?" Edna said.

"No, it's okay. Only family use this number." Cole lifted the receiver. "Hello."

"Cole," Cynthia said. "Sorry to bother you. I have a colleague with me. A third-year surgical resident. He needs to tell you something."

A combination of muffled and clicking sounds reached Cole's ear as the phone was transferred from Cynthia to whoever this guy was.

"Hello? This is Cole Nightshade."

"Hi, Cole. I'm Scott Montrose. I mentioned to Cynthia that I'd read the article in the paper this morning. And that I thought I knew who you were looking for. Cynthia was quite insistent that we call right away."

"Yes, she can be insistent." Cole could clearly imagine Cynthia strong-arming a surgeon. The guy probably didn't know what hit him. Or maybe he did if they worked together. "You must have some important information."

"Maybe. When I was in high school, I worked for a family with a five-year-old. Or maybe he was four. His name was David Fairchild. Anyway, my job was to entertain him. He was okay for the most part. I mean, he was a little kid. Then the little bastard stabbed me with a screwdriver. To this day I swear up and down that it was intentional."

"The father paid you big bucks to keep it quiet."

On the other side of the table, two pairs of eyes watched Cole intently.

"Interesting. You've heard about this?"

"Doctor, do you know Edna Willow and her daughter, Paula?"

Silence on the other end for multiple seconds. "I'll be damned. Mrs. Willow worked at the Fairchild estate at the time."

"She and her daughter are sitting right across from me in my office. They've been providing similar accounts. They mentioned you."

Both women gaped.

Cole briefly moved the receiver away from his face. "Dr. Scott Montrose," he said.

"Yes, Montrose was his name. He's a doctor?" An expression of delight replaced Edna's unease.

Cole nodded. He scribbled *surgeon* on a piece of paper and pushed it over to Edna Willow. Her smile expanded further. She showed her daughter, who nodded admiringly.

"Have you had any interaction with the family since then?" Cole said into the receiver.

"None. It was the reincarnation part that caught my attention. My high school girlfriend's mother used to work for those researchers. I recommended them to Mrs. Willow."

The call ended, but not before Scott told Cole to say hello to the women for him.

"I'm surprised he remembered us," Edna said.

"Right away. No hesitation. If you need surgery in Fredericksburg, you can check him out at Mary Washington Hospital." Cole smiled. "Is there anything more for me?"

Paula recognized the cue. "We should be going. You have things to do."

"Yes, ma'am. This has been extremely helpful. We'll need to check it out."

"Do you think David is involved?" Edna looked shaken.

Cole stood and both women followed his lead.

"I don't know. It may be nothing, but this is how investigations work. We examine every single lead. You did the right thing to report this."

Cole directed them to the secretary to leave their contact information before striding to Martin's office.

"I may have something. Can you meet me in my office and bring whatever names you've obtained from UVA?"

Cole summarized everyone's accounts. Then they started checking for David Fairchild on their lists of soccer connections. It probably took less than sixty seconds.

"Damn. He was a student at Fort Concord," Cole

said. "Graduated last year and played soccer with Zachary Tillman."

"And he's on the UVA list for students who are assistant coaches for kids' teams in Charlottesville. Along with Nadine Rudy. What are the odds?"

"Not high. Hey, wait. Does your list mention team names?"

Martin looked at his sheet. "Yeah. The woman at UVA gave me that info, too. You want the name of Fairchild's team?"

"Yeah."

Martin gave the name, and Cole sat back slowly. "I think that was who played Timothy's team when I went to Charlottesville. In fact, I'm almost positive."

Cole's mind raced. He recalled the college guy approaching him.

You're Agent Nightshade, right? Sorry to bother you, but those official guys over there asked for you.

"Holy shit. I know who he is. I talked to him."

The eighty-mile trek felt like it took hours when in fact Martin got them there in record time. Charlottesville PD in collaboration with UVA PD had already begun their search for David Fairchild. He wasn't in his dorm room—not surprising since he had two morning classes. The professor of his first class said he had been in attendance and had, in fact, turned in an assignment. There was a thirty-minute window between that class and his second. David had been absent from his second class. The professor, a little miffed initially when they interrupted his lecture, became concerned when he realized David wasn't there. That was not like him.

A systematic sweep of the campus commenced.

The police from both departments went from building to building, with greater priority given to higher-likelihood sites such as the library, the gym, and places to get a snack. Martin and Cole worked on his dorm.

The RA bit his thumbnail nervously as Cole searched Fairchild's room.

"Did you see him this morning?"

"Ah, yeah. Before his nine o'clock class. I had one too." His teeth clicked as he chomped through a thick section of nail.

"Did he say anything?"

"Nah, he just seemed zoned out. I was too."

"How did he look? Anxious? Upset?"

"David Fairchild? No way. The guy's always cool. Nothing shakes him."

Nothing struck Cole as out of the ordinary after exploring shelves and drawers. But on his desk, a book on Aztec culture opened to a chapter on human sacrifice.

That was interesting.

"Where's his roommate?"

"Um. He had to go home. His grandpa died. Or something."

Or something. Cole remembered one of his professors in college saying that college faculty were responsible for the high rates of grandparent deaths in the country based entirely on the scheduling of assignments and exams.

"Who's he closest to in the dorm?"

The RA shrugged again. Cole began to wonder how good the guy was at his job.

"He hung around with everyone on this wing."

The trouble was, everyone on this wing was gone.

"Everyone's in class, probably," the RA offered.

Over the next hour, students floated in and out of the dorm on an irregular basis. From them, Cole and Martin learned that David had definitely been present this morning, but no one had seen him since. While this increased Cole's unease, the students found it unremarkable. Such was college life. He was probably off studying somewhere or writing a paper. Or something.

"This isn't sitting well with me," Martin said over a late lunch.

"Me neither. I don't care if the students don't see it as a big deal. I'm suspicious."

There was little they could do, though. This was first and foremost Charlottesville's case, and they were as on top of the situation as they could be. Cole and Martin returned to their offices by midafternoon.

The street navigating through the future site of Chesapeake Park Homes was quiet, just like David had expected. The wooded area on both sides of the street showed some signs of activity. Little wooden posts adorned with pink ties—probably indicating lot lines—larger signs displaying street grids and lot configurations, and off-road tire tracks suggesting developers. Or maybe utility workers. It didn't matter—they weren't around now.

David pulled off the road and followed a previous vehicle's tracks. The tracks ventured only so far into the yet-undeveloped lot, but a lengthy path wasn't necessary for the next step in his plan. Opening the trunk, he pulled out the slapjack Regina had given him. He paused briefly to gently rub his fingers over the leather. Regina would be proud of him for taking this next step. It was destiny most certainly.

The slapjack and rope fell to the ground before the open trunk. Other camouflaging items were placed next to them: a cardboard box, a jack, a blanket. If anyone happened to drive by, it would look like he'd finished changing a flat. In the meantime, he waited.

The departure from UVA after his first class went like clockwork. It was overkill to leave so early, but it meant he could take his time and grab something to eat. Afterward, he went to a local park and sat under a tree reading a textbook for a class until it was time for the festivities.

Finding out where Nightshade's kid had soccer practice that day had been easy enough. Communities had to juggle which team practiced where and when, and the schedule for that team was provided without question. He arrived about fifteen minutes to spare before the end of practice—based on his scouting mission yesterday. Now he only hoped some busybody didn't come along and start prying into his business.

The scar lurched. Tug-tug-tug.

Showtime, young man.

David groaned. *Cool it, Dash.*

No, man. Look yonder.

David, who'd been leaning against his car, pushed off with his butt and scanned. Well, well. There he was. A glance at his watch said the kid was right on time.

Okay, get in position.

Shit. There was nothing to use for a gag. Too bad he didn't have tape, but he couldn't do anything about it now. No, wait. He'd use the kid's shirt. That solved that.

David glanced at the rope. He would need to move quickly with the tying. Fortunately, he had already thought ahead and cut it into varying lengths.

The kid approached on his bike. Out of the corner of his

eye, David could see that he'd caught the kid's attention. He leaned over to pick up the slapjack, making it nonchalant as if he were repacking a trunk.

Now, step out in the kid's path.

"Whoa! Sorry, man. I wasn't paying attention."

The kid hadn't been going fast so he braked easily. "It's okay. I saw you. Something happen?"

The kid looked at him curiously with his head tilted to one side.

He recognizes you, Dash said.

You're right, Dash. So Glo was here now, too.

"Not really. Minor car trouble. It's fine now." David play-acted a double take. "Say, I know you. Don't you play soccer?"

That came out dumb. The kid's status as a soccer player was obvious to any observer. He wore shin-guards and cleats, grass-stained practice shorts, and a T-shirt that was drenched after practicing on a warm day.

"Yeah." The reply was cautious. The kid squinted.

"Got it." David snapped his fingers. "You're Nightshade's kid. We played you guys in Charlottesville a couple of weeks ago."

The face brightened. "Yeah. I thought you were familiar."

David strode toward him, hand extended in greeting.

He is adorable. I can't wait. Glo was positively over the moon.

Forget that, Glo.

"Except he's my uncle. Not my dad."

At the last possible moment, David switched the slapjack to his right hand. He backhanded the stick across the kid's face.

The bike fell to the ground as the kid dropped silently.

"Doesn't matter."

13

Red

October 1977

"Still nothing," Martin said as he ducked into Cole's office.

"His parents' house?"

"Deputies checked late morning and just now. The mother says he's at school and they haven't seen him in over a week. He usually calls if he's going to stop over. They haven't heard anything."

Cole stood and stretched. It was after five.

"Why don't you head home?" Martin said. "Dominici will keep us posted." He stepped back as if he was ready to do the same.

The phone rang. Cole looked down—it was his private line.

At that very instant, a sensation of oily blackness covered him as if a huge grimy blanket had been tossed over his body.

"Cole?" Martin reentered his office with rapid steps.

"Holy shit." Cole plopped back into his chair. His vision returned, but the sensation of darkness circling him remained.

"You okay?" Martin coasted around the desk and placed his hand on Cole's shoulder. "You turned white."

Cole shook his head and reached for the phone. It must've been on the third or fourth ring. Martin grasped it before Cole.

"Cole Nightshade's office."

Kenny's voice projected loudly. Martin held the phone away from his ear. Still, Cole couldn't make out the words.

"Jesus. Hold on."

Martin held the phone out to Cole with his hand over the mouthpiece. "Your friend's son has been abducted."

"What?" Cole grabbed the phone. "Kenny, what?"

"Cole, someone's taken Timothy." Kenny's voice was amplified but remained remarkably collected. "It must've been within the past hour. Some kids found his bike off the road. Blood on the scene. I could use your help in the search."

The darkness hung on around Cole's periphery. But this wasn't something physical happening to Cole.

The remote viewing experience.

Being inside something dark and sort of rectangular.

The jostling movement.

Red door. A tunnel. Red shack.

Timothy on his front step eating potato chips.

Do you have children?

The fourth victim was the son of the lead detective on the case.

You're Agent Nightshade, right? Sorry to bother you, but those official guys over there asked for you.

"Cole," Kenny prompted.

"I know who took him. The guy we're looking for saw me at Timothy's game. He thinks I'm his father."

"You're not making sense, but I'm coming with you, whatever you're going to do."

"Are you home?"

"Yeah."

"I'm on my way to pick you up."

Martin stared at him. Cole could see the puzzle pieces falling together in his eyes.

"Shit. I think you're right," Martin said. "You go. I'll rally the troops. I'll be ten minutes behind you. Take a radio."

"Find out from Dominici what color the Fairchilds' door is. Contact me if it's red."

Mom probably wouldn't notice that he'd slipped in. If she did, she might be strung out enough on valium not to care enough to check on him in the garage.

Count on dear old Dad to get only the best when it came to products. The automatic garage doors were an example. They made almost no sound as they ascended on their tracks. He pressed the clicker to shut them just as soundlessly after pulling in.

Each heartbeat felt like an internal sledgehammer. David couldn't believe he was this pumped. The abduction had been chancy, and the risks were high. But damned if he hadn't done it with aplomb.

One cool dude, brother.

Thanks, Dash. Not bad if I say so myself.

How's our little cutie? Glo would not be outdone.

Fine when we checked fifteen minutes ago.

David had pulled over at one point to sneak a peek inside the trunk. The kid had regained consciousness and tried to retreat to the rear of the space.

Time to get moving. David exited the car. As he stood, his scar twitched and tugged almost to the point of flipping around. He pressed his palm against it. Pressure jabbed at him like rapid punching. The feeling amused him, and he smiled. His shirt on the scar felt like fine-grained sandpaper. He removed it and watched his twitching belly in the dimly lit garage.

You're getting excited, David thought.

You bet I am, Glo replied.

David popped the trunk. The kid tried to scoot away.

"C'mon. You can't go anywhere."

The kid mumbled something, but the gag kept it unintelligible. David mentally patted himself on the back for thinking on his feet earlier. His trusty blade had cut through the practice jersey easily, and he'd created a makeshift gag while the kid was still out like a light.

The slapjack's blow had produced a massive flow of blood. Streaks spread in all directions across the kid's face and hair, which now hung in clotted clumps. Not exactly attractive, but fitting for a sacrifice.

The kid must've caught his second wind. As David reached into the truck, flailing feet swung toward him. Pure luck saved David from a broken nose or worse as most of the boy's effort was wasted on the trunk lid. The rope tying his legs at the ankles likely contributed to his lack of aim.

David hated to do this because he needed the kid conscious and aware, but he reached for the slapjack and gave two halfhearted whacks. One hit its mark in the nose, and the kid wailed behind the gag. David poked him in the stomach.

"Shut up," he hissed.

Fearing the situation could unravel if he didn't act now, David hoisted the kid over his shoulder. He exited the garage through an access door.

"Rrriiddiirrrr. Rrriiddiirrrr."

Amazingly, David understood. "Yeah, man. Red door. We've got a red door."

David trotted as fast as he could toward the woods. The squirmy kid jostled with each step.

Kenny wore an olive-green fatigue vest that likely hid a variety of weapons when Cole arrived. Cole summarized everything as coherently as possible as he drove.

"Jesus." Kenny maintained a steely glare out the windshield. A sliver of sun remained above the horizon. "You're thinking in retrospect that Timothy's been connecting with you."

"A hunch," Cole said. His heart felt close to bursting for his friend. "But the red door..."

Minutes earlier, Martin had radioed. The door on the Fairchild house was red. "A fucking red door. From anyone else, I'd laugh this off," Kenny said. "But I know better coming from you."

"Goddamn. I just hope I'm reading this right." Up ahead, Cole saw the turnoff for the estate.

Kenny was focused and unemotional as he concentrated on finding Timothy. Only his narrowed eyes betrayed the violence that was poised to erupt should anything go awry. Cole was one of the few who knew it existed.

"Plan?"

"We don't have much to tie this guy to Timothy. Circumstantially we only have his relationship, tenuous as it is, with the other victims. We ask permission to speak to him or search the place. If necessary, I can bluff with the evidence gleaned from the reincarnation angle and telepathy."

"That's not much."

"We'll also look for some probable cause to enter."

Kenny nodded his approval.

The driveway was long, more of a country lane. They were approaching the house when the driveway curved to the right.

"I wasn't expecting that."

Kenny pointed ahead. "Curves around the house. Main entrance must be in the rear. Strange layout."

Cole circled an extension that had to be the garage, likely big enough for three cars. A heavily wooded area loomed on his right. The driveway ended, as Kenny had predicted, at the main entrance.

The center door was red, even in the dusk.

"This is it."

They jumped from the car. The passenger side door remained ajar. Cole pushed the doorbell multiple times, then paused. After a second, he pounded three or four times. As he lifted his hand to bang the door again, it opened.

A tall woman answered. Her hair was cut short but hadn't been combed in a few hours. It looked as though it had been blown around by the wind. Her eye sockets were puffy and dark. She was likely under fifty, but worry lines and microscopic fidgeting movements presented her as older and considerably frail.

"Mrs. Fairchild?"

"Yes?" A hand clutched her shirt collar.

"I'm Cole Nightshade with the FBI. This is Kenneth Augustine, a federal agent. We'd like to speak to David."

Mrs. Fairchild's eyes darted between both of them. "I'm sorry. He's at school. I mentioned this to—"

A piercing scream shattered the stillness somewhere

deep in the house. All three froze for an instant. The scream resumed.

Kenny turned to Cole. "Probable cause."

Cole, however, was already moving. He grabbed Mrs. Fairchild's elbow. "Where's that coming from?"

"Basement," Mrs. Fairchild mumbled, her eyes darting in panic.

She ran with greater intensity than Cole anticipated.

"Juanita? What's wrong?"

Juanita screamed a third time, embedding undecipherable words in the shriek.

The location of the screams became obvious as they pursued the woman through the house. In the kitchen, Cole saw a doorway leading to a basement. Juanita was yelling high-pitched words. While Cole could identify the language as Spanish, he didn't speak it, so the meaning was lost.

Juanita had perched at the bottom step. She looked up and saw Cole leading the charge. He displayed his badge. At the same time his right hand rested on his weapon. "What is it?"

Juanita pointed farther back in the basement while words her tumbled among sobs.

Heavier footsteps pounded down the stairs, probably passing Mrs. Fairchild. "Head, Cole. She said there's a head."

Oh shit.

Cole leapt the last two steps and sprinted into the basement. The lights were illuminated and the reason for Juanita's outburst became clear. A chest freezer, lid open, stood against a near wall. Packages of wrapped cuts of meat and other leftovers were placed there. Juanita had probably gone downstairs to select something for the next day's meal.

She'd stumbled on an object that looked unfamiliar to

her. Something roundish that should not have been there. She unwrapped the package.

A severed human head.

Cole inspected it long enough to see it wasn't Timothy—and to recognize who it was based on pictures he had seen of the victim. Zachary Tillman.

"Fuck, Cole." Kenny's voice contained both confusion and relief. "This is our second freezer. You and me."

Mrs. Fairchild snuck up behind them and retched. She pushed down the gag reflex after a rush of dry heaves. A short whimper escalated into a keening wail.

"Mrs. Fairchild, we need to talk to your son."

Her head rocked furiously from side to side while the wailing continued. Cole grabbed her upper arm and forcefully pulled her from the basement.

"Kenny, help. Let's get her out of here."

Kenny took her other arm and pulled the woman even more vigorously.

At the base of the steps ascending to the kitchen, Cole was slammed by a neurological sensation that sent his perceptions spiraling. He fell to his knees on the steps and vaguely felt the painful impact somewhere in the back of his mind. Kenny's grip on Mrs. Fairchild was the only thing that kept her from spilling off-balance onto his collapsed form.

"Cole!"

The impact was like being hit with the backside of a snow shovel, except there was nothing physical. His visual and auditory senses were overwhelmed with a blasting stimulus of sight and sound.

Mental sensations coalesced into words while images emerged and vanished amid rocking and swaying motions.

Red door.

Remember red door.

Woods.

Dark.

Straight.

Straight.

To the tunnel.

No, not a tunnel.

Flat floors. Sides. Roof.

A covered bridge! Red. A red bridge.

A fucking red bridge!

Dash. Who's Dash?

Glow. Glow what?

Cole scrambled to his feet as the internal pressure eased. Blood dripped to the floor. His hand flew to his face. A bloody nose. He gave me a bloody nose.

"Cole!" Kenny continued to drag Mrs. Fairchild into the kitchen. Juanita, still sobbing but more under control now, supported Mrs. Fairchild on the side vacated by Cole as they approached the top.

"He's here, Kenny." Cole's voice sounded hoarse. "They passed a red bridge. A covered bridge. I've seen it."

Kenny turned to Juanita and spoke rapid-fire Spanish. She responded with the same intensity.

"She said the bridge is in the woods. We follow the path outside the main entrance. Follow the path after the bridge and we'll run into the kid's clubhouse. Also painted red."

Right outside the red door. Of course.

Cole removed the radio from his jacket pocket and contacted Martin, filling him in. At the top of the stairs, he spied a flashlight attached to the kitchen wall by a magnetic holder. Cole snatched it on his way to the red door. Kenny followed.

℘

Once in the woods, David felt relieved. He no longer stuck out like a sore thumb for anyone in the house to observe. Nightshade's kid—or nephew, as it turned out—was like a bag of sand. The weight cramped his shoulder, which surprised David. The kid wasn't exactly ripped with muscle. Just lean and angular. That may have been the problem. The little shit kept flopping right and left as David half walked, half ran along the path.

Darkness continued to settle in, and while there was a nearly full moon, it wasn't enough to illuminate the uneven terrain. David had thought he knew every inch of this forest. The circumstances, however, forged a landscape of unpredictable footing.

The kid mumbled, softly at first, then louder. He was regaining consciousness again. His body became animated. The bound legs began kicking, awkwardly for sure, but knees and feet landed painfully on David's gut and thighs.

David dropped him on the ground, mostly due to necessity. He was losing his grip. The kid moaned deeply into the gag.

"That hurt, huh? Stop kicking, you little shit, or there'll be more."

Two forced groaning noises that could've been "Fuck you."

I like this kid. He's got spunk.

"Yeah, Dash? I think he's a pain in the ass."

C'mon. Pick him up and get moving. Carry him in your arms. It might be easier.

"Give me a break."

I'm just telling ya. That's the way to go.

"Shit."

Still, David took the recommendation, picking up the boy so that he laid in his arms. It was easier. He resumed his steps.

See?

"Shut up, Dash."

The kid's eyes bugged out.

"I'm talking to Dash, you little shit. He's part of me."

David ran forward, no longer stumbling but still unbalanced. The kid's eyes remained round disks, staring in unmasked fear.

Give him a kiss.

"Screw that, Glo."

Or bite him on the neck. Right now. Let me feel it.

We've got to keep moving.

Just a little one.

David paused and gazed at the neck only a foot away. He could see a pulse throbbing under the exposed skin. No longer in control, David elevated the kid higher while he lowered his head. His mouth settled on the neck.

His captive jerked his body furiously. Bound hands tried to push David away. David could feel his own personal power. He was invincible. Immortal.

Beneath his lips and licking tongue, David felt the kid's neck muscles maneuver to produce a garbled wail. The salty taste of sweat filled his mouth.

Fantastic. Succulent.

David bit down but not hard. No marks. At least not yet. The kid squirmed in his arms. A muffled yell followed. David smiled at the boy.

"What do you think, Glo?"

The young are more flavorful.

"Okay, enough. Let's roll."

David resumed his ungainly run. The kid's face turned away from David and looked forward. He started yelling again behind the gag when he saw the covered bridge. Over and over the same words. The extreme darkness within the bridge quieted the kid for maybe a second, and then he started up again. Once on the other side, the words changed.

"That's right. A covered bridge. Smart kid."

David's scar tugged so hard it seemed to have leapt for joy.

The kid noticed it too. He stopped his complaining and gawked at the movement spreading across David's belly.

"Yeah, I know. Cool, right?"

Cole bounded into the woods. Dusk had settled more deeply within the shade, but the path was still visible. None-theless, Cole switched on his flashlight. The beam cascaded over bushes, shrubs, and saplings with his swinging arm.

"How far?" Kenny pulled up beside him.

"Can't be much. The clubhouse was built when he was a little kid."

Their pace was steady but cautious. Cole resisted the urge to go full out for fear of missing something or running into a trap. Kenny's long legs threatened to overtake Cole at any moment.

"Here!" Kenny stopped short.

Cole almost slid past, but caught his footing. A small piece of torn garment.

"Timothy's?"

"I think." Kenny pointed. "There." A splash of blood and footprints. The dirt had been disturbed. Possibly by some-thing dragged across it.

"Let's go." Cole took off, shinning his light back and forth across the path and sweeping the woods on either side.

"What's that?" Kenny called from behind.

Cole had seen it, too. A cut-out opening in a structure. His light revealed the red paint job on its broad side. Underneath, the trickling of a narrow stream.

"That's the covered bridge."

Cole entered. At first glance it looked like the tunnel. His tunnel that he saw weeks ago. Not cylindrical, though. Wooden plank floors. Unpainted interior walls.

Two eyes reflected his flashlight beam. On a ledge near the interior roofline.

His step stuttered, and he nearly tripped but caught his footing. An owl? Was that a fucking owl? Didn't matter. It wasn't human. He kept running.

Bursting out the opposite end, Cole found the path easily. Behind him, the sounds of Kenny's footsteps grew duller when he left the planks and returned to the dirt.

Off to the left, a gray streak rushed into Cole's peripheral vision. He glanced, initially perceived nothing, then noticed a figure farther beyond where it should've been.

Colorless and with no substantive depth in its form, the figure still appeared human. It swerved and faced Cole.

Dark, slicked-back hair. Scruffy beard. Dash Grymes charged. Mouth etched with a lifeless grin. A face desiring carnage.

Cole accelerated, trying to avoid Grymes.

Faster. Faster.

Grymes increased his speed to maintain pace with him. And closed the gap between them. Quickly.

Cole wouldn't make it. Grymes was closing—arms raised.

I'm gonna get you!

Grymes launched from his feet, swiped at Cole.

Cole weaved around the outstretched arms. Grymes flew past.

Cole shifted his attention to the path. He saw the four-inch-diameter tree branch at head height a split second before slamming into it.

The collision sent his feet rocketing forward, and he fell backward onto his side.

"Cole!" From behind, Kenny's face appeared.

The pain was like a jackhammer pounding his face, with the focal point at the bridge of his nose. His nose clogged rapidly. Sitting up sent the world spinning, and he fell back again. Kenny's grasp kept him from falling back to the ground.

"Get up, Cole."

"Shit, Jesus." Cole shifted to his hands and knees. He got his left foot under him and pushed. The motion produced additional vertigo and his stomach lurched. He shook his head in an attempt to stop himself from puking. More flares of pain shot off like fireworks, but his stomach held on.

"Let's go. You first, though. Don't wait for me."

Kenny, weapon in one hand and flashlight in the other, disappeared down the path.

The kid kicked and rocked. David was thrown off balance twice, staggering into the woods both times. With the second stagger, the kid fell from his arms, and David remained upright only after clutching a tree trunk while nearly keeling over.

The kid roared behind the remnants of his shirt. Screaming something over and over.

"You little fuck," David yelled back.

David picked up the kid under the armpits and dragged. His kicks were ineffective now, but his bound hands swung around like a baseball bat. Each swing resulted in a hit somewhere. Finally, David dropped the kid again in disgust and kicked him in the ribs.

"Stop messing with me. You little shit. I can make this a hell of a lot worse."

After three swift kicks, the kid stopped swinging his arms and curled up, groaning.

"That's better." He grabbed the boy's arms at the wrists and resumed pulling. The coarse ground was raking the kid's bare back nicely. It had to hurt. Served him right.

"Dash, you never said this would be this hard."

Silence followed. Dash was speechless. A rarity.

"Dash, where the hell are you?"

The clubhouse appeared on the left as David walked backward. The kid noticed it and moaned sharply.

"Rrddshk. Rrddshk." Over and over.

"Yep, red shack."

Twilight for sure now. The light would hold for a bit longer. He had time.

C'mon. C'mon. Just ten more steps.

His scar was jumping like mad. Holy shit. The kid's face turned upwards, his eyes watching. He certainly had a bird's eye view of the twitching. It probably was freaking him out.

David glanced behind him to see the altar area, the stake at the ready.

"First, I'm gonna impale you. Then cut out your heart." David swooped down and grabbed the kid in his arms. Knees were bucking near his face. Arms swung chaotically and hit David repeatedly. Too many blows to count, but no big deal.

The sacrificial offering turned to see the stake. Realization dawned on its face.

A sturdy branch, straight and an inch in diameter. One end buried with the point sticking up. The point whittled by him with his father's knife. The very one that would cut out the heart.

Three feet of agony in position.

"Bombs away." David, nearly on top of the stake, tossed the kid.

Except the kid didn't drop the way he was supposed to. He managed to grab David's upper arm long enough to throw his trajectory off kilter. Just above the hip, his side caught the point enough for a jagged tear of skin to appear. He fell against the stake, tilting it back.

You didn't secure it deep enough, jerk. He practically knocked the damn thing out of the ground.

"Shut up, Dash."

Forget the stake, man. Cut him. Now. They're coming.

"Someone's coming?"

Can't you hear them?

David's heart was beating like a big bass drum, drowning out all other sound. He couldn't hear a damn thing.

"Shit." He reached for the kid's bound hands. The fight had gone out of him, so David was able to loop them over the stake. It was done before the kid realized what was happening. He tried to yank his arms free. The stake held, but David could see it wouldn't for long.

After pulling the kid's legs taut, David sat on his pelvis. He found his switchblade and released the blade.

"Time for the heart."

David inserted the point right below the ribcage. He

started his incision, careful not to cut too deep. No use killing him before reaching the heart.

The kid screamed.

David understood the word "stabbed."

Nearby, a voice cried out.

"Timothy!"

Shit, kiddo, make yourself scarce. You gotta overpower them. Take 'em by surprise.

Cole should've been knocked on his ass. His face was swelling up like a grapefruit. The pain had subsided a little, but it wasn't much of a consolation. His vision still swam, and he suspected he had blood in one of his eyes.

Following the path, now outlined by the beam, remained his one focus. Fleeting images of shadows, snippets of voices, reverberated from one side of his brain to the other. When he shook his head to clear them, electric flashes of pain circled his head.

RED SHACK. RED SHACK.

Okay, Timothy. Red shack coming up.

Cole scanned as best he could. Didn't see it. Bushes swept his ankles and legs. He'd wandered off the path.

Damn.

He reoriented and kicked something metal. A god-awful stench billowed. The beam of light showed a medium-sized cooking pot (cooking pot?) on the ground. The contents had been ejected when he kicked it.

Sticks of varying sizes. Mixed in were slabs of flesh. A finger. Animal carcasses, too. Trinkets. Morsels. Temporary sacrifices. To appease the gods until the finale. The great climax.

And flies. A lot of flies.

He swallowed back a vile taste in his mouth.

Cole stumbled forward, to get the hell away.

Find Timothy.

Somehow he made it to the path. Bushes rustled in a breeze. Fallen leaves scattered among his stumbling feet.

A red clubhouse stood before him, appearing like a magic trick.

By God. There it is.

Ahead, Cole heard Kenny yell his son's name.

Goddammit, move.

Cole broke into a loping run. Adrenaline rushed into his midsection, turning the pain down multiple notches.

A cracking branch to his right. Cole rotated, his .45 and flashlight extended. A rock the size of a tennis ball connected with his right shoulder. The joint seized in response, and the weapon dropped.

"Shit." Cole collapsed to his knees, frantically searching for the handgun. Thundering footfalls crashed through the woods.

He'll be on me in a second.

But no, they were running away, not toward him. He spotted the gun, just beside his right foot. How did he miss it?

Cole came up ready to fire, aiming frantically in front of him. The light swept the tree branches and trucks. Shadows flitted from tree to tree.

"Where are you?" A whisper.

Cole scanned increasingly broad swaths of woods. Where was the bastard? The red clubhouse stood multiple yards back. Had he gone there? That would not be a smart choice. No. Fairchild was in the woods. Hiding in the gloom.

"Timothy! I'm here, buddy." Farther down the path, Kenny had found his son.

"Jesus," Kenny said, anguish in his voice. Cole had never heard that depth of distress from his friend.

With his shoulder still on fire from the rock's impact, Cole lumbered his way toward Kenny.

An urgent groaning noise escalated from around a curve in the path. Cole stumbled forward and came upon the site when the groans became words.

"Dad, Dad." Timothy's voice remained muffled even with the gag removed.

"It's okay, T. You're safe."

Cole saw Kenny working over Timothy, who was prone on a slight mound of earth that lay on a patch of elevated ground along the path. He holstered his weapon.

Timothy's feet hung over a ledge comprised of a long slab of rock. His legs were bound at the ankles; Kenny feverishly hacked at the rope. His arms were already freed; sliced sections of rope lay scattered below his hands. Still, Timothy kept his arms extended with his hands around a stake embedded in the ground a few inches beyond his head. Cole figured they'd been stretched painfully, making movement difficult.

Timothy was also covered in blood. Cole stepped as quickly as he could to help Kenny with the rope securing his ankles.

"Timothy," Cole said. "We're almost done. We'll get you out of here."

"There's a sick guy here. I was sending you the message."

"I got it." Cole tried to smile, but his face, in swollen disarray, wouldn't respond.

"Ah more telepathy stuff, huh? I'm gonna have to watch

you two," Kenny said. He'd adopted a playful tone, but Cole noticed that his hands were trembling.

The center of Timothy's abdomen had an incision of about three inches. Blood cascaded down his sides. His face had been battered, and his swelling looked like Cole's felt. Mucus and saliva dribbled over the bottom half.

A hard crack disrupted Cole's observations. A tennis ball–sized rock lifted skyward, then fell with a thud outside of Cole's vision. He glanced sideways. Kenny looked bewildered. A stream of blood surged from the crown of his head. With a quiet "Huh," Kenny slumped to the ground.

"Dad!"

Cole swung around. Something that felt like a hot poker glanced off his shoulder blade.

This guy is good with rocks.

David Fairchild was right on top of him.

Not a rock.

Fairchild was reaching behind Cole for something solid and sharp.

Jesus, a knife.

Cole pushed up with his arms. Fairchild swung with his other hand but missed, and his fist pounded the ground. Fairchild roared, his face an inch from Cole's. Jaws opened and closed in rapid succession behind snarling lips, with teeth clicking unnaturally loudly. His eyes were red coals.

Trying to bite?

Raising his left hip, Cole got Fairchild off balance. Fairchild swayed back, and Cole pummeled him with his left hand.

Fairchild pinwheeled his arms to remain upright on his haunches. A portion of his exposed midsection extended forward. A well-defined scar on his skin took the brunt of expansion. It looked like something was trying to punch out of his torso.

Fairchild's face stretched with shock, eyes and mouth so wide, it appeared as though someone was pulling them open.

From over Cole's head, the wooden stake sailed like a missile, guided by two blood-smeared hands. The sharpened point, more blunt than razor sharp, tore into Fairchild's torso. The tip penetrated an inch above the protruding mass. The splitting skin sounded like the tearing of wet newspaper.

Timothy screamed and released his hold on the stake.

Fairchild fell backwards. The stake tumbled out his mid-section and clattered to the ground.

Cole fumbled for his pistol, his hands feeling clumsy. He took aim and waited for Fairchild.

The young man gasped. The bulging mass was literally tearing from his stomach. The wound had given it an escape hatch.

Fairchild sobbed. Words came and went, but they made no sense. "Glo…Immortal…Regina." Cole stopped listening.

"Cole." Kenny was conscious and on his knees. He aimed his pistol at Fairchild.

"No, Kenny."

"Move. Please."

"I said no. As long as he's alive, the others stay in his head."

Kenny glared at Fairchild, then Cole. His weapon lowered.

"Dad." Timothy's voice was hoarse. "What is that?"

Whatever had been pushing from inside Fairchild had emerged. He was trying to cradle the thing in his dirty hands. Though smeared with bodily fluids, its characteristics were identifiable.

There was a head, with tufts of blond hair.

The head contained eyes, a nose, ears, and a mouth. All were discernable but appeared unfinished, premature.

The body was shriveled but well-formed enough to contain floppy limbs extending from below the neck. Arms.

There were no legs.

As Cole watched, the head flopped backward, its eyes falling on him.

Its lips parted and the thing wailed.

14

What Do You Think?

Late October 1977

THE SUN WAS SETTING BEHIND their neighbors' houses to the west. Cole sat on the chaise longue in the backyard patio. The pattern, chosen long ago by the couple who'd rented the house to him and Cynthia, wouldn't have been his choice— the bold vertical lines in royal blue and white drove his eyes crazy. It was comfortable, though. He just had to avoid looking at it too closely.

The temperature hovered near seventy, but sitting under the awning made it feel cooler. Cole's chills had hung on after his fever came down. He wore a hooded sweatshirt over a sweater. A blanket covered his legs.

The patio lights came on.

"Here you go." Cynthia rejoined him, carrying his cup of tea. One of Agnes's blends.

"Thanks. This'll be great." He sipped the warming liquid. It *was* great.

The four individuals in the woods had been carried out

on stretchers. David Fairchild was whisked away to a secure hospital setting, surrounded by a mass of heavily armed law enforcement officers. Cole, Kenny, and Timothy were rushed to Mary Washington Hospital. Cynthia happened to be with another patient at the moment of their arrival, but she caught wind of the new admittees soon enough. She was at Cole's side frequently that night, only departing long enough to check on the other two periodically. Stitches for all three. Concussions for all three. Assorted sprains and pulled ligaments. All healable.

Unfortunately, Cole developed an infection that led to a fever. Which meant he stayed in the hospital a few days longer than the other two, coming home this very afternoon. The culprit was likely the knife, although Timothy hadn't come down with a fever. Still, he got the same dosage of antibiotics that Cole did as a precautionary measure.

Cynthia sat in a folding chair and reached for his hand. "You're looking better."

"I feel better. Really."

Cynthia shook her head and sighed. Then she smiled slightly.

"I'm sorry I do this to you."

"You don't *do* this to me. It happens. It's just you. The finest folklore medicine practitioners in the country say you're a healer. I think this is what they mean."

"So are you. We're a matched pair."

"Well, we lead intense lives. We can't forget who we are."

"Never." He sipped some tea. "With this blanket, though, I feel like an old man."

"For God's sake, Cole. You've been ill. And you're on sick leave. Relax and take it easy."

"Yeah, old man. Just relax." Kenny strode into the backyard with boxes of pizza. Timothy followed with a bag of chips.

"I was thinking something healthier than pizza, Kenny," Cynthia said.

"Nah, the hell with that. He's been craving it."

"Yeah, he said," Timothy added.

Cynthia looked at Cole.

"It's true."

She rolled her eyes in exasperation. Cole smiled to see it. It meant she cared.

"Timothy, can you run inside and get the paper plates? They're on the table. Oh, and the soda in the refrigerator."

"Sure thing." The boy disappeared in an instant.

"What's this about you guys taking a short vacation?" Cynthia said.

"Yeah, we are. Time for a father-son exclusive getaway. Spend some fun time together. And he needs a break."

"You do, too," Cole said.

"Yep, I do. We're both a little shaken."

"Cole said you're going to Sanibel for the week."

"Timothy has no school next Thursday and Friday. Teacher conventions or some shit like that. I thought, what the hell, I'll take him out for the other three days. I contacted the school and got all his assignments."

"He's going to love you for that."

"Of course."

"Anyway, I have some connections and got a house right on the beach. Secluded, quiet, and peaceful."

"Sounds ideal," Cynthia said.

"What's ideal?" Timothy rejoined the group with paper plates under his arm, a pitcher of iced tea, and cans of soda.

"What? No napkins?"

"Dad."

"Your dad was just filling in Cynthia about your vacation."

"I can't wait."

"So, what kind of pizza?"

Pizza was distributed. Conversation stopped and started around mouthfuls of food.

As they slowed down, Kenny nudged Timothy with his elbow. "Go ahead. Ask, She's the expert."

"Um. That baby thing that came out of that guy. It was screaming. How could that be?"

"Ah. Cole wondered the same thing. He thought he was the only one to hear it. You did too?"

A single nod.

"That…thing…is called a parasitic twin. When Mrs. Fairchild became pregnant, she was going to have twins. Fraternal twins—a boy and a girl. But one twin didn't separate and develop. The other one did and became stronger. That's called the dominant twin. Sometimes a parasitic twin becomes absorbed into the other twin and disappears within the tissue. Other times, the parasitic twin develops somewhat. They may grow legs or arms or a head. But they're entirely dependent on the dominant twin for life. They don't have the organs to survive on their own. They're really just skin and tissue."

Timothy scrunched up his face.

"The scar that he had? That was from surgery done when he was a baby. There were legs sticking out of his belly."

"Eww."

"The other portion of the parasitic twin was still inside. You can see it didn't grow much."

"No, but it was alive. It screamed." Timothy frowned.

"Honey." Cynthia leaned closer. Her face was about two

feet away. "I explained this to Cole, too. You didn't hear it scream. It had no lungs. No heart. No brain. It just had the outward form of a baby."

"How...?"

"It's hard to grasp, I know."

Timothy turned to Cole. "What do you think?"

"What she says makes sense. You need lungs to scream. It was just a clump of tissue."

Kenny slung his arm across Timothy's shoulders. "Sometimes you have to keep wrestling with the idea. You'll make sense of it after a while."

"It's true. Weird things happen," Cole said. "You've got to live with the weirdness sometimes. It's like the Fairchild kid. The researchers I talked to say he's a reincarnated mass killer who was directed by his past life to commit these crimes again. That's one explanation. But there are others."

"Like..."

"He was fascinated with human sacrifice and this long-dead killer, Dash Grymes. He read books about him. Saw a movie about his crimes. He may have just been a sick kid who was influenced by what he read and saw. Who knows?"

"Which do you think it is, Uncle Cole?"

Cole thought for a long time before he answered.

About the Author

ANTHONY HAINS IS A PROFESSOR emeritus of counseling psychology with a specialization in pediatric psychology. He retired in May 2018 after thirty-one years at the University of Wisconsin–Milwaukee. His novels include *Sins of the Father, Nightshade's Requiem, Sleep in the Dust of the Earth,* and *The Disembodied.* Anthony lives with his wife in Whitefish Bay, Wisconsin. They have one daughter.

www.ingramcontent.com/pod-product-compliance
Lightning Source LLC
Chambersburg PA
CBHW060413180626
46817CB00007B/2571